Spells and Bindings

Krista Eviota

Ukiyoto Publishing

All global publishing rights are held by

Ukiyoto Publishing

Published in 2023

Content Copyright © Krista Eviota

ISBN 9789359206615

All rights reserved.
No part of this publication may be reproduced, transmitted, or stored in a retrieval system, in any form by any means, electronic, mechanical, photocopying, recording or otherwise, without the prior permission of the publisher.

The moral rights of the author have been asserted.

This is a work of fiction. Names, characters, businesses, places, events, locales, and incidents are either the products of the author's imagination or used in a fictitious manner. Any resemblance to actual persons, living or dead, or actual events is purely coincidental.

This book is sold subject to the condition that it shall not by way of trade or otherwise, be lent, resold, hired out or otherwise circulated, without the publisher's prior consent, in any form of binding or cover other than that in which it is published.

www.ukiyoto.com

To the little girl who knew fairy tales to be her only haven—the stories are still keeping us safe today.

Contents

Chapter 1	1
Chapter 2	8
Chapter 3	15
Chapter 4	27
Chapter 5	36
Chapter 6	43
Chapter 7	50
Chapter 8	56
Chapter 9	62
Chapter 10	71
Chapter 11	77
Chapter 12	86
Chapter 13	94
Chapter 14	100
Chapter 15	105
Chapter 16	112
Chapter 17	119
Chapter 18	125
Chapter 19	129
Chapter 20	138
Chapter 21	144
Chapter 22	151
Chapter 23	156

Chapter 24	161
Chapter 25	171
Chapter 26	181
Chapter 27	185
Chapter 28	195
Chapter 29	201
Chapter 30	207
Chapter 31	218
Chapter 32	225
Chapter 33	232
Chapter 34	239
Chapter 35	246
Chapter 36	257
Chapter 37	262
Chapter 38	275
Chapter 39	280
Chapter 40	286
Chapter 41	294
About the Author	*301*

Chapter 1

The flames are dancing and bowing toward mama, reaching out to her as if drawn by her presence alone. Her eyes are the color of worn leather and they glitter as she watches the motions of the fire. She's holding the small cupcake we decorated in the kitchen earlier tonight.

She smiles down at the lone blue candle on top. The warm light flickers over her skin, bathing her. Softening her features even more.

My mother has a sweet face, her cheeks are full and this gives her face a youthful roundness. Her eyes are framed by wispy eyebrows that are only ever furrowed in concern. Her lips are plump and fuller at the bottom. She is beautiful in the most radiant ways. I once heard papa describe her as sunlight which I think accurately describes her presence. I have not met a lot of moms in my life yet, but I know mine looks the most beautiful.

A smile stretches across her lips as she leads her three daughters in a fit of hushed giggles.

I beam at her now and she rubs my head. She presses her finger on her lips to keep me and my sisters quiet. My cheeks feel tight as I fight the giggle that threatens to escape me. My excitement bubbling over the fact that I'm sneaking around with my mother and sisters in the dark.

2   Spells and Bindings

My older sister, Zoha, nudges me with her elbow and a soundless "*Oof.*" comes out. I shoot her a look, my eyes narrowed. She returns the glare with one of her own. This only lasts a second before the corner of my lips twitch and we both concede. Grinning at each other like fools instead.

The morning light barely seeps through our small windows so the hallway is dark save for the small candle on the cupcake. We walk on the tips of our toes and huddle in the middle of our corridor. The image of our hunching bodies flashes in my head and it encourages another bout of giggles. I just know that we look like a bunch of troublemakers. For the sake of stealth, I try to distract myself as we continue along the hallway.

There is a chill in the air, like a soft dew kiss and I shiver as the cold reaches me. I'm still in my favorite night shirt, the edges fraying and the material worn from the wash. Zoha is wearing a matching one, the hem of her shirt crumples and stretches around a small fist—Zafiya's.

Our youngest sister stands close beside her. Their bodies press against the wall and we make it to the front of the closed door to our bedroom. I look over at both of them and they meet my gaze, mischief light their faces and I know it reflects mine, too.

I push open the door and we all peek inside to find papa still snoring in bed. His arms are thrown out as if waiting for a hug to come from above. Mama grins and motions for us to come in.

Zafiya is the first to give in to the excitement. She breaks into a run toward the bed, squealing. She launches herself on top of papa and we hear him grunt.

With laughter and mirth, Zoha and I follow suit. We crowd him. Our small bodies slotting with each other as we tumble on top of our father. He lets out a sleepy laugh and his chest rumbles with his laughter. His arms, long limbs, reach out and envelope all three of us in an embrace of laughter and sheets.

"Happy birthday, papa!" I breathe out and he tightens his arms around us again. A sound of pure satisfaction rumbles in his throat and he nuzzles the top of Zafiya's head. He looks up at mama who is still standing with the haphazardly decorated cupcake in her hand. His gaze softens even more, his green eyes lighting up at the sight of his wife.

"Is that for me?" He asks, gaze still trained on her. His eyes trail her, cataloging her features. The corners of his lips quirk up as they continue to stare at each other. Words being exchanged through eyes.

Without breaking stride, mama walks up to the bed and situates herself by the edge. Papa sits up, bringing us along within the bear of a hug still tightly secured around us.

"Make a wish, my love." She raises the cupcake to him. Zafiya wiggles in papa's arms and he looks down at her. She bites her lips, physically fighting the urge to blow out the candle herself. He kisses the top of his youngest daughter's head before looking back at mama.

"I only need you and the girls." He blows the candle in one quick huff of breath and leans in to kiss mama on the cheek.

Gross.

My sisters and I groan at the very affectionate display and squirm in our father's arms for release. He bellows in laughter at our reaction.

"There's more kisses to go around!" He declares and then places big sloppy kisses on top of our heads. We fake disgust and it eggs him on to tickle us with renewed vigor until we become a screaming, laughing mess on the bed.

Mama stands up and tucks the cupcake away for later. She takes a moment to watch us tackle one another. A wide smile pasted on her face. Her hands are clasped over her chest as the very image in front of her warms her heart.

I know she wanted to get papa a bigger cake but she had just used the last remnants of her salary for groceries. We were with her then and I remember too well how she hid her concern with a stiff smile. She watched the cashier like a hawk as the total continued to go up.

With only a few coins to her name along with two bags of food to feed a family of five tucked under her arm, she was set on just going home. She told us we'll get papa a cake next year. We just stepped out on the parking lot when Zoha and I suggested we decorate a cupcake for him instead. She had lightened marginally at the idea and had scraped up her measly change to buy one.

He doesn't seem to mind that the cupcake is an explosion of pink. Topped with a mixture of glitter, frosting and gummy bears—courtesy of Zafiya. His laughter eases some tension in my mother. There is no question that papa is perfectly content with the humble gift we offered at the crack of dawn.

He continues terrorizing us with tickles until we concede with tears threatening to escape our eyes.

Zoha and I are tasked with flipping pancakes while Zafiya busies herself with the small fruit toppings on the counter. We don't do a very good job at it. Some pancakes were a bit overdone—bordering on burnt. The stack of dark pancakes grows, each piece varying in thickness. Papa wouldn't complain and Mama would simply laugh a little before taking a bite.

We spend the rest of the morning in the kitchen, making a mess of our breakfast while mama and papa dance within the cramped space near our dining table. It doesn't bother them, with how they flourish and dance, one would think they'd have been dancing in a grand ballroom hall.

With joint hands, they sway along to the music playing from the radio.

We look at our parents and shake our heads, mimicking adults looking over errant children. I conceal a smile when they twirl and laugh against each other. It's a sight we always saw at home.

For as long as I can remember, my parents always held each other in whatever means possible. Small touches throughout the entire day, hand-holding, hugs, and kisses here and there. They act as if they would both float away if they weren't touching, it's sweet, really.

Papa slides his hands around mama's waist and dips her low to the floor. When they come up for air, my mother is giddy and blushing. He grins at her and he brushes a calloused thumb over her flushed cheek.

Papa uses his hands a lot, not just to show such affections with mama and his daughters but he uses it for a living as a landscape gardener. He loves to keep his hands dirty, tending to flowers and nourishing them to life. His hands have grown rough as he continued to use them for labor but they remain gentle. I love tracing over the rough patches in his hands and we make a game out of making shapes from them.

They make their way over to us, finished with one of the many dances of that morning. Mama slides her warm hand around my chest keeping my back flushed against her front in a hug.

"How's breakfast prep going?" I lean my body towards her and look up at her.

"Uhm..." I smile sheepishly. "Crispy pancakes are a thing, right?" Mama laughs and rubs her hands up and down my arms in a comforting gesture. I sigh at the contact.

Unlike papa, her hands are smooth and soft, not having used them for arduous work. Instead, she uses them to nurture. When we were much younger, she had used them to bathe us and to scrub dirt from our bodies. She had used her hands often to tie intricate braids in our flaming red hair and to tuck away loose curls through the day.

Eventually, she had used them working odd jobs like waitressing, forcing her to take more time away from home. Yet, she had always used her hands to smooth away our worries and to gently lull us into the night.

"Go wash up, it's almost time for school. I'll take over." She kisses the top of my head and sidesteps me to do the same with my sister. "You, too, Zo."

"I'm almost done here, too!" Zafiya exclaims sliding the sliced fruits into a bowl before she steps up toward us and we make our way to our room. We've perfected the art of preparing at the same time without stepping over each other in the bathroom.

"Be back here in 10 minutes for breakfast, the last one back will wash the dishes!" Mama calls from the kitchen and papa's laughter echoes through the hallway as my sister and I break into a sprint.

Chapter 2

"Gave you an extra piece of chocolate in your pack, Zelle." That extra piece was only for me—she knew Zoha or Zafiya wouldn't enjoy it as much as I would. Mama whispers before she kisses the top of my head. I shoot her a pleased grin and she mirrors it, pinching my cheek. Then she does the same with my sisters.

As much as my sisters and I are close, our tastes are wildly different from each other. That even with how we style our hair and clothes, we have our own distinct identities.

Zoha climbs the car first—our eldest. She wears her auburn hair in a tight high ponytail, not a strand out of place. The chill bites at her skin making her cheeks grow pink. She pulls her blue coat all the way up to her chin. She really doesn't like the cold.

"Come on, we're going to be late!" She calls after us as soon as she settles into her seat. I boost Zafiya up our family SUV, and she scrambles on all fours to get herself seated. She tugs on her yellow knit sweater to straighten it. Her curly hair is pulled into pigtails on top of her head and it whips around with her as she moves. She is a bundle of energy barely able to contain herself.

I sidle up next to her and close the car door after me. I have my favorite black bomber jacket on and my hair is loose around my shoulders. None of us had managed to take after our mother's beautiful raven black hair, instead we all had fiery red hair courtesy of papa.

Papa says that our distinct hair is our best feature and continues to brag about it at home while mama argues that it was our sharp eyes. They were a reflection of mama's upturned leather brown ones, aged and yet bright.

"Let's go, papa." Zoha urges with a slight annoyance in her voice. She's only a year older than I am, me at fifteen and her at sixteen. Her decisiveness and firm decision make it feel like we are years apart in age, though.

Papa is already used to her moods and he simply laughs at her tone. He looks over his shoulder to give us a wink before he starts the car to drive off. Mama's hand laced with his—of course.

During the drive, we're mostly silent. Only my parent's hushed murmurs fill the air. I've always enjoyed looking out the window to watch as the houses and trees speed by. We had taken this route countless times to school so I knew when I need to look out to see Mrs. Lavine's lawn.

She's one of papa's clients and he often boasts that it is the prettiest lawn in the neighborhood. Teeming with life and flowers—one of his proudest works, I remember him calling it as such. I've always loved her lawn among all others but when we drive by this time, the grass is not as green.

The flowers look limp among the bushes. I immediately point this out.

"Mama, look, Mrs. Lavine's lawn!" I lean around mama's back seat to ask her to look but the tight grip she and papa has on each other's hand is enough to stop me. It wasn't a casual touch, their knuckles white from the effort. "Mama?" I whisper and she looks back at me.

There's a brief moment of terror on her face, one I have not seen on her before. It makes my heart jump but she is quick to mask it with a smile. With her free hand, she twists over the car console and tucks my hair around my ear.

"Sit back, Zelle. We'll be there soon." I look over at my sisters after I nod, Zafiya is resting her head on Zoha's shoulder. Their faces reflect the same concern over the sudden tension in the air.

I sit back without a word—reaching over to hold their hands in mine, too. My father's shoulders tense as he starts speeding up. His eyes dart from the road and the side mirrors. I crane my head to look behind us but I stiffen when mama stops me.

"Eyes forward, Zelle." The grim tone in her voice leaves no room for arguments.

Papa takes turns that are outside our normal route and I know this road no longer heads towards school. Papa's normally calm and collected demeanor is at odds with his behavior now.

He's jittery and the car jerks harshly at every turn. His knuckles have grown white as he grips the wheel.

My throat runs dry as my heart hammers in my chest.

I look out. The day started out with bright skies but now it had grown dim. Thunder echoes nearby and thick clouds start rolling in. The road darkened under its shadows.

"Mama?" Zafiya speaks up then, the shake in her small voice is hard not to notice.

"We'll be okay, little warrior, we'll be okay." She coos to our youngest. A nickname that has stuck to her because, out of the three of us, she's always been the fearless one. Unbridled youth and energy. The brave one. Even now, despite her voice breaking, her eyes are clear and set on our mother. Not out of fear but of interest. Mama doesn't look back but she starts muttering under her breath.

"I call now the words in dire need,

no harm shall pass this is my creed."

Her voice carries over us, growing louder as she utters the words. Her voice takes on a somber timbre, one I barely recognize as hers. It's melodious and deep, pulling from her throat.

A current stirs in the air kissing my skin with electricity. This makes the hairs on my arms stand on end and I shudder at the sensation. I tuck my hair behind my ears as wind picks up inside the car making my hair gently sweep across my shoulders.

Papa steps on the gas harder and the engine roars. We jerk at the sudden speed, our heads slamming back into our seats. Zafiya lets out a soft grunt and Zoha draws her closer.

"Protection come upon my family,

let light hear my plea.

As I will it, so shall it be."

Mama continues to chant these passages under her breath, each time more urgent. I strain around to look at her and I could have almost sworn her skin glowed. The car enters another back alley with barely enough space to fit the vehicle. Papa curses under his breath and makes a sharp turn into another narrow road.

At the movement, my shoulder slams on the car door. I choke back a sob as pain blooms down the side of my arm.

I keep my grip on Zoha's hands. At this point, our joint hands are the only thing holding Zafiya down to keep her from careening off.

With an effort, I turn my head to look behind us and my breath catches at the sight. A rumble of dark clouds is coming straight towards us. Covering everything else from sight.

"Zelle! Eyes. Forward." Mama turns around and grabs me by my sore arm through the space between her chair and the car door. I whimper at the sharp sting that shoots up through me from her grip. I avert my eyes to my lap and my lips quiver. "Keep driving, Gab. We've almost lost them." She instructs him before she resumes her chant.

Papa grunts as he lets his foot off the gas and we start to slow down. He makes a couple more turns and he lets out a long breath once we exit into a busy highway. He drives up a couple more miles before he relents and takes the nearest exit.

I don't even know where we had stopped and I don't dare ask.

He eases the car to the side of the road and stops. Neither of my sisters move, still as I am. Our hands linked on Zafiya's lap. Sweat slicking our grips but none would let go.

We keep our eyes on the back of mama's head, not daring to look anywhere else. The rhythmic clicks of the car's hazard lights are the only sound accompanying our thundering heartbeats.

Mama lets out a shaky breath and she turns to face us again. Her olive skin is a little flushed and her lips pale. The smile she has on is strained and her brown eyes are ablaze.

"Just a little adventure." Her voice is breathy now. Scratchy from her repeated chanting. She tries to lighten the mood with her smile and little joke. It was anything but comforting and she sees this when none of us return her smile.

She drops the facade and reaches over the console instead.

Her hand goes to the top of my sisters' heads. As soon as she touches them, their eyes close. Their shoulders slump forward. Their breathing deepens and they fall asleep in no time.

Despite the adrenaline coursing through my body now, she's going to block me out. I don't know how but she'll force me. Make me lose consciousness at her will.

When her hand hovers over my head, I swat it away on instinct. Her eyebrows shoot up in surprise at my reaction, alarm making her eyes go wide as she looks at me.

"Zelle—" Papa turns around and meets my eyes. His brows furrow forming a gentle line between them.

Papa and I usually don't need words between us. As much as Zafiya and Zoha were Mama's favorites, I was his. He's the one to calm me and talk me down when I step out of line.

The look on his face now is enough to let me know I should let my mother do what she needed to do. I swallow, my throat dry, and I nod at her.

Mama rests her hand on my head and at the contact of her warm skin, a blanket of calm covers me. My eyes immediately grow heavy and my head starts swimming. I lean back and let myself surrender to this unnatural slumber.

No questions. For now.

Chapter 3

The days that follow are nowhere out of the ordinary. We wake up and sleep, going about our routines and roles at home. The ease of normalcy too tempting to resist and no one talks about the events that happened that day.

I have very little memory of what had happened after we fell asleep in the car, only that we woke up at home. Mama and papa were already in our room waiting for us to open our eyes. We ate dinner with forced conversation and it was then that I knew this was our way of agreeing never to bring it up. To pretend like it never happened.

Mama is careful with me though, more so than with my two sisters. Afterall, I'm the one who had resisted at first. She often peeks into our room to find me in bed with a book

I know she knows that I have questions that I wouldn't dare ask her.

What bothers me most is that she didn't sound like she was praying then. She was chanting and her voice carried an essence in the air. Was that a spell? I couldn't wrap my head around it and I keep turning the memory in my head trying to dissect it. Nothing about that day was normal and I seem to be the only one that's bothered to point that out.

16   Spells and Bindings

She's standing in the doorway now and I try my best not to look at her.

I'm not scared of her. Of that, I am sure. She's still mama. The woman who holds me in her arms through tears. The one who takes away pain and never inflicts it on purpose. Although, a part of me wonders what she's hiding from us and why she feels the need to do so.

She was able to force us to sleep then. To follow her will without much of a fight and it makes me wonder if she's ever done that before.

My skin prickles at her attention and I know she wouldn't leave until I look at her. I relent and peek at her now over the top of my book. She's wearing a small smile on her lips. She's worried. About what—I wouldn't know. With the way she's standing and shifting on her feet, something tells me I'll find out soon.

"What are you reading?" She asks lightly as she sits at the edge of my bed. I close the book and tuck it under my arm. It's a book on witches and I bite down on the guilt.

"Nothing good." She senses my discomfort and pulls the book from me. I watch her face darken as she reads the title.

"What—" She frowns and looks up at me. Eyes accusing and hard. "What is this?" Taken aback by her anger, I shrug.

"It's just a book, mama." I grumble. "I just thought…"

"No." She shakes her head and she grips the book tight before setting it aside, sliding it particularly farther away from me. I guess I'm not getting that back. "You shouldn't be reading things like this, Zelle. They'll bring nothing but trouble." Her strong disapproval further fuels my suspicion. I had only picked up the book one day when I was sitting on my thoughts on the incident. Although the book sounded so farfetched, part of me recognize that this was a possibility worth looking into. Mama takes a cleansing breath before clearing her throat.

"I actually came here because I needed to talk to you." She looks at me like I'm some animal ready to pounce on her. Her eyes are wary and watching my every reaction. The unease grows but I don't break the silence. "We're moving."

"Moving where?" I respond quickly, almost reflexively. It didn't make sense. Out of all the things I had expected her to say, this was not one of them. "And why now?"

She lets out a long breath and she scrubs her face with her hands. I've always seen my mother as radiant. Like she was the only person that could outshine the sun with her warmth. This is not the case now, somehow her energy had dimmed. She holds dark half-moon bruises under her eyes. Their pallid color standing out more under the light of the room.

These cracks in her armor make my chest tight with guilt. I've never seen her so desolate. I'm sure the space I've deliberately put between us since the incident is part of the reason why she's out of her mind in worry. I remain silent then, not voicing out the protest begging to be uttered.

"Things came up and we can't stay here anymore." Her tone and the tired look in her eyes left no room for argument. I shake my head before I can stop myself.

"I don't understand."

"I know, Zelle. It'll be hard to understand but I promise it will be alright." She takes my hand and holds it in hers. I fight the urge to pull back.

"Is this about those things chasing after us? Are we not safe anymore? Please tell me." My voice is shaking now. "Please talk to me, mama." She squeezes my hand and her lips press together tightly.

"No, there was nothing chasing after us." My eyes widen, she's lying straight to my face. "We can't afford the house anymore. I've lost my waitressing job at the diner and papa is not getting enough clients here."

"What about school? Linc is here. I can't–" She stops me with a look and all remaining argument falls off from my lips. The words fizzling out and leaving nothing but a distasteful aftertaste.

Linc Benson and I have been the best of friends for years. I have not been one to make many friends at school because no one wanted to befriend the girl in hand-me-downs so he is special and rare. The thought that I'd have to leave him behind breaks something in my chest and yet, I do not argue.

"I'm sorry, Zelle." I hug my knees to my chest and I look away from my mother. Not wanting this pain in my chest to be associated with the woman I loved with everything I am. Her reasons didn't feel right but I don't question them. Her lies tastes bitter on my tongue and I don't want to hear more.

She wouldn't give me answers. Wouldn't bother explaining to me why we must uproot our lives just because she said so. She rests a warm hand on my head and it makes me wince. Comfort was the last thing I feel from her touch now.

"We'll leave in a week." I balk at that.

"That soon?" Mama doesn't answer and just sighs looking at me. She looks even more tired than when she came in. Aas if this conversation sucked so much energy out of her. I push off the bed and I mumble under my breath without looking back at her.

"I'm going to see Linc." I silently walk down the stairs and take two steps at a time. My breath is coming in rough hitches. I look around the house and I fight the stinging in my eyes.

I believe myself old enough to understand that my mother would always act with our best interest in mind but as I walk through our tiny house and see the worn walls that hold memories of our lives, I cannot help but feel dejected. When I reach the door, Papa's head pops from the living room doorway and his eyes soften as he finds mine wet from unshed tears.

"Be back by curfew." He comes up to me and crouches to level his eyes with mine. I look down and avoid his gaze. "Hey." He whispers as he tilts my chin with his fingers so I have no choice but to meet his eyes.

"I'm okay. I get it." I clip out, hating the shake in my voice. Hate that the tears I fight against makes my throat thick and my voice small.

"When we get the new house, do you want to work in the garden with me? We can make it prettier than the one we have here." I bite down on my lips as my chin starts to shake. The small garden behind our house is my favorite place in the world and we're leaving it behind like it means nothing.

"Whatever the new house has, it won't be the same." I mumble.

I've watched papa in that garden for years, giving life to a small patch of land. It held the best flowers that made our house smell like spring the entire year. I've constantly pestered my father to let me help out but mama would stop me most of the time, telling me yard work is not for ladies.

I know papa's invitation was an attempt to make the move appealing to me so I feign a small smile. I cannot find the voice to object to a move they've most likely already set in motion. There was nothing else to be done but to follow because that's what good children would do for their parents, right?

"We'll make it better, you and I. I promise you that." He was a man of few words and even more so, a loyal man to his wife. I'm sure if I ask him for the truth, he wouldn't give me the version I want to hear. "It's not the house that makes the place home, it's the people in it, Zelle. We'll be okay." His eyes soften as he sees my losing battle with my tears.

"Okay, papa." He ruffles my hair slightly and kisses the top of my head.

"I love you, you know that right?" I cannot answer. My throat thickens and I only nod before I turn to leave. I feel his gaze on my back even from across the street.

The walk between my house and Linc is short, it was barely enough time for me to shake off my unease and to wipe away the escaped tears. I look up at their house fondly and the first memory of our friendship blooms in my mind.

I first saw him from outside my window when they moved into our neighborhood. He was a lanky kid with a mess of dirty blonde hair jutting out in peaks to top off his height barely covering the wide forehead and plump cheeks. I remember thinking he was handsome then and I had allowed myself a hefty amount of time to observe him behind our curtains.

Even as a child, he had been tall and looming then, with long arms and legs that should have made him look awkward in his movements. But he moved slowly and with ease as he pointed out directions and furniture for the movers to pick up and bring into the house. He had watched grown men with his round stormy eyes, it made me wonder how much older he was than I am. He intrigued me.

It had taken no prompting for me to walk over to him so I could introduce myself. I had put on my brightest smile, brushing away my auburn hair as he looked over at me with those careful eyes. His indifference eventually melted away when I offered him the chocolates I always had tucked in my pockets and he accepted them with a thin smile.

He lived with his mother, Dianne Benson. She had the same blonde hair and steel eyes. She immediately welcomed me into their home as my friendship with Linc grew. My parents had done the same with him.

Dianne had often said we were the only family they had. Linc's dad was no longer with them—whatever that means. Dead or gone, we never asked because mama said it would be rude to.

I dig my worn-out sneakers on their mat, hating that all I could think about is that this would probably be the last time I would do this. I knock softly and it takes but a minute for the door to swing open.

The flash of dirty blonde hair welcomes me.

In the years since we've met, Linc had grown into his lanky stature and had filled it in slowly. He still had a lean build and had only gotten even more taller. His cheeks have lost their plumpness and his jaw has grown narrower, sharper. His round eyes, still stormy as always, now hooded and cutting. He'd skipped his awkward stage and dove straight into handsome teenager. Although his mop of hair is always at disarray but it only adds to his youthful charms.

Girls at school *swooned* over him. He barely talks to anyone but me or my sisters and his quiet nature added more to this allure. I have not particularly looked at him that way mainly because if you've seen a boy in his natural element. Then you'd see how filthy they can get, it's hard to erase that image and see him as anything more than a friend. He greets me now with a lopsided grin.

"Took you long enough. Where have you been?" I haven't seen him since the episode in the car. I shrug at him, opting not to answer. His brow furrows once he sees my expression. "What's wrong?" I shake my head, not trusting myself to speak up without crying in front of him. He grabs me by the wrist and pulls me inside. "Come on, Mom's out back tending her garden."

I follow along, too familiar with the layout of their house. The front door immediately opens up to painted white walls surrounding the den, cluttered with knitted throws over plush couches and littered books left open on any available surface. Their house brimmed with activity. Despite only being the only two people to occupy it, Diane and Linc always made the house feel full.

Their home had better furnishing than we do, wider hallways, newer bits and bobs, and shinier floors. I used to feel out of place or conscious of my thrifted clothes and worn sneakers. Linc always looked like he was dressed to the nines—as much as any kid our age could.

Our contrast is evident no matter how much I try to dress up around him. Linc never seemed to mind and Dianne never looked at me in anything other than fondness so I stopped trying to impress. The niggling insecurity about my state of dress smothered by welcoming arms. I take another sweeping look at their house and I whimper as I start missing the place even as I stand here now.

Linc looks back at me and the crease between his brows deepens. When we reach his room, he turns to me and he cups my damp cheeks. I hadn't even realized my tears had spilled until then.

"Talk to me." I look up at his stormy eyes. Linc is safe, and he is part of what makes this place *home*. My heart stutters in my chest as I speak.

"We're leaving." My voice was nothing but a whisper and my face crumples as I wrap my hands around his neck. "Just like that. They're taking me away because of what?" Linc's arms wrap around my waist as he leads me further into the room. Leaving his door open.

Dianne has a strict no locked doors policy whenever I come over. She often points out that young men and women shouldn't ever be left alone in locked rooms. I'm sure she'd throw a fit if she sees me locked in a teary embrace with him now but I couldn't find the strength to care.

I hug him tighter to me, trying to force his skin to stay on mine. To let his scent envelope me. He smelled of the ocean breeze. Sharp, yet warm and comforting.

"Start from the beginning." Linc's voice is muffled as he buries his face in my hair. "What happened?" I cry harder, all the pent-up frustrations of the few days crashing down on me. The stifling feeling of not being able to speak up in my own home just to *ask* my parents. To talk to them about what I had just witnessed.

Now, it's this. A move. An upturning of my life and I couldn't even bring myself to question them. God, I couldn't find the voice to talk to my parents.

"I don't know, Linc." I look up at him and he wipes the tears that keep flowing. "Something happened. Something changed at home and now we're moving away." Linc settles me into his bed, his arms coming around me as he lets me rest my head on his chest. He blows out a breath.

"Did they say where you'd be going?" I shake my head and I laugh at my ludicrous reaction. I didn't even ask them where we'd go and just agreed to it.

"They're running." I mumble, the restless energy that had festered since the incident taking over. It sounds ridiculous coming from my mouth, I immediately want to take it back as soon as I let it out. I scrub my eyes with the heels of my hands and groan. "They're running from whatever was chasing us in that car a few days ago." Linc doesn't say anything as I recount the events of the incident. I chew my bottom lip between my teeth and I sit up.

"It sounds like a load of bull, I know." I look up, expecting to hear Linc laugh at my foolishness but his eyebrows draw together in a frown.

"Look, Z." He places his hands on my shoulders and he pushes me up so we can sit, facing each other. "Don't think about things like that too much. It won't do you any good." I frown at his response. Ridicule, I expected. But dismissal?

"Don't think about it?" I huff in frustration. "Linc, they're literally packing up our lives and running with their tail between their legs. I'm going to be far away from you and all you can say is don't think about it?" I couldn't keep the shake from my voice and Linc winces as he reads my emotions clearly.

"I'm sorry, that's not what I…" He trails off. "I promise we'll stay in touch. I'll text you everyday and wherever you go I'll ask mom to drive us there every weekend." I feel cold suddenly as realization dawns on me. He's not fighting this move either. He's already come up with a solution as if we've already left.

I look at him with a frown and he refuses to meet my gaze.

For the first time since I met him, Linc is not siding with me and I feel utterly broken. I haven't even moved yet and things have already changed.

Chapter 4

It took just a week for us to pack up the house and to move to the new place. We had measly belongings and most of them fit in our SUV and Dianne's car. They had helped us dump our lives into moving boxes and leave the rest in a cloud of dusty memories and sentiments.

To say things have gotten better, would be a lie. After the move, mama and papa kicked into high gear trying to maneuver our lives. New school, new neighborhood, new life.

Now, a few months into all this *newness*, the shiny fresh life had not lost its luster on my sisters. Both of which were happily getting themselves whipped up in the whirlwind of change. They were *excited* to move. I feel betrayed just thinking about it.

I had turned towards my curiosity to appease the melancholy of leaving a life behind. What started out as a simple peek into that one book—which I really hadn't seen again after mama took it from me—had turned into a fascination. I didn't kick up a fuss, not wanting to further burden my parents with my mood and attitude. Instead, I had used what remained of my time to read about magic and witches. It's mighty avoidant, I know, I'm pretty sure this was not a healthy way to deal, but my family seems to be doing the same.

There was comfort in thinking that there was a higher reason for this upturning of my life. That it was simply something I could not fight because there were beings we needed to run away from. The other alternative of that reason being: it's just *life* or us being too poor to keep the house I grew up in. Those sad, albeit more realistic, reasons are something I refuse to swallow.

The more I read about magic and witches, the more I find myself entranced. Like something clicked inside me and I couldn't stop trying to dig deeper. It was addictive, finding an alternate reality and piecing things together in my mind.

I close *The Green Witch's guide to Earth Magic* after I finish scribbling notes on its pages. I found it in the budget bin at the bookshop when I snuck out to the mall yesterday. I get out of bed and on silent feet make my way in front of our shared closet. It was a lot smaller than the one we had before and I look at it with disdain.

It's bursting with clothes and coats shared between three young girls. It's a mess to say the least, but it's the perfect place to hide my stack of books. I push aside the coats and move around some of the boxes I've put in place to further cover my collection. It's gotten quite expansive.

A dose of magic in such a bleak reality would make life so much easier. People wouldn't have to learn how to scrape measly earnings to live comfortably. People wouldn't have to leave their homes and friends. I make a mental note to try and look for a book about this.

Was it necessary for me to go through such means just to hide my interest like some dirty secret? It shouldn't be.

Once, mama caught me with one of my books and had thrown a fit.

"I told you to stay away from books like this." Her cheeks were flushed as she grabbed the book straight from my hands. It was one of my favorites because it talked about how witches are more attuned to the energy of nature.

I had been devouring it and taking note of how it says witches can then channel this energy into their spells. It sounded much closer to fiction than that of reality, but oh, how I loved it. I had been uttering the spells and pretending to see the magical lights in the air in my room. Nothing had happened, of course, but I had the grandest time.

"It's for a school project! I need to write a paper on the topic." I defend myself. She narrows her eyes at me, absolutely not buying my lie but she didn't say another word before she left my room. I thought the matter was laid to rest but she called the school that very night to tell them how harmful this type of topic was.

To my absolute horror, not only did she find out I lied about the school project. She was also informed of the classes I've skipped claiming to be sick in the infirmary. In truth, I was in the school library's pagan religion section.

She grounded me for a week after that and I've learned to hide my books better. Her constant need to stifle it makes me want to dig deeper. If she wouldn't tell me about magic and her spells then I'd find out on my own.

I shove the book at the back of the small space, making sure it only fell behind my side. I straighten and brush my knees before I close the door to our closet.

I nearly jump out of my skin when Zoha clears her throat. I stiffen my back and turn to look at her. She taps her toes impatiently.

Tap, tap, tap

I cringe at the sound of her shoes against the floor. She purses her lips and I swear at that moment, she looks exactly like my mother. I struggle to fight a shudder.

"You're not exactly hiding those well." Her voice laces with disdain. She knows how my obsession grew and she'd been clear about her opinion on the matter.

"You're not going to tell mama." I say, keeping my eyes on hers. It's both a statement and a request. I know well enough that even if she did not like my fixation on this topic, she'd still have my back. She wouldn't like it, but she'd still lie for me. Sibling loyalty and all that.

"You have to stop this. You're being weird about this. It's been forever since that happened and you're still digging around it?" I sigh, this is a conversation we'd had over and over. The outcome would not change even now.

I know she remembers what happened but happily keeps the memory locked away like my parents wanted. I keep pointing out that mama was uttering a spell in the car but she chooses not to comment on it. Even going as far as rolling her eyes at me as I told her of my theories.

"Maybe magic exists in the world and we can make spells. Wouldn't it be cool, though? We can get our house back." She snorts and rolls her eyes at me. "I'm serious. Humor me for a second and—" Her raised eyebrow stops me mid-sentence.

Zoha isn't judging me, but she also would choose not to talk about things she found ridiculous. I give up trying to implore her.

"I'm not doing anything wrong, Zo." I spread my hands to show her they were empty. Her frown deepens and I sneer at her. "I'm just reading about it." My guilt is always best covered with annoyance.

"You know that's not true. You saw how mama got so upset about your book of energies, what do you think finding your collection would do to her, huh?" She steps closer, preparing to say more but stops when our little sister bursts through the doors.

Her curly pigtails of red hair swings wildly as she bounces on the heels of her feet. We both break out into smiles at the sight.

Zafiya is our neutral ground. Even if she were only a year younger than I am, she was our baby. Zoha and I are often at odds which I've accepted as our normal dynamic as siblings.

One thing we both agree on is the fact that our youngest sister needs to stay away from the argument, whatever it is. She is to be kept safe and untouched by our anger.

Never caught in the crossfire.

"Papa says it's time for dinner." She angles her head looking at the two of us, "Mama isn't here yet so he ordered pizza." She turns around and is gone as quickly as she came, leaving the room a bit warmer than how she found it. Zoha looks at me, her eyes glinting with something between a plea and a warning.

This would not be the last time we would talk about this.

On our way down the stairs, we hear a crash. A screeching sound echoes from the dining room. The sound of glass shattering on the floor.

Zafiya's scream follows and it makes my heart lurch in my chest. I scatter towards the room and I have to bite down the scream.

Papa is on the ground beside the pile of broken glass. He must have fallen while he had it in his hands. Zafiya is pressed up against the wall while looking at him, her face pale. I rush to my knees beside him, my hands landing on the glass cutting them.

"Papa!" I shake him. "What's wrong? I'm here." His eyes are squeezed close and I shift on my knees to hover over his face. I couldn't even feel the sting of the glass as they dig deeper into my knees. My heart is hammering in my chest. Adrenaline flooding my system.

Papa clutches his chest and groans. Gab Scott never shows pain, so seeing him slicked with sweat and hearing his labored breathing feels like someone poured ice down my back.

"What's happening to him?" Zoha asks, she stands frozen by the doorway to the kitchen.

"Call mama!" I scream at her. She jumps at my voice. Zafiya walks toward her, shaking as she clutches herself. "Zaf, run to the neighbors now. Get help!" Neighbors we barely knew, neighbors who probably wouldn't run as fast as they can like Dianne Benson would've. The same thought must have passed her and I shake my head. "Just call anyone, anyone that can help."

Her face, streaked with tears, grows determined. She forces her lips into a line, her chin shaking but she nods without saying anything else. She bolts out of the house in a flurry of steady steps.

For a brief moment, the show of bravery from my youngest sister keeps me stunned. I take a second to look at the spot she occupied only a moment ago. I jolt out of it when I hear papa take a shuddering breath. My bloodied hands are on his face, tapping his cheeks to wake him.

"Papa, it's me. Can you hear me?" He opens his eyes to look up at me. His eyes that remind me of green gardens are glassy and unfocused.

"What's wrong with him?" Zoha's voice is frantic and her hands shake around the phone she has clutched to her ear. Mama isn't picking up the call. She's probably driving, already on the way here. Zoha kneels across from me.

Mama should be here soon, I pray. It must have only been over a minute or two since we found him on the floor but why does time seem so slow and yet it also feels like it's going a hundred miles an hour? My ears are ringing and I can't seem to keep air inside my lungs.

What do I do? What do I do?

"There should be someone in this neighborhood that would be in their homes." I reason out and Zoha nods to agree. They may not know us, but maybe someone would help. "Surely, they would come once Zafiya told them what was happening, wouldn't they? If the Bensons were still here…"

"I don't know. God, I don't know." Zoha is crying now. "We have to do something!"

"I know." I bend my head down and breathe deep, the air feels thick against my throat. Papa had gone still under my hands. I refuse to look anywhere else but at the shallow rise and fall of his chest. Watching as his breath turns erratic. His fingers are starting to grow limp in my hands when only a moment ago he had been clutching them. I blink as I watch tears bloom over the cotton of his shirt, mixing with the blood from my hands.

There's so much blood pouring out of my wounds but I barely feel them. Instead. there is nothing but ice in my veins. This cannot be happening. I wrack my brain for a solution and magic is the only thing I could think of. I pray to all that is good that my hammering heart can speak so loudly into the universe that my intent will be heard.

Save him.

"Let him be alright." I pray to the air and Zoha follows suit. I squeeze my eyes shut and pray in earnest. My arms start to shake as I grip his hand tight in mine and a numbness start to tingle my fingertips. Is this due to blood loss? I don't relent my hold on him, let me bleed out for all I care.

Save him, please!

Someone, something should be listening. If those books had any semblance of the truth something is bound to answer my plea. The tingling feeling at the tips of my fingers grow stronger, sharper, like bees have materialized under my skin and are wreaking havoc in my system.

Still, I don't let go. I close my eyes. Focus my attention on our breaths and the wind. In my mind, I see the air in the room. The way it carries my internal pleas through the space. The bees in my skin grow frenetic, concentrating on the little cuts on my palm. They grow strong enough that I hiss in pain.

Then I gasp as my mind starts seeing threads of light burst out those cuts. The threads flow from my blood and they drip over my father. That light seeps into his shirt and into his body.

My eyes snap open and I frantically squeeze my wrists, urging blood to flow out of me. Zoha grabs me.

"What are you doing?" Her voice is shrill and panicked. I shrug her away and continue to squeeze. Although I don't see it with my eyes open, I remember the threads of light bursting out of me.

Save him Let my blood be the key. Please let it keep him alive.

A different kind of coldness covers my body as those threads latch onto him. I don't even have to squeeze that hard anymore as the blood flows generously out of such small cuts. It shouldn't have been possible for it to bleed that much and yet–it's working.

Papa's face is relaxing, the furrow in between his brow disappearing as his breathing evens out. I whimper and clutch my own chest as pain spears through it–my insides feel like they're freezing over. Zoha grabs me by the shoulder and shakes me.

"Stop, Zelle!" Her eyes, the color of earth, are wide in horror. I give her a weak smile and I continue my prayer, now certain I'm saying it aloud.

Let my blood be the key,

Don't take him from me.

"No!" Zoha screams and she shoves me away from papa. As soon as I break contact with his skin, it's as if those threads snapped, too. Immediately, the pain and ice in my veins dissipates.

I try to reach him again and I scramble over the floor but I stop when the backdoor slams open and Zafiya comes rushing in. Her cheeks are stained with tears and dirt. Her knees banged up and covered in soil. She must've tripped on one of our neighbor's lawn somewhere.

"I knocked on every door." Her voice is small and scratched. "Only one of them answered. He–" She swallows trying to catch her breath. "He said he'll call for emergency services for us and just wait for them to come."

"No one is coming because they don't know who we are." I say now, defeated. They are strangers and they don't care. Zafiya falls to her knees beside me, almost crumpling straight into my lap. I hug her close to me as exhaustion pulls at my consciousness. I fight against it. I refuse to look away from papa and we sit there listening to our father's breathing.

It sounds so empty, his breathing. As if not enough air is being pulled into his lungs and I block out the sound.

I refuse to look away even as his chest stops rising and the siren rings far off the distance.

Too far, too far.

Chapter 5

A police officer drives us to the hospital in silence. Nothing but the faint roar of the car's engine filling the gaps in the air. We closely trail the ambulance and I keep my eyes on the doors that held my papa inside.

Zoha is still holding my hand in hers. Rubbing warmth into them. The gesture was anything but soothing. Her gentle touch feels wrong against my skin, I don't need comfort now.

I need to see papa open his eyes again, I need him to be okay because somehow a part of me already knows that he isn't.

It feels like someone punched a hole in my chest.

We make it to the hospital and Zoha keeps her arms around me as we walk inside. I'm certain I'm swaying on my feet. Someone ushers us into a waiting room and my skin feels foreign under the light.

I lose all thought until Mama bursts into the room, frantic with red-rimmed eyes. She's still in her waitress uniform and she looks very much like how I feel inside. Broken, somehow.

"Mrs. Scott." The police officer meets my mother by the doorway, not even letting her enter the room fully. She is shaking like a leaf and she glances at us before she lets the officer lead her out the hallway to talk out of earshot. Most likely so that we won't hear my mother sob as he tells her what happened.

Zoha looks shell-shocked beside me. Her usual pristine hair falls around her face in a blur of red streaks. It looks like she ran her hands through them and pulled incessantly.

Zafiya's head is on her lap. Knocked out from exhaustion. I don't even know what time it is. How long have we been here?

"Does it hurt?" Zoha's voice takes me out of my stupor and I see her eyes glued to my hands. I look down, too. I had been picking at the bandages on my palms. The nurses had come earlier and tended to them. I shake my head and stare at them.

I'm afraid to speak. It feels like when I do, it would feel too real.

Zoha reaches over to lace her fingers through mine, grounding me. We all stare at the door, willing someone to come in and tell us papa is okay.

When it does, it isn't a doctor who steps in but mama and I see the officer tucking his cap under his arm as he watches us from outside the room. Mama walks with steady strides to us and I wonder where she had gotten the strength to even stand on her own.

She would not let us see her weak—cannot. She crouches in front of us and places a hand on my knee and Zoha's. Zafiya sits up, bleary-eyed.

"The doctor is going to be here soon." She says in a soft voice.

"You have to heal him, mama." My voice sounds sharp as it echoes in the room. Mama's eyes snap to mine and she frowns.

"I can't do that, Zelle." I grit my teeth and clench my fists until they shake.

"Yes, you *can*." I remember the images in my head and the cold feeling in my bones. The phantom pains still echoing in my gut when my blood flowed out of my hands and on papa's skin.

It wasn't enough.

"I tried but I wasn't strong enough." Mama startles at this and her eyes fall to my bandaged hands. "You can do it, can't you? You're stronger than I am." I ramble on and her eyes grow wide at the string of statements I let out. "You're a witch, why don't you use your powers to heal him? You're only thinking about yourself. About your stupid secret." At the mere mention of the word witch, mama winces as if I slapped her.

She grabs me by the wrist, almost yanking me out of my chair. Her warm healing hand now feels like burning vices on my skin. I let out a sound close to a whimper and she leans so close our noses almost touch.

"You don't know anything, Zelle. Don't talk like you understand because you don't." Zoha who is half in shock pulls me towards her, putting space between mama and me.

"She's only worried about papa. She didn't mean what she said." Zafiya is crying over the exchange and I hate myself all the more for causing her distress. Mama's muddy eyes, the one all three of her daughters carry, widens.

She lets go of my wrist as if she didn't realize what she had done. The guilt crumples her face as she sees the red marks she's left on my skin.

"I'm sorry. I'm just—" Before she could finish the sentence, the doctor comes through the door. Mama gives us another look, one full of regret and worry. She stands up to meet him by the doorway.

All three of us follow. Without looking back, she stretches her hand behind her, instinctively reaching for a hand. When no one takes it, she clutches it to her chest.

"You can see him now." The doctor says in a flat voice. I look up at him and I detest the way his eyes shine over at me and my sisters. There is pity there. Sympathy so thick that it makes me sick. He's waiting for one of us to crumble.

None of us say a word when we follow him out onto the hallway.

We stand outside papa's room and the doctor tells us about what we should expect to see inside. My eyes fixate on the doctor's collar, wanting to look at anywhere else but his eyes.

His coat looks like it had been worn in a rush, the collar upturned. Did he have to rush out of his office while they took papa out of the ambulance? Did he run as fast as he could to chase after the time that seemed determined to slip through my father's fingers?

I clutch my hand tight, thankful for the searing pain brought on by the wounds reopening at the pressure. I try not to hear his voice when he tells us how my dad's *body* would look inside that room.

I refuse to hear it.

Zafiya, our young soldier, grabs my shaking hand. Although clammy, they are solid against mine. Zoha takes my other hand and we stand there outside the door. We form a chain between us, each one anchoring the other.

We don't let go as we step into that frigid room together.

I feel like I would float away if not for my sisters holding me. When I see the scene inside the room, my chest hollows out even more. I take a deep breath and resent the air the fills my lungs. It only takes a moment for anger to fill the hole inside me.

Witches be damned.

Magic be damned if it couldn't save us from this.

Chapter 6

Three Years Later

Zoha is coming home for Zafiya's 18th birthday. She had left for college two years ago and she rarely comes home anymore. She left just before papa's death anniversary and had thrown the house on its axis.

The first few months after the funeral, Zafiya had been a mess of tears. Her grief had been heavy and prominent. With sobs that filled our walls and were salt to our festering wounds. She would often lay awake at night and cried until she had exhausted herself enough to sleep.

I had been content to let my anger take the reins during the blurry aftermath. To don this armor of thorns so that inside I can remain empty. Being the eldest, she was the grounding force of that chaos. The balm over our hurt.

She had soothed Zafiya and had met my fury head on so that my anger had a place to go until I ran out of fuel. We became a team and had taken care of the house while mama took multiple jobs to keep us afloat. What shaky stability we've established is rocked once again when Zafiya left for college.

"Please, Zo." I pleaded. "There are other options for university that's much closer."

"I don't want to go to those schools." She had barely lifted her eyes to meet mine as she continued to pack her clothes into the singular suitcase we all used to share.

"Just wait then." I reasoned. My heart raced as I watched her slowly fill it with clothes, it signaled her leaving sooner. "Wait until we're okay, until mama's okay again." She scoffs at that.

"She's never going to be *okay*." She punctuates her point with air quotes. "She'd rather work than stay here with us, we barely see her and even then, she wouldn't talk to us."

"Just wait another year, please." I had implored her, ignoring the guilt of wanting to keep her in our pool of grief because I didn't want to deal with it alone.

"No." And that was it. Her final answer before she left, with no promises to visit or stay in touch. I can't say I blame her. If I had the chance, maybe I would have left, too.

I'm in our backyard now, toying with the pink Pieris shrub that grows flush against the side of the house. The petals are gorgeous against the chipping paint of our walls. I've taken up gardening and have poured all my energy into keeping papa's garden alive.

I used to say I tended to this garden just to keep a part of him still with me but I've also mostly fallen in love with nature. I brush the petals with my fingertips, feeling the velvet texture against my skin. I ignore the way the bulbs seemed to breathe and blush open at my touch, chalking it up to wind.

"Hey, you. I've been looking for you." The familiar timbre of Linc's voice brings a smile to my face. I had seen him sparingly through the years but our friendship remains present in my life.

"And I was sure you were going to find me soon enough." I look over my shoulder and Linc is by the open doorway.

He's wearing a gray shirt that compliments his eyes. I fight a grin when I notice that the smoke in his eyes shimmer when he looks at me. His hair is longer now, the dirty blonde falling over the sides of his face, framing them perfectly.

My gaze skims over his body, noting that he had put on muscle since the last time I saw him but remains lean. He looks very much like an agile hunter.

My heart does a little flip at the sight he beholds but I look away.

Our boundaries as friends are clear enough. They are never to be dallied with. Not that I want to, really. I value his friendship in my life more than anything and that takes precedence over my loneliness.

"Here." He tosses a velvet box my way and I catch it with both hands. He shrugs when I raise my eyebrow in surprise. "Got myself a part-time job these days. No big deal." I carefully pull away the black ribbon surrounding it.

"It's Zafiya's birthday, not mine." I say even as I smile at the box. He runs his hand through his hair and shrugs again, a nervous tick of his.

"I got her a present, too. I wasn't able to get you a present for your eighteenth, so consider this a delayed one." I snort at him and hold my hand on my hips.

"I'm nineteen. Almost twenty, Linc. Should I expect a present for that missed birthday, too?" I tease and he scoffs at me. He had been here then when I opted out of another party and instead, he had let me try my first taste of beer. He was already twenty-one at that time and had no issues buying alcohol for our escapade.

"Just open the damned present, Z." He mutters and I oblige him. A soft gasp escapes my lips when I open the box. A stone the size of my thumb winks at me, the light shining on its surface. It has an iridescent blue sheen against pale white.

It's a moonstone. A stone that embodies feminine energy and promotes tranquility. I cringe as the knowledge about crystals embedded into my brain supplies unwelcome information at the sight.

I take it out of the box and feel the smooth weight on my palm. It's cold to the touch and if I hold it long enough, I could feel a steady thrum of vibration coming from the rock. It's beautiful.

"Is this your way of telling me I need to act more like a woman now?" I tease and Linc sputters, losing his cool demeanor for a bit. He clears his throat.

Was that a blush creeping up his neck?

"Stop teasing, Zelle." He deadpans and I laugh. "It's for protection." He takes the stone from my palm. It's attached to a simple black leather rope. He slips it over my head, brushing away my sunset hair. I fight a shudder when his fingers skim over the skin of my neck.

I look down at the necklace. The stone sits perfectly snug on my chest, still cool to the touch.

"You know I don't believe in that stuff." I mutter under my breath despite the smile that breaks out on my lips. "But thank you." He smiles back at me and we both turn when mama pops out from the back door. Her eyes immediately land on the stone around my neck. A flicker of recognition flashes in her eyes but is gone as quickly as it came.

"Zo's here." She doesn't wait for a response before ducking back into the house. She's been busy all morning and couldn't bear to stay put. Cooking meals while cleaning out the rest of the house on her down time.

"She's buzzed, want to go sneak around and find her stash?" I quip at Linc and he laughs.

"As much as I want to, knowing how well you can handle your liquor…" He rolls his eyes with a shake of his head showing exactly what he thinks about my alcohol tolerance.

"Okay, next time." I offer and we laugh again.

"I promise to get you enough beer that you'd forget your problems and be giddy with bubbles in your stomach." He grins at me before tucking my arm around his so we can walk inside.

Zafiya is already seated at the table. She opted to wear her favorite yellow sundress today. Her curly mane tumbles around her shoulders.

I mourn the loss of her cute pigtails.

My eyes dart to my other sister right beside her. Zoha is more than happy to fuss over the birthday girl. Her years away from home had turned her into more of a woman than I am. Her cheeks have lost their bulk making her look sharper. I note that this loses some of her resemblance to mama, who's face remains rounded and youthful.

Zoha is wearing a dark blue shirt underneath a cream cardigan. She painted her lips red and it matches our fiery hair so well. Her hair is still in the impeccably tight ponytail. Looking every bit as put-together as ever.

Zoha looks ethereal, beautiful in her savagery. In her presence, I feel a bit conscious of myself. I smooth out the hair that I continue to wear loose in a mass of waves that run down my back.

"Hey." She looks up at me. A flash of uncertainty in her eyes. We haven't spoken much since she left, and when she visits—although sparingly—she does this. Gauge my reaction to her presence and looks over at me as if she'd see all my thoughts written on my face because she's too afraid to ask.

"Welcome home, Zo. We missed you." I bend down to hug her, admittedly, a little bit stiffly. Zafiya joins in on the hug and lets out a sigh of relief. As if having all three of us in the same room together was such a big weight off her shoulders.

I'm inclined to agree on that. It feels good to have both of my sisters here. Awkwardness, aside.

"You should come home more often." Zafiya mumbles under her breath but our eldest chooses to ignore it. I straighten and take my seat beside her as we settle into comfortable chatter. Linc sits across from us and welcomes Zoha with a small incline of his head.

The lamp flickers and the room turns dark, but is soon bathed in a warm light. Mama steps into the room with a cake burning bright with candles. Store bought and huge, I force a smile as my mind immediately takes me back to the time where we had only gotten a measly cupcake for papa.

I know the same memory urges mama to give us *more* whenever she can, but I stifle the thought. Now isn't the time to rehash regrets.

She sings the happy birthday song under her breath and we sing along with her. She takes slow steps and I smile at the image.

I look over at Linc who slips a hand under the table to hold mine. I squeeze his hand back but only look at him when he takes a sharp breath.

The blood that started to warm my cheeks drains at the ghosted expression on his face. I look to where his eyes landed.

"Mom." Linc breathes. I let out a scream as Dianne stumbles in from the doorway covered in blood.

Chapter 7

Everyone in the room stops breathing. Zafiya scrambles out of her chair with a scream mirroring mine. Zoha lunges toward Dianne who sinks to her knees.

Her shirt billows loose on her body in tatters. Her right arm hangs limp at her sides where deep cuts shredded her exposed skin. Her free hand clutches her stomach as more blood blooms on her shirt.

"I couldn't stop them, Aria." Her wide eyes, grey as Linc's, drifts to mama. She has bruises on her face, but her eyes are clear. Mama, who was still standing at that point, drops the cake and rushes toward her.

"How close?" Mama asks as she rips from her own shirt to tie it around Dianne's arm.

"Here, *now*." Those two words made my skin crawl. Before my mother could answer, the ground starts to rumble.

The concrete walls of the house shake along with the tremors until our windows shatter. The screeching sound of bending metal pierces the air. It rings so loudly it feels like nails are scraping inside my head.

A scream tears out of me when more glass shatters and some of the shards cut my skin. I bend over on the floor in pain. Linc's hand closes over the back of my head as he guides me under the table.

My sisters are both huddled under the table and I make a move to reach over to them as the ground shakes beneath us. The chaos of glass breaking and plates falling from cupboards has both of them curling up to protect themselves.

Strong wind whips through the air, flipping the table away from the ground. Someone screams again.

"Out of the house now!" Mama's voice booms amidst the chaos. Linc stands to his feet pulling me along. The floor starts to split open at my feet. The tiles crack open as the ground below moves. I lose my footing and my knees hit the ground hard.

I curse under my breath and Linc is quick to pull me up. I look over at him and he has Zoha's arm gripped in his other hand. His face is pale and grim. Jaw ticking from the strain as he grinds his teeth.

He is stable on his feet as he guides me and my sisters out the house. Wood and rock are falling over us, blocking our path. I duck just in time as the photos start flying off the wall and more glass and splinters hurl my way. Is this an earthquake? No, this is too long—too strong. If not that, then what?

The sound of our ceiling crashing to the floor fills the air and I could barely hear my own voice when I turn to call for mama. Dust and wood splinters are flying in along with the wind.

"Mama!" I scream.

She stumbles out with Dianne's arm slung around her shoulders and a wall of fire bursts from behind her. My eyes widen at the sight. She turns toward me, her eyes aflame, too.

Run.

She mouths before Linc pulls me again to drag us further away from the house. The air whips harshly around us, almost sharp against my skin. We make it to our car and my sisters huddle close to me as Linc tries to open the door.

Zoha is losing most of her composure now, her eyes staring at our crumbling house in fear. She has her arms around herself and Zafiya tucks in close. I don't need to look back to know that the fire I saw behind mama grew. I could feel the heat radiating from it.

My heart hammers in my chest and breathing feels like taking in sharp knives down my throat. Something addled the air with a current, it spears my system and I feel my fingers tingle. I chalk it up to fear and climb into the car as soon as Linc opens it.

"Get in!" He screams over the howling wind. He doesn't wait for my sisters to clamber inside before he runs toward my mother.

She still has Dianne limping alongside her. My shoulders relax as they come closer.

My eyes strain to see them through the smoke coming from the fire. It burns with intensity swallowing everything in its path. Zoha gasps as two figures emerge from the fire raging from our home. They do not even flinch away from the heat and they walk through it.

These figures are that of a man and a woman, if I can even call them as such. Both dressed in flowing black cloth that whispers in the wind like smoke. Their skin graying and pasty hanging from humanoid bones. Not a single hair on their head and it makes their black eyes that much more terrifying.

They are nightmares walking on two legs and they stalk closer and closer.

The female snarls, showing razor sharp teeth. They move in unison, floating off the ground. They lift both their arms and the wind lashes out harder. I see this when mama's dark hair whips around her face.

Mama flicks her wrist and directs her palm toward the two figures. At that motion, sparks form out of nowhere and more fire comes to life, setting everything ablaze. The creatures shrink back a fraction and this allows her and Dianne to rush to the car.

Mama climbs to the driver's seat as Linc helps his mother to the passenger seat. She groans as he buckles her in.

"We need to hold them off." Mama says and she shares a look with Linc. He nods and closes the door before we speed off without him.

"No!" I bang over the glass window and I see him watch us drive away. "Mama, you can't leave him there." I sob and when I attempt to reach over her, Zoha stops me.

"Say the spell, Zelle." I look at my sister with wide eyes.

"I don't know what you're talking about." Renewed fear entering my system as her words register.

"Yes, you do." Her eyes are clear and her lips set in a thin line. I look over at my mother and her eyes meet mine over the rear-view mirror. She nods.

That moment breaks my resolve. My world stopping for a second. This is it, isn't it? Her admission to my suspicions all those years ago. Along with it, her permission that I say the spell. What does that make me then?

I start crying even as the chant forms on the tip of my tongue without much thought.

"I call now the words in dire need,

no harm shall pass this is my creed."

I start the chant that had since been ingrained in me despite my efforts to bury it. As soon as I say the words, Zoha releases a breath and Zafiya whimpers in her seat. Her eyes clutched tight as if in prayer.

"Zo, Zaf." Mama calls as she makes a sharp turn. "Say it with your sister. It's stronger when all three of you say it." We let the moment hang silently until they echo my words fervently. There's warmth blooming inside of me, a current forms underneath my skin and it purrs as the words flow out of me.

"Protection come upon my family,

let light hear my plea.

As I will it, so shall it be."

As the last few words snake out of our lips, the car starts to shake and the sky above us darkens before the world flips upside down.

Chapter 8

The road in front of us crumbles and Mama jerks the wheel away from the gaping hole from the ground. The quick jerk catapults the car and everything turns and turns and turns.

The car violently rolls over, glass and metal flying in the air. Someone screams, I can't tell if it was me. My body slams against the door—or was it the roof? Pain blinds me.

Part of me thinks we would keep going, but it's over in a second. Before we roll one last time, I succumb to a darkness that takes me away from the chaos. It's a welcome reprieve.

When I open my eyes, it's quiet. I make a small movement and I groan as pain blooms through my body. I'm hanging from my seat upside down and the blood is rushing to my head.

I scan the wreck and Zoha is no longer beside me in the car. Mama hangs limp from her seat and Dianne's upper body pokes through the open windshield.

I avert my eyes from the gore. Zaf is still in the car and she's splayed on the roof, her back on the ground. I try to call out but only a croak squeaks out of me, my seatbelt is putting pressure on my throat. I need to release the lock so I can get down.

Oh god, please let them all be alive. I attempt to squirm again in my seat and I grit my teeth as new waves of pain radiate from my body.

"Zaf." My voice is barely a scratch of a whisper, but she starts to stir. I call to her again and she groans. She's turned away from me, but she moves to face me.

"Zelle?" My heart seizes at the sight. Blood is running down one side of her face and she has way too many small cuts blooming on her skin. "It hurts." She groans again and her breathing starts to quicken as her wounds register. Her chest shakes with the rapid motions.

"Look at me." I urge her and her eyes meet mine. Tears already rim her bloodied eyes. She stares at me, her gaze glassy and unfocused. I would take note of her wounds later, I tell myself as fear threatens to push me over a precarious edge.

She's alive, that's what matters now.

"Come on, get up, help me." There's glass and blood—God, please let it not be too much blood everywhere.

She tries to push herself up on her arms, careful about the glass around her. I let out a whimper of relief as she has enough strength to move. She takes a steadying breath and then another before she asks.

"Where's Zo?" Her voice low but steady. A wave of pride washes over me at the sight of our youngest. Wounded, but still asking about Zoha. This proves that our little warrior has more fight in her than any of us combined.

"I don't know. We'll find her." Not a promise but a plea, to whoever or whatever might hear me. "Can you get me out? The lock's busted." A chill runs down my back when the wind starts to pick up. The same eerie howl grows louder around us again. "Faster, Zaf. That's it, keep it steady."

My sister, knowing full well what the wind meant, picks up a big shard of glass with bare hands. She crawls on her knees, wincing as she cuts them further. She doesn't stop until she's in front of me. She uses the glass to shear the seatbelt trapping me to the seat.

The car starts shaking from the wind. Familiar black smoke rolls from the street and at this sight, she quickens her pace. They're coming.

She's already halfway through cutting the seatbelt when she freezes. Her eyes widen as she looks at me. Before I can ask her what's wrong, she jerks back as if yanked by invisible hands. She screams, the veins on her neck straining at the effort. She kicks and shrieks until she is effectively pulled out of the car and away from me.

She throws the shard my way before completely disappearing from my sight.

"Zafiya!" I call after her, knowing she's gone. I dart my gaze around me and all I see is the dark smoke snaking its way around the entire car. I couldn't hear her anymore; I couldn't feel her presence nearby. I let out another scream now prompted by rage.

I cannot stay here, I need to get her back. I ignore the way my body protests and I reach for the glass Zaf threw my way.

I grit my teeth and I let out a sob once my fingers wrap around the glass. I take it to the frayed belt and continue sawing through the edge. Sweat builds and trails from my back.

My vision turns fuzzy at the pressure building inside my head, but I continue to hack my way through the belt. Whoever took Zaf would surely be back for me.

I cannot let them. I could barely feel my fingers and my breathing is too sharp. I groan and drop the glass with a weak curse.

"Pick it up." A soft gravelly voice comes from in front of me. I almost missed it, barely hearing over the blood roaring in my ears. I recognize that voice, though, and I whimper at the first sign of life she's exhibited since I woke up.

"Mama." She turns her body towards me, the best she could while hanging. Her olive skin is pale and clammy, but her eyes are arresting. As clear and piercing as any other day.

The wind around us starts to pick up and her black hair flows from her face.

"You have to stay together, you have to get your sisters." I raise my hand towards her, they feel like dead weight. Needing to touch her, to feel her comfort. I know she'll make me feel better. I'm sure that if she can hold me, she can take away the pain now flooding from my chest.

If only I can get to her.

"Mama." I call again, my voice shaking. I hear her mumble a small chant under her breath and fire sparks on me. Panic shoots through my system and I yelp. I use my hands to pat down the fire but stop when I see it's only localized on the seatbelt. She's burning it off of me, freeing me.

I look back at my mother. Her brows furrow and her eyes remain on the seatbelt, watching it break under her power. Sweat beads on her forehead and I know whatever she's doing takes up every drop of energy left inside her.

The belt breaks and I fall hard on the ground. With a grunt I turn to crawl towards her. The flames sizzling out but her eyes remain ablaze with them.

Find them.

I startle when I hear her voice inside my head. She didn't speak. No, her lips didn't move even as I look at her now.

Find your sisters. You are stronger together. Look for Ava.

My eyes widen when the wind starts howling louder.

Close, those two figures are close. I need to get her out. I need to—

A force grips my entire body and flings me out of the car. A sharp scream barely had time to escape from me. I tumble a few feet away, landing on my stomach. All air knocks out of me.

I turn my body with a wheeze. Mama is looking at me, her eyes glowing even brighter with flames. It's so bright, this power burning inside of her.

She smiles at me and the expression breaks my heart into a thousand pieces. Resignation, apology, and regret all wrapped up into that one smile she sends my way. Her eyes glow brighter until I had to look away.

Once I do, the car bursts into flames.

Chapter 9

It consumed her.

Consumed.

That's the only word that runs in my mind as I stare at the fire bellowing and growing. The smoke thick and dark that I could have sworn soot was coating my throat and my tongue even from this distance. My eyes water from the heat but I couldn't look away.

Strong fingers grip my arms and pull me to stand. I had been on my knees, how I'd gotten on them, I couldn't remember. They cup my cheeks and peel me away from the burning sight.

Cold steel eyes met mine. A woman with high cheekbones housed in a pixie's face is studying me. Her brows furrow when I don't speak and move my eyes back to the burning car. Her hair is a stark white waterfall cut blunt around her chin.

"Are you Ava?" Surprise flickers in her eyes and her brows shoot up.

"No, but I will take you to her." Her response is clipped and I nod, looking back at the fire. "Snap out of it." Her voice has a lilt that draws my attention away from the rising pyre. "Where are your sisters?" The mere mention of my sisters brings a wave of guilt. For a moment, I had forgotten about them and all I felt were the flames on my skin and the tears burning my eyes.

"They took Zaf." Shadows roll behind the stranger's steel eyes, her lips pressing into a thin line. She looks like she's about to lash out in anger over that fact, but she just nods. "And Zoha…" I trail off because I don't even know. I hadn't seen her since the car stopped flipping over.

They must have taken her, too. Maybe she didn't even survive. I don't know which one would be worse. Pressure builds on my temples, and I shake my head to make the feeling go away. Both my sisters are gone. The reality of that statement polarizes all my thoughts. What should I do?

My limbs start to feel numb as ice rushes through my veins. My heart is beating wildly in my chest and it's making it hard to breathe. The stranger senses my panic and hushes me when I start to mumble incoherently.

"You are connected as sisters." She takes my hand and places it on my chest, her hands on top of mine. "If she's close, we can use that to find her. Repeat after me." I only stare at her when she starts a spell.

"Bound by blood,

I call to thee.

I seek thy path,

Show unto me."

With much less vigor, I mimic her words and finish the chant. Nothing happens.

"Try again. Dig deep and pull all your thoughts, your emotions, all your wants into a singular goal. Use the words like you would a prayer, like it will give you the very thing you want at this moment." I breath deep again, considering the stranger's words. "Want and think of nothing more but to find your sister." I chant again.

My chest floods with bone-deep warmth and something grows tight. A singular point of force draws my attention like a thread unspooling from inside me and out into the world. It demands to be followed.

I sprint, clutching that thread within. I know that Zoha is on the other end. The stranger follows me, waving her hands over us and I feel a force envelope us as we run.

"What did you do?" I ask, winded but still running.

"A glamor. We shouldn't be seen, they're still looking." Too many questions started to brew in my mind. A glamor? What does she mean? Who is she anyway? Should I trust her?

None of these questions I voice as we turn a corner. I find my sister unconscious on the ground with rocks jutting out of the earth encasing her in a shield of stone.

"Zoha." I reach for her and she stirs with my voice. I touch her arm and her skin feels cold against my fingers. "Zoha, let's go." Save from a few scratches she looks okay and I release a shaky breath. My blood continues to hum with adrenaline.

"We need to go. Now." The stranger behind me grasps both of our wrists and she looks behind me, her expression grim. Then the world blurs into smoke. I look down at my hands—no, it wasn't the world that turned to smoke, it was *us*.

Our non-corporeal forms blend into each other as the wind picks us up in its current and blows us away. I feel weightless and cold. Such a strange sensation, but it helps me breathe, at least just for a moment.

It takes us a few shadow jumps—as the stranger calls it—before we reach what looks like someone's study. Our feet hit the ground with soft studs. She lets go of our wrists and calls out to the room.

"Ava, we're here." The stranger calls to the room before stepping away from us. Zoha, who regained her consciousness during our travels, inches closer to me. She grabs me by the arm and pulls me behind her. Shielding me from the stranger with her body.

Not feeling the same trepidation as my sister, I take the small silence to look around the room.

Rows of books line almost all sides of the walls with a thick tapestry covering one side. Large arching windows allow the dusk sky to illuminate the study. Plush mismatched couches are angled in front of a steel framed coffee table. The lush cushions make me want to sink my knees into them. My exhaustion comes on strong at the sight of comfortable places to deposit my aching body into.

Lit candles are on top of almost every available surface of the study, making the room smell strongly of cedar and burning wax. The room feels warm but cramped. Papers are strewn on desks, tables and floors. Open books are left thrown about as if in haste to get to the next one. This was a well lived-in study, like scholars could have allowed themselves to surrender all hours of their days to this place alone.

As my gaze continues to roam, it lands on a woman with brunette hair standing by the huge doorway. I can only assume her to be Ava. She has a sharp nose and full lips that make her look like she's purposefully pouting. Her cheeks are a bit flushed and the small pointed chin brings back some softness in an otherwise sharp and severe face.

She dons a stark white silk dress that flows to the floor. The sleeves are cut from what looks to be the softest chiffon and it drapes over her thin arms. The fabric shifts as she moves, making her look like a wraith in motion. As she comes in, she brightens the room.

She tilts her head as she looks over me and my sister. Tucking away small details but never commenting. I feel oddly exposed under her calculating eyes and I shift on my heels. I wait for her eyes to trail up from my toes until she meets mine. Mud brown eyes against emerald ones.

"Zelle, Zoha." She inclines her head in a shallow bow. My sister stiffens and she pushes me further behind her, blocking this woman's view of me.

"Where are we?" Zoha demands. Her voice stern and cold. I remain silent, I couldn't trust myself to speak. "Where's Zaf and our mother?" Ava's mouth hardens into a thin line. She walks around the room avoiding our gaze as if finding her words on the spines of the books that line the walls. The books look old, worn and beloved. Each one exhibiting character and history.

"They were able to get to Zafiya before I could." The white-haired stranger shakes her head, disappointment painting her pixie face. There are shadows dancing in her eyes. "Aria knew we were coming. She—" Her eyes cut to me and my sister. At the mention of my mother's name, Zoha takes a sharp inhale as if to ask about her again. Before she could, I cut in.

"Mama saved me and burned herself in the process." My voice feels foreign. As if the sound came from somewhere else. Like my own ears didn't want to believe whatever words I just uttered. "Mama told me to find you."

How long has it been since the wreck? The flight and the strangeness had distracted me enough to ease away the memory of my mother's face.

Looking back now, I know she had a chance to save herself. Knowing makes it worse. Whatever remaining power she had could have been used to break herself out, but she chose not to. Instead, she made sure to get me out and to reassure me with that one smile before she burned.

Would she have felt her skin boiling? Felt it searing her flesh and her beautiful raven hair? Did she survive until her lungs melted from the heat and she suffocated from the soot?

"Decoy." Ava speaks, her voice gentle, interrupting my thoughts. As if she knows the haunted expression now ghosting my face is a sign that points to my oncoming hysteria. "She needed to burn the car to destroy any trace of your escape. Her matter-of-fact tone does not make it easier to swallow that truth, so I don't respond. "She needed to stop the Comendeti from looking for the both of you. To buy you time to run."

"Comendeti?" The word is foreign to me. I wrack through my memories from the countless stories I've read but come up empty.

Seeing my confusion, Ava pulls a book from the shelves and sets it on the desk at the corner of the room. She gestures for us to come closer. She opens it and the page somehow lands on an image of the twins that had stalked us from the house.

Their image brings the familiar cold chill down my skin. My throat dries and I wrap my arms around myself as shivers threaten to wrack through me. I turn away and look out the window.

"They're magic eaters." She explains as if that was the answer that would make our situation any less confusing.

"Why were they chasing us?" Zoha speaks again, her eyes flitting to the book briefly before pinning Ava with a stare.

"These parasites sensed your magic and wanted it for themselves." It's the stranger who speaks this time, she pushes herself off the wooden wall and stalks towards the desk. Her hair falls around her face as she leans into the book with a sneer. "Your unprotected and raw power surged when the youngest turned eighteen. With all the three of you together, your power awakened and we felt it all the way here in Meridian. Even through Aria's bindings."

"What power are you talking about?" Zoha raises her hands in the air in exasperation. "We have no power." She looks at me to urge me to agree but I don't.

"We... we said that spell together, Zo." I say defeatedly. She shakes her head and lets out a hollow laugh.

"How do we know you didn't send them to us?" Zoha bites back and I clutch her arm. No matter the situation, it does seem that Ava and this stranger saved us from the monsters. Riling them up wouldn't be the best move, not since we have no idea where we are now. Mama also named her so trust comes easily.

"I sent Valera your way to save you, child. It won't do well to question my intentions." Ava's face is a blanket of bored expression, but her voice conveys a warning. Valera smiles at Zoha. The gesture was anything but friendly. She remains unfazed with whatever curses my sister is trying to convey with her eyes. Valera points to the book.

"They're cursed beings that have walked this earth for far too long Leeching off of every poor soul they come across. "They take anyone and anything that has even an ounce of magic inside them. Mostly witches, to... feast on." The first sign of hesitation enters her voice.

"So Zafiya—" My hand shoots to my throat, feeling my pulse hammer underneath the skin. The face of my sister fills my mind. That bloodied face that was so determined to free me instead of running away. She should have been saved. Valera might have found her first. I should've—

Ava touches my arm to stop my thoughts from spiraling again. Zoha glares at the contact.

"They won't harm her." *Yet*. I shudder at the thought. "They need her to complete the Triune." Ava's eyes land on Zoha and then to me. "Three sister witches that are rarely seen within any coven. Witches are normally only blessed with one child. Two if the Mother is feeling generous." She leans on the desk and flips through the book still open in front of her. "They're greedy and insatiable. They have gone through great lengths to get their hands on less powerful beings." She juts her chin in our direction. "I would imagine if they have all three of you in their possession, they'd have an enormous supply of magic. Any other witch would pale in comparison and they'd gorge themselves to oblivion." Her words clang in my mind, she couldn't surely be talking about us?

"We're not who you think we are. We're no one." Zoha counters and she pulls me by the wrist to storm out the room. Valera raises a brow as she watches us walk out the room. Ava sighs but lets us go.

Chapter 10

We enter a long hallway, the same dim light of flickering candles illuminate the varnished walls. Tables that are bursting with different blooms of flowers fill the carpeted pathway. I take a second to breathe in their earthy scents. Undeterred, Zoha strides forward without pausing.

I follow shortly as I continue to gape at the details of the manor, the wood walls are tall and they end in a concave ceiling giving it even more height. Aged copper fixtures hold the candles that mixes the earthen air with the smell of wax.

There are too many doors for us to go into, too many options and outcomes for failure, so instead we stride forward in search of the way out.

It doesn't take us long to reach a stairway at the end of the hall. I look back and note that neither Valera and Ava are following us as we bound down the stairs.

"Where do we go?" I ask her but she doesn't answer. She tightens her grip on my wrist.

"I don't know, but we can't stay here." The stairs are expansive, and it meets with another flight of steps on the other side of a flat carpeted landing. Right above it hands a huge crystal chandelier that reflects fractured twinkling lights everywhere.

The joined steps lead down toward an empty hallway where the walls are now made of marbled stone. My eyes sweep over the thick columns and polished floors. The high ceilings make it look more like half a ballroom instead of a den where there are more open archways on each side.

"We have nowhere else to go." As if she didn't hear me at all, Zoha continues walking. Her stubborn streak on full display. "Zo." I call again but she doesn't turn around. Her back is stiff and her chin tilts upward. To any other onlooker, she is the image of strength and pride. I know better though. I see the way she swallows and takes deep steadying breaths every chance she could. She's as nervous and fearful as I am. "We don't know what we're up against and we need to find Zafiya."

"Better listen to your sister Zoha. Now's not the time to throw a tantrum." I bump into Zoha when she stops on the landing. That voice—

Zoha's brows furrow and she lets out a sharp exhale of air. I follow her gaze only to have my heart hammer in my chest as I see a familiar mop of blonde hair. He turns around and familiar smoky eyes meet mine.

"Linc." It was the only thing that I could say at the moment. The shock of seeing him here undoing more of the resolve I had in my system. A small flicker of guilt comes over me as I remember the last time I even thought about him.

He'd stayed behind to try and buy us time from those creatures. Somehow, he knew what he needed to do despite his fear at that moment. The image of him and my mother communicating silently flashes through my head.

He knows a lot more than we do, apparently.

He shoves his hands in his pockets. I look at his stance. To anyone else he would look nonchalant and arrogant, but I know his tells well enough. His tapered jaw ticks and I know he keeps his hands hidden because he would have been tugging on his fingers otherwise.

He searches my eyes with his now—reading me as well as I read him. He's trying to peer into my thoughts. Fearful of my reaction to his presence here.

When I don't look away from him, this bolsters his shaky confidence. He finally starts to walk up the stairs to stand in front of us. Zoha is the first to speak up.

"What are you doing here?"

"We all need to talk." He doesn't look away from me. Zoha leers at him.

"You're working with them?" She asks through gritted teeth.

"You're safe here." He assures me with the gentlest of tones. Zoha scoffs but he ignores her. His eyes soften a fraction as he takes in my countenance. His eyes land on the the cuts on my arms and my bloodied hands. I look at them, too. Inclining my head because I'm numb to the ache they should be giving me. "Let's get you both washed up so we can all sit down and talk."

"I don't understand, Linc." I look up at him, finding my voice in that moment. "How do you know these people? Why are you here?" He averts his gaze and sighs, running unsteady fingers through his blonde locks.

"Settle and we'll explain everything to you." He walks towards the stairs at the opposite end of the landing. He doesn't look back and keeps walking, expecting us to follow wordlessly.

"Are we prisoners here?" Zoha voice shakes and her knuckles grow white from how hard she's fisting her hands, either in fear or with anger. Most likely, both.

Linc throws his head back and lets out a humorless laugh. He turns and looks over his shoulders.

"Far from it, Zo. Need I remind you that my mother also lost her life to get you out of there." His voice breaks on that word. *Also.*

There it was.

The fact so ugly it takes up all the air around us. I look away from him, not needing to see the way his sympathy and pain muddles his grey eyes. Does he know how his mother died? How mine burned the car with both of them still inside it?

"Valera also risked heading straight to Meridian just to get you out of there." The muscle in his cheek twitches, his temper threatening to spill out. We don't respond and he struggles to keep his sneer down.

"We'll make plans to take your sister back from the Comendeti, and we could do without the attitude." His tone levels into boredom. A perfect mask to the ice in his eyes.

The need to defend Zoha takes over and my lips curl over my teeth. His eyes widen. I've never been one to rise to an argument with him and the surprise is evident on his face.

"You're out of line. Our lives are up-ended, we have every right to be on edge." He clears his throat and nods. Temper dissipating into shame. He lets out a shaky breath.

"I know and I'm sorry." He frowns and turns his face away from us. "We *are* on your side and we can start talking and explaining everything if you let us. We can answer those questions, if you listen." Without waiting to hear a response, he continues and this time we follow him.

A similar long hallway welcomes us and Linc stops in front of one door. He leans a shoulder by the door frame.

"You can use this room for now, rest and wash up. The water should heal some of the wounds. Clothes should already be available for you." He opens the door and steps away, "Call me when you're ready." On instinct, my hand goes to my pockets and my heart drops. My phone isn't there and I deflate. My phone held photos, memories of my parents that I need right now. The thought of losing even that small piece of them hollows me out.

"I don't have my phone." My eyes burn with more tears. It feels ridiculous to be looking for my phone at a time like this, but the panic starts bubbling up again. "Linc, my phone I need to—" Linc steps up to me and I trail off. He cups my cheek so I can look at him.

"Shh. I know." He swipes a thumb against the tear that escapes me and he gives me a shaky smile. It was such a sad, broken smile and I want to hold him to me. Maybe he'd help fill this empty space in my chest. "Just call out, I will hear you." He leaves without letting me beg him to stay. Feeling raw, I stand there dazed watching his retreating figure go back down the hall.

I jolt when Zoha takes my hand and pulls me inside the room.

A large bed with four wooden posts sit in the middle of the room. The clean white linen sheets beckon to me. Without caring about the dirt and blood still caking on my clothes and skin, I climb between the sheets. Letting the blanket shut everything out. The world is too bright, moving too quickly and leaving behind a reality I once resented for its simplicity.

With nothing else to hold on to but my weary body, I let myself empty out the tears threatening to drown me in tides.

Chapter 11

I hadn't allowed myself to look in the mirror. Until now. My eyes are swollen from crying. There are angry bruises on my cheeks and forehead. They bring back very vivid memories of my body slamming inside the car. I shiver and grip the edge of the sink.

My hair, damp from the bath I had soaked in for God knows how long, falls over my face. Zoha is standing beside me while she combs through her own and ties it into a tight braid. We stand there silently; she doesn't speak until she puts the brush down and she's satisfied with her work.

"No better time than now to get those answers." I couldn't agree more. So, I lift my face toward the ceiling and call Linc's name. Feeling ridiculous but oddly trusting he'll actually hear me

Not a second later, a knock rasps on our door. We both jump at the sound.

We pad our way to the door and I take a shaky breath before opening it. Linc is leaning on the door frame with a small smirk on his lips. His white button-down shirt open enough to expose the pale skin of his chest. He sends me a sheepish grin and he doesn't even need to speak for me to know what he's thinking.

See that, I told you I'd hear you. Not finding the strength to take his bait, I walk into the hallway with Zoha close behind me. I briefly glance at Linc as his boots make muted thumps on the carpet while he matches his strides with mine.

We continue down the stairs and Linc strides past me to lead us toward the large expanse of the den at the bottom. He lifts his left hand to gesture towards the first open archway and we walk through it with mostly silent steps.

My nerves are singing inside me again. Buzzing with anticipation. Whatever truths we are about to be faced with would change the course of our lives. Be it for better or for worse, that's yet to be seen.

We enter an expansive dining area. One filled with bright hanging lights. The large wooden table in the middle of the room is already filled with food and the smell makes my mouth water. Ava is sitting at the head of the table, a wine glass swirling in one hand. Valera is on her right.

Linc takes the seat beside Valera and so the only place we could sit would be beside Ava. Zoha takes the closest seat next to her putting me farthest from the rest of them.

Ava's eyes sharpens a bit as she watches Zoha's protective stance, but she doesn't comment on it. Instead, she sits still sipping from her wine glass. Valera barely glances our way before she starts shoveling green beans and meat on her plate.

"You said we'll talk, so talk." Zoha's tone makes me wince. Although I can tell she's trying to be far more subdued than earlier, I doubt everyone else would notice.

She's always been unable to dull the sharpness of her own tongue.

I shift in my seat when Ava puts her glass down and crosses her hands in front of her. My veins feel electric with the emotions coursing through me, so I can't help but speak up. Partially to ensure Ava couldn't say anything in response to Zoha's tone—which would make matters worse and we haven't even started talking.

"You said we're witches. I had suspicions..." I clear my throat when my voice breaks but I keep my gaze leveled, not wanting to meet my sister's when I say, "I know now that our mother is one." I meet Ava's gaze and she nods.

"She was my sister." The use of the past tense is not lost on me. I wince and crumple into my chair, winded. "Not blood sisters." Ava's voice is softer seeing the physical reaction I have when talking about my mother. "We were in the same coven, trained together and practiced under the same mentors. We were friends." Her green eyes dart between Zoha and me. Her expression somber—there's respect there. Admiration. "Your mother was one of the most skilled witches that our coven had ever taken in." She brings out an old book and opens it to an earmarked page before handing it to us. On it is a picture of twelve women all dressed in long white robes. They all looked so young, barely out of leading strings, I bet. Despite being posed in what looks like a formal class photo, each one of them were laughing.

I spot my mother instantly. Her round face was beaming at the camera, while her arm was wrapped around a much younger Ava. Her hair was cropped short, almost up to her chin, it was frazzled and windblown. She looked so care-free, so untouched by worries.

I look closely at her now, at the young woman who would grow up to be our mother. She looked happy and loved. She was accepted and was part of what looks like a very close coven. Why turn away from all of this?

"She looks just like you." Ava says to Zoha and I see the way my sister stiffens further at the statement. Out of all three of us, Zoha was the one who looked most like my mother. She used to love that fact a lot but I've noticed her conscious attempts at making the resemblance less noticeable. A change here and there, nothing grand but the thought behind it is not lost on me. When Zoha doesn't respond, Ava seems to have sensed her misstep and continues. "We were friends early on into our training, found our way together."

"I don't understand. If you were so close that you call her you sister, why don't we know you?" I had not meant it as an accusation. If they were friends then I'm sure, we would have heard about her from our mother at least once.

"We lost contact after her exile from the coven." Zoha frowns and speaks up.

"Exiled?" Ava nods. Her eyes fall towards the wooden table as if reading the pattern of the wood. Finding the story of their history there.

"There are certain covenants to uphold as a witch. Rules that are the very foundation of our sisterhood. The failure to uphold them results in a witch's exile." Valera cuts in when Ava's voice dips a little low.

"They are banished and removed from the protection of the coven and its sisterhood." Valera explains now. She's pushing around the food on her plate as if the topic made her lose any of the appetite she had been nursing just moments ago.

"Why was she exiled?" I ask, my voice small.

"Witches are not allowed to marry outside of the wiccan line." Valera looks at Ava and her expression dims a bit more.

"The need to keep the magic within pure bloodlines was a covenant all witches and magus have taken with each other." Ava grimaces showing exactly how she feels over that rule. "Every suitable maiden in a coven is offered to wed a magus—a powerful male sorcerer—for them to wed and be fruitful. This was agreed upon to ensure our kind do not go extinct."

"And that *offer* is just a euphemism for forced." Valera grumbles and Ava's eyes darken.

"That's barbaric." Zoha mutters under her breath. I don't even bother apologizing for her choice of words because I agree. "You're telling me, witches are nothing but breeding mares?" The fire in her eyes burn bright as she directs them to Ava.

"As the new high priestess, I'm working on overruling this covenant but it takes time to change people who have been set on their ways since the dawn of time." She rubs her temples and lets out a long breath. "Aria was a visionary and a contrarian. She never wanted to bear children and wanted nothing to do with the magus picked for her." Ava looks at us again, observant. A small smile reaches her lips before she looks away. "Maybe now I realize she just did not want to bear *his* children, but she was more than happy to bear Gab's"

"You knew our father, too?" This makes my skin clammy. Their secrets are piling on top of each other, the fact remains true now. Our parents lived a life so apart from our reality, do we even know who they really are?

"Gab was our custodian for Meridian Manor—our hearth. This is where members of our coven hold our rituals and witches can choose to live here." Ava raises her hands and gestures toward the large expanse of the manor. "It has housed generations upon generations of witches. This is where we teach and nurture the young ones, this—" She catches herself in her digression and brings the conversation back to our father.

She takes the book again from us and flips it to a different page. One where the same twelve witches were out on the field of flowers. My mother was wearing white trouser pants, her raven hair was longer now but it was still wild around her face. Ava points to a figure far off into the background, it was a blurred silhouette of a man barely visible to the camera.

"There was connection between them, one so strong that all our sisters felt it. At first, we just teased them about it, really. In a house full of young women, it was not unlikely for one of them to be curious of the handsome custodian." Ava smiles down at the photo, seeing so much more than we could. Part of me is jealous now, for her to have shared so much with my parents. "Gab tried to stay away, but Aria was persistent. He was helpless against her schemes and they just…fell." She turns away from the page then, "It was against the rules, of course. She was a witch in line to be wed to a magus and he was human."

"What happened then?" Zoha's sharp tone has dulled into a breathless wonder, forgetting her animosity. She is as lost and as captured as I am hearing about our parents. It makes sense now that our parents never talked about how they met, even if we begged and begged for the story. It had never occurred to me that they've been keeping it from us out of necessity.

"I helped them keep it a secret. Stood guard for anyone who might pass by and see them together. It hadn't been easy for the two of them, having to hide and sneak around but they tried their best." Ava sighs and rubs her arms with her hands. Tears burn my eyes again and my throat feels tight.

"On the day set for her wedding with the magus, they had a plan to break out of the wards to escape. They were caught soon after and were exiled immediately. I know it wouldn't have been easy. Gab had no family outside Meridian and Aria was taken here as a child when both her parents died. They seemed happy enough to accept the punishment despite what trials they would have to face together out there. They never really looked back." My parents have always seemed so content even as we struggled in our finances.

Leave it to my parents to have some grand tragic love story. It's hard for me to not believe any of it. They must have suffered greater troubles even before we were born but had stayed with each other. The memory of how they danced in our humble kitchen holding each other makes my heart yearn. I bite the inside of my cheek to keep from falling into a heap of tears.

"We had not known about her daughters until more than a decade after they left. When the three of you gradually grew up and your magic grew with you, we felt it in the air. Your powers. The signal was strong enough for your keepers to find you." She juts her chin toward Linc.

"Keepers?" I ask.

"Keepers are witches' guardians. They are born into their roles. The sacred affiliation goes back generations and centuries. Valera is mine and the Bensons are yours."

My eyes slide to Linc. He's watching me, gauging my reaction over the discovery. My hand shoots up to the necklace that was under my sweater, the moonstone. For protection, he said.

"So, all this time, you knew where we were and you let those *things* find us." Zoha's voice laces with enough venom that I find myself impressed that Ava didn't even wince.

"I am the high priestess and even so, I could not remove the decree on her exile. It didn't seem like your mother wanted to, either. Dianne spoke to me years ago when the Comendeti almost found you. She told me Aria used a protection spell and had managed to escape by driving away with Gab and you three in the car. They thought it was enough and so asked me not to step in." The sudden speed chase that started my theories about mama being a witch.

That was the first time they had attacked and we had retreated. Moved away on the off chance they would lose our trail. I close my eyes against the guilt that surfaces when I remember how I had resented Mama over this move.

"Through Dianne, we discovered that your mother bound your powers. Kept them muffled and dormant as long as she could. Deterring any way for us or the Comendeti to detect you. Your parents are exiled but you are still children of the coven and we would have protected you if she had let us." Zoha shakes her head. Not believing this tall tale unwinding in front of us.

"That's impossible. I can accept that my mother's a witch, but *I* am not." Ava raises one brow and leans back on her chair to level my sister with a hard gaze.

"The thrumming in your veins, the vibrations that you feel under your skin." She looks at me, too. Knowing full well I could feel it buzzing. "With your mother gone, her bindings no longer have their effects on you. Whatever she's been keeping down is.... unfurling."

I look at my fingers, feeling them pulse as if in rhythm with my thundering heart. Whatever humming in my nerves I felt earlier was not the adrenaline I thought it was. It hadn't dissipated since. I know exactly what Ava means now.

Something—something deep down—is waking up.

Chapter 12

"I don't want to hear any of this." Zoha stands up in a rush. Her chair falls back from the motion. She whirls on her feet and leaves the room in a huff.

I keep my eyes on her until she disappears towards the stairs. I let out a sigh and scrub my face with my hands. Wishing away the chills on my skin.

This is all too much and I could feel a headache starting to build up. I look up to see Linc still watching me over the rim of his glass, wary and guarded.

"You knew, all this time. You *knew*." It isn't a question, but he nods. "Why couldn't you tell me?" He regards me carefully and he releases a long breath.

"Your mother made a deal with mine. We were to keep this secret, this binding, for her. And in turn, she wouldn't turn us away." He spears a green bean with his fork but doesn't bring it to his lips.

He stares at it, eyes seeing something else.

"It would be a disgrace for keepers if they are turned away by their charge, we would lose our status and powers." The image of my gentle and warm-spirited mother flashes in my head again.

I don't recognize the woman they're all describing in their stories, this *witch*. But somehow, I could see how these are things that she would do. Not doubting that my mother would be protective and powerful. But to go through such lengths just to keep part of our identity a secret?

"I have a headache." I murmur, not to anyone in particular. I stand up slowly and meet Ava's gaze evenly.

"How do we get Zafiya back?"

"We will use your power to track her and get her back. Valera needs to visit other covens. We need as much information about the Comendeti's current whereabouts. We start tomorrow." Her shoulders lift a little and her back goes even more rigid. She is tense, waiting for me to respond or to decline her offer. As if the statement presented me the option to deny them and leave instead.

I pull my shoulders back and nod in their direction before leaving. Burying what we've uncovered and accepting these events as some fever-dream would not be an option.

I'll do whatever I have to do to bring Zafiya back.

Instead of heading towards the bedroom upstairs, I head to the main door. I'm surprised when the thick wooden door opens without much struggle. The door barely registering any weight as it willingly lets me out.

Once I exit the manor, the night chill bites into my cheeks. I wrap my hands around myself in an attempt to chase away the cold. I crane my neck to look up.

Wired and polished arch windows grace the bricks. The Manor was what one would closely call a castle, albeit a smaller, more humble version. It has long spindling towers on each side, with the tips almost hiding in the wispy clouds. My jaw slackens as my eyes trail its height.

The front door has massive wooden oak doors with metal handles. Torches light its perimeter casting it in a glow that spoke of old lore and history. It looked untouched by time and yet so very *aged*. I smile as my eyes find strong thick vines trailing one side of the manor. Much like the hallways inside, nature softens the harshness and coldness of the place.

I peek over the looming windows to see the lights inside flicker, I wait a beat to see if anyone would peek out. I could almost imagine my mother pushing herself up on those glass panes to peek at the forest just waiting right outside the manor's doorstep.

She had lived a life here that we had no idea existed. She had molded her ideals and her foundation within these walls and how odd that we're here now without her. It makes the place feel full of her and yet so empty.

There are soil plots and a fenced garden right by the walls of the building. Had my father been tending to those plants when my mother saw him through those windows? Had they stolen glances and shy smiles over those glass panes while their relationship flourished under secrecy.

If they'd known how their lives would have turned out, would they still have run away that day? If they knew they would both end up dead leaving three daughters in the dark, would they still do it? With that sobering thought, I turn away from the manor.

Directly in front of me, a path opens up. It leads from the front steps illuminated by floating orbs. I chose not to think too hard on the rationality of those small pyres floating on thin air. This world is strange and disconcerting, I don't even know if I'm still in the same country.

I walk down the path toward a thickening forest. I'm careful to look back at the manor every now and then, making sure that I could still see it on the horizon. I know full well how easy it would be for me to get lost in the night. I'd rather not do that now.

I find a dry patch of ground near an oak tree and sit down. I lean my back against the rough bark. I wish I had more tears to drain myself of whatever gloom is suffocating me. Instead, all I do is tilt my head back and watch the moon disappear behind wispy walls of clouds.

Magic and witches.

Things that I have read upon and researched before, things I had hoped to be real and obsessed over. I had fallen in love with magic then. I should feel excited and curious that this whole other world is opening up, shouldn't I?

Shouldn't I feel *something* just knowing I have powers inside me that I can use? That I can use these powers to save my sister and to find her.

I raise my hands above my head to watch it block out the moonlight. Such thin hands that I have used to tend to gardens and to cook. Hands that failed to reach out to touch my mother for the last time. I turn them over and I see the scars on my palms.

A permanent reminder of the time I had wished my father to hang on a little longer. When I prayed a little too hard and had bled all over his skin just to will him awake but nothing happened. If mama hadn't kept this a secret would I have known what to do to save him?

The way they spoke of my mother's death was sign enough for me to know that no magic I possess could bring her back. If anyone, the high priestess would have already offered by now.

"Say the word and I will come get you the moon." I jump and a small sound escapes me. I withdraw my hands to myself and curl closer towards the tree, the rough bark biting into my back.

"It's me." Linc steps out of the shadows and angles his head my way.

"Can you really do that…" I trail off and look back up at the moon which is in clear view. "With your powers, I mean." He sits down next to me on the ground. I note how he puts distance between our shoulders.

"No, I don't think anyone can."

"What do you do then?" I don't meet his eyes. Happy to keep my gaze on the moon peeking behind the clouds. It's easier to talk to him without seeing that haunted pity in his eyes.

"My powers are meant to protect you from harm, mostly." He waves his hand in front of him and a blue sheet appears in front of us. It glows softly in the night. It illuminates us both and I stare at it in awe. He throws a rock towards it and it bounces off, rippling the sheet in the process. "A shield." As quickly as it appeared, it winks away at his will.

If they had shields, wouldn't they have been able to shield us from the Comendeti? He knows me well enough to answer without needing to hear me ask this aloud.

"Mom was injured before she could reach us. She'd been scouting the town that day. We've been doing that since your dad died " His tone is quiet, subdued. Guilty.

"So that's the real reason why you found us again after we moved." A cheap shot, I know. Whatever role he had to play in this life, it looks like he didn't have much of a choice but I wanted to lash out.

"We knew that Zafiya's eighteenth birthday would have heightened her powers. Completing the Triune." His choice to not step up and answer my accusations is confirmation enough for me. He'd been duty bound as my keeper, not as my friend. He wraps his arms around his knees. "We had to make sure that if Comendeti started sniffing around we'd be able to get you out. She couldn't fight them off and I couldn't..." He shakes his head, clearing away what memories haunts him too. "They got away from me and had already tracked you down, so I had to call for Valera to take you and your sisters away from the wreck."

"Couldn't you have done that?" I could feel him studying my face now, trying to find a hint of anger and blame. He would have found none. As broken as I am inside, I don't think I could ever blame him for whatever happened.

"No, Valera is much more skilled than I am. Mom was still training me with shadow jumping but we couldn't do much under the guise of normalcy. We also had to tamper our magic to keep any trackers from sensing you in the new neighborhood so we weren't—" He paused and clenched his jaw. "We didn't have enough power to take them on, to protect you." I turn away from him and sigh.

I don't blame him or his mother for whatever happened. Dianne had lost her life trying to keep them from finding us and her warning had allowed us to at least get to safety before the Comendeti arrived. If she hadn't warned us we had been caught unaware and we would have all probably lost our lives then.

The headache I've been nursing blooms into a full-on migraine and I sigh, exhausted. Linc reaches inside his pocket and he produces a packet of painkillers. The ones I always had with me because I get headaches so often. I smile at that. Of course, he would have that with him.

I take the pill and tuck it into my own pocket, uncertain if such a small thing could take away my pain.

"I wish I was dreaming, Linc. I wish I can wake up and find both of them in their beds tomorrow." His hands links with mine, reluctant at first but grows firm when I don't pull back. He doesn't say anything, and his silence is enough to keep me from tumbling into the dark depths of my mind.

I'm teetering on the edge of madness. Trying to grasp the realities I face: my mother's gone. Zafiya's survival relies on our ability to use our untapped, untrained, and unknown powers.

Yes, I'm pretty sure I'm going to go mad.

Chapter 13

Find her.

Mama's voice echoes in my mind and I wake with a startled gasp. My sleep had been empty and dreamless, but I had tossed and turned enough times for me to work up a sweat. The bed was so soft, it was unlike anything I have ever slept on and somehow that just reminds me that we're no longer at home.

Zoha slept like a rock, barely moving in the night. I groan at the light seeping through the curtains. I slip out of bed and into the bathroom. I need to brush my teeth, hoping the bitter taste in my mouth would leave. I want to throw up but come up empty, my stomach nothing but a gaping hole. When was the last time I had even eaten anything? Zafiya's birthday, I was supposed to have cake but we hadn't even gotten that far before—

I bend down to splash my face with cold water. Willing away the nausea and the thoughts. I strip away my clothes to change into a pair of gray sweatshirt and pants.

The bruises blooming on my ribs are healing far too fast than they should have. I throw the clothes on and opt out of doing anything with my hair aside from using my fingers to smoothen it out.

I walk back to the room only to find Zoha still in bed, she had pulled the covers over her head blocking the rest of the world out. Her pain is my pain, too. Despite that, I don't know how I could comfort her—I don't think I could.

If I were to function under these pretenses, I need to steel myself against what is haunting me. I don't have the luxury and Zaf needs me. This thought guns me with determination.

I leave the room without saying a word to my grieving sister. I bound towards the front door only to find Ava already waiting for me there. She'd exchanged her robe for what I could only assume as her work clothes.

White linen pants and a loose muslin shirt. Her chocolate hair pulled in a single braid behind her. She looks more ready for a sunny stroll instead of training for witchcraft.

"Expecting a pointy witch's hat?" I school my expression immediately.

"No, that's not…" I trail off when she smiles. She starts towards the path away from the house. I follow closely behind, watching the braid sway behind her.

"What are we going to do?" Ava continues to walk down the same path I took that led me to the clearing with flat lush grass last night. Valera and Linc are already waiting for us there. Linc is leaning against the same tree we sat under yesterday. His hair casts a shadow over his eyes.

He kicks a rock with the heel of his boots when I come closer. He spares me a moment's glance—the rock seemingly more interesting than I am. Valera is lounging on the ground a few feet from him under the shade. She's wearing a razorback top that exposes her midriff. Her arms exposed and tanned. She has lines of what appears to be swirls and lines of an old language straight down the back of her arms. Her white hair is loose and blowing in the wind.

Something lodges in my throat then. Seeing them in regular clothes does not make them look like they'd be as powerful as the beings that took my sister. We might as well have been a group of friends going out to a nondescript brunch.

Will their training be enough so that I can get my sister in time? I'm resigning my sister's fate in their hands and yet–

Valera flicks her wrists and the same smoke that had absorbed my form now brings out a thick book beside her. Ava crosses her legs and sits beside the book. I take a seat and look up at where Linc chooses to stay watching us.

"We could have done this inside but given your lack of practice... being closer to nature would be the best way to access your magic." Ava reaches out for my hands and turns them to face skyward. "Magic exists everywhere, seen and unseen. As a witch you will act as a conduit, to summon and call upon these forces to listen to your bidding." She hovers her hands on mine, barely touching skin. Yet, heat and vibrations radiate from them. "Your blood is humming." She whispers almost to herself.

I take a sharp breath as I feel hands crawl under my skin, surveying and roaming the surface. I have to stare at

Ava to know that her hands aren't the ones I'm feeling—or at least not anything physical that I could see.

Her warmth seeps into me, sending shivers as I feel phantom limbs dig deeper. Something inside my chest squirms at the attention, it's a foreign weight that I do not recognize. She tries to touch it and I feel her hands grow warmer against my skin. The heat coming from Ava's hands reminds me of Mama, how she always had those warm healing hands. Hands that are as hot as the fire—

The image of my mother's face before she was engulfed by flames sweeps through my mind. Dread grabs me by the throat and everything goes cold. I could sense metal gates clamping down my mind. I'm inside my head, searching for any other memory of her, any other moment to see of my vibrant mother.

I run towards the different packets of my brain, but she's gone. I see nothing but her death and the cold suffocation that comes with it. I want to scream for her, to find her. There was nothing, nothing but her blood. Her flames.

Get me out. Get me out!

There was nowhere inside my mind for me to hide from the images. So visceral. So clear. They hone in on her hands. The ones that hung limp around her even as she swayed in that car seat.

I scream. I try to pry myself out of the torture that my brain is subjecting me to. The cloud that looms behind my eyes would not clear. The memory of my mother's last moments amplifies. A torturous movie that's making my ears ring.

Hands grip my arms and shake me. Wet streaks stain my cheeks and I try to take in deeper breaths. The air is not reaching my lungs fully. The smell of soot is so strong. It's laced with something else. Something strong and pungent—flesh.

I could smell her burning flesh. Bile burns my throat at the image.

"Zelle, release it." Ava's voice booms in my head and I realize she's trapped in my mind with me.

In my head I see her now—her green eyes bearing the same clouds that I can feel on my own. Whatever cage that crashed on us both breaks loose and I'm back in the forest with her.

Her eyes clear out and she watches me come back to my body. She has a sheen on her forehead which is the only evidence of any strain of our activity.

The arms that are holding and shaking me are Linc's. He's breathing hard and my weight is on him. Not having the energy to fight it, I sink further into his chest. Grateful for any warmth that he could pass through my quickly numbing body.

"What happened?" He asks Ava, alarmed. Ava stands up and takes a step back swaying slightly. Valera is quick to catch her by the elbow, taking a protective stance.

"Normally this is how we show young witches how to find their core." Ava says, breathless. "We do this to show you where it is by following the path to where your magic is strongest but your shields seized up. I couldn't break through it." Valera takes a step closer toward her and my eyes slide to the keeper as she watches me.

"My core?"

"Yes, a witch's core stabilizes your magic. Allows you control over your powers and to let energy course through you as a conduit to fuel such magic. It would usually be easy for you to open up and find out…" Ava trails off.

"I didn't do anything." I tell her, as if to ease the cold expression on Valera's face. I look at Ava and she is more winded than I had initially thought to be. Valera has an arm around her and a sneer directed at me.

"No, not intentionally." Ava presses on as if to tell Valera to stand down. "Something triggered your emotions and caused your powers to act on instinct to protect you." In turn, keeping Ava hostage with me as I went through the whirlwind of my grief tenfold. I don't have to say this when she nods, knowing exactly where my thought turned toward.

"Well, way to make our first lesson a lot more interesting, Zelle." Linc's lighthearted attempt to cut the tension is feeble but welcome.

Chapter 14

"Again." Ava murmurs and I raise my hands to the sky. We've been trying to let her back in without me caging us in my head so she can help me find the path to my core.

Each time she tries though, my mind shuts us both inside. Refusing to let her near whatever it was that my mind is guarding. We end up reliving my mother's death in vivid detail. I had lost to nausea at one point and had gotten sick. Sweat dampens my sweatshirt and it clings to my skin.

We also tried scrying with the use of a crystal quartz pendulum over a map. She was hoping that some innate part of my magic would come out and it would help me with it but nothing. The hum in my veins have not relented though, but my limbs hurt. My mind feels like a liquid flame is burning me from the inside.

When Ava took breaks, Valera stepped in for spell-casting lessons. We tried various spells and had me repeat them but the air around us remained still. Although, I much rather enjoyed spells. I loved the cadence and the rhythm that came from speaking them out loud. They feel right on my lips and yet I'm starting to feel like we're getting further from the goal and we were losing such precious time.

"It's not working." I grunt and fall on the ground, weary and tired. My legs screaming for relief.

"You're putting up more walls when you should be pulling them down." Ava crosses her arms over her chest, obviously perturbed. Her braid has started to unravel and loose brown hairs are sticking out which makes her look younger. Albeit, weary.

Witches do not simply conjure powers but amplify the ones around us. We can tap into energies and life. Ava had told me using our magic always came with a cost. It surges through our bodies and the physical limitations are often evident.

Hence, why my body feels like jelly after hours of trying to do *anything*.

"I'm not even sure how I do that, you're being awfully vague about this." I mumble under my breath, my attitude slipping through. Defensive urges coming up. I've been trying so hard. Following whatever instruction they ask me to, they tell me to breathe in, I suck in air like a good little *witch*.

If anyone here knew how much I needed to use whatever power I could to find my sister, it was me. Linc puts a hand on my shoulder, a comfort and a deterrent for my temper.

"Maybe we should try again tomorrow. She's worn out, she won't be able to do much in her state now." As much as those observations sting, I couldn't even bring enough energy to argue. Valera nods, agreeing. She places a hand on Ava's arm and shadow jumps the both of them out of the woods back to the manor.

I have to walk and I groan. Boo, Linc can't do that yet.

"Can you stand?" I let out a breathy laugh. Isn't it pathetic how I woke up believing I could actually save my sister today? I can't even stand on my own two feet after a couple of hours of training.

"No." I admit and without waiting a beat Linc hoists me up. I wrap my arms around his shoulder to balance myself. He grips me by the waist to keep me from falling forward. "I don't think I can do it."

"A day. It's been a day, Z." We start walking back to the manor. As we get closer, the more bitter my mouth tasted. The disappointment too strong for me to swallow.

"I don't think I have much of those left, Linc. It's not like I can have this movie montage of myself becoming the most powerful witch." He laughs a little at my reference, but his face turns serious.

"Just survive the days, Zelle. Survive them with all you've got and you will get where you need to." He pulls me closer against his body when I started to slip further. "Work with Ava. Rest. You cannot do it all in one day, Z." I don't tell him that it's not a matter of wanting, but *needing* to get there. The last time I saw Zafiya she'd been injured. Would the Comendeti even dress her wounds? Would they be making more instead?

The doors to the manor swing open and Zoha peeks out. When she sees me, she starts running towards us. Almost shoving Linc away so she can duck under my arm to help me up.

"What the hell did they do to you?" Her voice is sharp and her eyes shoot daggers toward Linc.

"We tried tapping into my...powers so we can find Zaf." Her brows bunch together and she looks down at me. Before she could say anything else I counter. "Do you have any other ideas on how else we can find her?" She flinches at my tone. A flush creep up her cheeks and her eyes mists.

I mentally berate myself for being snappy.

"I'm sorry, Zo. I didn't—I'm just tired." She looks away and helps me cross the threshold towards our room without another word. She helps me into the bath that she must have already prepared knowing we were coming back.

The water is milky and warm. I sink with a sigh as my entire body relaxes into the water. I dip my head under. The sweat and the pain seeping out of me in waves. When I come up for air, Zoha pulls a chair behind me.

"Sit up, I'll help wash your hair." I take a second before I oblige and her hands find purchase on my scalp, scrubbing away the day's work and I groan. "Thank you." She murmurs.

Knowing better than to turn around and face her, I stay still. She's put herself behind me for a reason. Whatever she is planning to say, she doesn't want me looking at her when she does.

"I know you're trying while I'm on my ass crying about it but—" Her voice breaks. I squeeze my eyes against the sting of tears brought on by just that sound.

"You don't have to thank me for anything, Zo." I pull my knees up to my chest and rest my chin on them, cradling myself. "It's my fault they were able to get her, you know." Zoha's hands never stop working. She moves on to rinsing my hair with more warm water. "If I had told her to run and find you, those Comendeti assholes would have gotten to me instead."

"And you think that would make the situation any better?"

"I don't know, but at least she would be safe here. If anyone, our little warrior would have been able to save both of us without this much trouble."

"If you're going by that logic, then it would have been best if *I* was taken." My words fail me, my mind tired. The bitterness in her voice is sharp on my tongue but I don't refute her.

I sink back into the water and the next time I come up for air my sister isn't in the room anymore.

Chapter 15

I awoke with a jolt and the room is still dark. My skin slick with sweat and my breath shallow. I couldn't recall if I had dreamed, only that I felt like someone had punched a hole through my chest.

I swallow the lump in my throat. Zoha was on the other side of the bed with her back turned to me and I resist the urge to sink into her. Not knowing how I could ask her to ease my grief over hers.

She and I had not always been expressive in our affection, that was all Zaf. What Zoha and I have is sheer love wrapped in unbreakable—albeit very cold—loyalty towards each other. Her absence in the last two years makes it even harder to break this boundary. So instead, I choose the coward's way and slip on a thick robe so I can make my way out of the room.

The corridor is as dim as the night that we came here. Only lit by flickering candles. The carpet is soft under my feet.

There's a hum in the air that pricks my skin while I walk towards the staircase. My fingers run over the cold wood railing. Weary. I'm so tired that my head feels like it's swimming in water and my legs drag over each other. The front door was left open and without hesitation, I slip out.

The night is silent. I look up towards the moon covered by the clouds. It brings a muted light to my surroundings. Making the trees look like they were lined with silver. The chilly air blows over me and I shudder. I rub my hands over my exposed arms attempting to warm them against the cold. The leaves rustle along with the wind.

I stop for a second straining my ears against the air. I could have sworn a soft melody is building into a crescendo around me. For a moment, if I refuse to let my mind think of where I was and why, a kernel of peace wiggled its way into my system.

I continue down the dirt path, away from the house and deeper into the woods. I hum along the faint melody ringing in the night and my steps feel light against the grass.

I've been walking for much longer than I thought. I look over my shoulder and I could no longer see the manor. A trickle of anxiety makes its way into my system but I shake it off.

I'm sure I'll find my way somehow.

I continue walking past the path. I step over rocks, dodging thicker plants until I find an opening.

I'm welcomed to the sight of an expansive brook with streams wide and roaring. The fierce current had slowly eaten away at the land encasing it and had grown wider and wider. The water roars and splashes over jagged rocks and jutting land. I tentatively make my way closer, carefully dipping my toes in the chilly water.

I feel the current then, steady and forceful against my skin. Goosebumps rise along my arms as the chill works its way into my body. Through the moonlight's shy light, I see that the terrain is uneven. There are small streams and craters of deeper pools—separate dipping areas where the water goes eerily calm in its depth.

The water invites me. Such a luminous invitation, if I may say so. I climb down the rocks, nearly stumbling over. I strip the robe I wore around my shoulder that had grown damp with humidity and sweat and toss it towards the land.

Foolish as it is, I make my way to one of those cratered areas and I continue to strip away my clothes for a dip. As my skin breaks through the surface the water ripples, it shines silver under the stars. I slowly sink the rest of my body into the water, the chill suddenly chased away by a warmth from the depths.

Underneath the surface, I feel lighter. The chill that had clung to my limbs flows out of me and through the current around me.

The notion of anyone seeing me naked in a pool of water makes me laugh a little. If someone ends up calling me insane, I probably won't argue. Zaf would have joined me or rather would have been the first to jump in without testing the water's temperature.

She loved the ocean. We used to drive hours out over holiday weekends so our family could take trips to the beach. Zafiya would barely be able to sleep the night before in her anticipation. Zoha and I would have to force her into bed just to get her to shut her eyes.

She'd end up sleeping the entire drive there, alternating between sleeping on my shoulder or Zoha's. Mama would pack us snacks and lunches to eat by the water. Zafiya would scarf hers down in a minute and run still half clothed to meet the salty waves with her laughter.

I break the surface and push the hair away from my eyes. I take another deep breath and dip my head underwater fully expecting to be welcomed by the dark. Instead, I see fiery red hair. My mind goes alert. My heart lurches when I see her silhouette in the water. Her yellow dress is like a beacon in the dark.

"Zafiya." I call out and she turns to look at me, her eyes widening when she recognizes me. The alarm in her face is evident as she takes a moment to look around her surroundings.

I reach my hand over to her, but I know she's not in front of me. This was a vision, a projection of her in my head. Have I completely lost my mind? Is this a hallucination? But she turns because she can see me, too.

She leans closer and when I attempt to touch her again the image wavers along with the ripples of the water.

"Zelle!" She sobs my name. "What's going on? What's happening? Why are they keeping me here? Where are you?" She shoots me the questions as she wraps her arms around herself. I cringe at her panic. Of course, she has no idea what's happening. I barely have a clue myself and the urge to comfort her floors me. She's wearing the same yellow dress from the last time I saw her.

She must be so cold now. Soot and dirt are caked on her nails and her hair is a matted mess on top of her hair.

She's not being cared for, that much was evident, but she is alive. It's only been two days but the uncertainty had been like a dead weight in my chest.

I welcome the relief.

"Zaf, we don't have time. I'll explain later, I promise." She takes a breath and nods. The promise of an explanation was enough to calm her for a moment. I try to look around her but the vision is dim. "Where are you? Where are they keeping you?" My voice grows frantic as I see her shift her glance.

"I don't know. I just woke up here after–" She pauses and stiffens. Her eyes grow wide as she looks back at me.

"You need to go." She whispers, her voice steady. "I think that's them." She warns me, her hands clutch tightly into fists. She huddles in a corner and crouches making herself smaller but her whispered voice still remains strong. "They're looking for you. They've been asking me to call for you. To trace you because they don't know if you were alive and where you could be hiding. And now—" She trails off when the water ripples, the surface disturbed. My skin prickles in awareness, something is in the water with me now.

She turns to me as if sensing the same thing I am. She grits her teeth.

"They're coming. I love you, please go *now*." Zafiya's image disappears in a blink, the water now suffocating me. I rear my head back and out of the water gasping for air.

I sense another movement from behind me, causing the water to shift. I whirl and see white fog rolling in towards me. My limbs ache but I trudge back towards land as fast as I could. I pull myself into muddy soil where my robe and clothes are and I quickly put it on. Keeping an eye on the fog that's inching closer and closer. The same melody that led me here is so much stronger in the air.

I was lured to it. It had wanted me to come here. To trap me.

It's almost at my back so I run into the woods. My skin breaks when it catches on the twigs and branches. The sharp small cuts drawing blood but I don't stop until I see the path back to the manor.

I stumble and fall hard on my knees. I shriek. Bone meets sharp rocks. Stars bloom in my vision. I grit my teeth and force myself to get up on shaking limbs.

I take two steps toward the path, but the fog reaches me first. When it makes contact with my skin I scream. Pain shoots through my arm—sharp and agonizing. Searing cold and bites into my limb. It feels like claws are digging into my wrist pulling my entire body into the fog to consume me.

The claws have made their way up unto my elbow and I can't pull away or move. I scream for help. I can't see what has me in their hold. There's only ice and hurt. Nothing but pain, pain, pain.

Help, someone. Help!

I try to scramble away, my free hand finding purchase on the damp ground and I crawl. Breaking my nails as I grip rocks to pull me away from the fog. Where do I go?

A hand grabs me by the shoulders and pulls me away from the fog. My back hits warmth, flesh under soft cotton. They drag me towards the clearing for the path.

I hear a hiss come from the fog and the sharp chill on my arm grows worse and I scream. My skin is being torn from my limb and whatever has its claws on me does not want to let me go. It's going to tear my arm clean off.

Whoever had grabbed me keeps pulling despite my screaming until we heave and fall on the path. I scramble back as the fog threatens to come close, but it doesn't. An unseen barrier causes the fog to hiss and reel back. To disappear.

"Where the hell have you been?" Linc's ragged voice echoes in the air. We are on the ground and I was practically laying on top of him now. I'm shivering and his warmth could barely chase away the cold.

His arms tighten around me and his eyes rake over me to check for injuries He curses loudly when he sees all the cuts on my face. All thanks to my rush through the forest.

"My hand." I croak. I couldn't find the strength to lift it and look. Linc shakes his head, his expression dark. He stands up, lifting me up into his arms. I lift my eyes to him as he runs toward the Meridian.

"We need to go. Now." He doesn't even strain over my weight and I snuggle closer to his warmth. I slip away into inky unconsciousness.

Chapter 16

Ice pricks my skin. My hand is breaking from within. The flesh darkens and I watch it turn into a sickening purple. I open my mouth to scream but I don't hear my voice over the sound of my bones splintering.

My flesh is falling off and my nerves are on fire. I want to scream. I want to pull my limb off to stop it from hurting. I clench my hand in a fist and it disintegrated into a fine dust.

Oh, it hurts.

Nothing but pain shoots through my body, frying the nerves in my spine on its path. My hand continues to freeze over. The cold crawls from where my hand once was, until the sensation creeps up to my neck, cutting off my scream. My vision blurs. The world is starting to disappear.

This is it. My end. My failure. Inevitable and painfully helpless.

"Come back to me." Zoha's voice clangs in my mind, the echoes filling my senses. She calls my name and I feel air in my lungs again. I could feel something grip my mind and anchor me back to my body.

In a gasp, my vision clears and my eyes meet hers as she's looking down on me. Sweat rolling down her forehead and her eyes are filled with tears. She's shaking but she smiles at me and I see only her.

"Hey." I turn my head and let it burrow deeper into the pillow. I'm back in our room. The robe that I had donned earlier now replaced by a loose shirt that's soft against my skin. I look around me.

The lack of pants would have alarmed me in other circumstances. Especially in the presence of a man in the room but I have no energy to protest. My hands feel warm and I look down. Zoha and Linc are holding one hand each, both clutching a bit tightly, willing feeling back into them.

"You were attacked in the woods." Linc is the first to speak, seeing the confusion I wear on my face. "Your arm was badly hurt but we were able to heal most of it for now." I slip my hand from his and hold it above my face, turning and flexing it. Trying to erase the image of it falling off in front of me.

"Something *took* my hand." I croak out. The hoarseness of my voice proves that I had not just been screaming in my dream alone. I make a move to sit up, Zoha stands beside me to take on most of my weight in the process. The blood drains from my face at the effort and I have to bite back a sob when nausea comes barreling through.

"The *Hala*." Linc explains. His face pales several shades of gray. "The fog demon, close relations with the magic eaters. You had managed to get away from the wards around Meridian. It sensed you and lured you. It touched your skin long enough to cause damage, but I was able to pull you away before—"

"Before it killed me?" Linc couldn't suppress his wince.

"No." His eyes churn. "It wouldn't have killed you. It would have taken you to the Comendeti first." His jaw ticks as his emotions battle him for control. "As your keeper, I should have been there to protect you sooner." His cheeks redden and he bends his head lower. "I'm sorry." His shoulders slump forward and his voice is soft with defeat, the shame radiating off of him in waves.

"Sorry?" Zoha cuts in before I could say anything. "Clearly, you're not capable of doing the sole thing you're supposed to be good for." She seethes. The earlier tremble in her voice replaced with venom. The lack of retort from Linc is proof enough that she landed a solid hit.

"It's not his fault." I counter weakly and shake my head when Zoha starts to say more. "It was my choice to leave and wander off into the woods. To find air and think." I rub my face with my hands, a headache is starting to build at the base of my skull.

"He should've protected you." Zoha's voice shakes and she swallows against the lump in her throat. I slide my hand back into hers and squeeze. The anger, all that venom, sneaks out of her and she slumps beside me. Looking at our intertwined hands. "I didn't even know you were gone until…" She trails off.

Her anger for Linc roots from her anger with herself. Guilt spikes from my gut. The thought of waking her up so she can come with me then didn't even come into mind.

Her time away had affected me more than I thought it would because it never occurred to me until now that my absence in bed would have affected her this much.

I lay my other hand over our joined ones and I bring it to my lips.

"I'm sorry. I should've woken you up, I didn't realize…" If it had been Zafiya beside me, I would have woken her up. Told her how suffocated I had been feeling and we would've cried together.

Before papa died, Zoha had been cold, but she was still someone I would turn to. Now though, I would much rather deal with it alone than bother her with my grief. This fact makes my heart tighten in my chest.

She shakes her head and slips her hand away from mine. Not wanting to acknowledge the gap in our relationship as sisters. She busies herself with fluffing and tucking the blanket around me, actively ignoring Linc who stayed by the edge of the bed.

We're not going to talk about it. Not now.

"I spoke to Zafiya." I change the subject. At that, Zoha's eyes shoot to mine. Wide and hopeful.

"You made contact?" Ava speaks from the doorway and she steps in without waiting to be invited. She's holding a tray of soup and the smell alone makes me acutely aware that my stomach burns with hunger. The loud grumble of said stomach is loud enough for everyone else to hear. Ava gives me a tight smile and lays the tray on my lap.

"Eat while you tell us exactly what happened." And so, I do. Recounting the events that led me to seeing the image of our youngest sister and speaking to her.

While I spoke, Zoha paced the room and settled by the window to look outside. Purposely putting space between herself and the rest of us on the bed. Needing the distance to breathe and separate herself from the absurdity of our reality.

I polish off the soup and the bread that came with it. The fullness of my belly eases some of my discomfort. Although the pit of my stomach bubbles with dread when I remember how Zafiya looked in the vision. The image of her pallor and the wounds on her skin is enough to bring tears to my eyes.

"The water would have been the perfect root of energy for you." Ava holds her chin in her hand, in thought. Turning my tale in her head. I'm sure she's trying to find answers to why this unguarded act allowed me to make contact with Zafiya. "You came in unaware and opened your mind to the thought of your sister. In turn, bringing down your mental guards and acting as the perfect conduit for energy to flow and feed your magic in the process. Your magic listened to your sole intention and allowed the connection to take place. Doing it outside the wards…" She trails off, stopping herself from saying more.

"I didn't intend for it to happen, but will I be able to do it again?" Doubtful that there is anything more for me to offer in my previous training. Tonight was a lucky shot and what could very well be a one-time encounter.

Those odds aren't as easily replicated.

"We'll work on finding your triggers." Ava looks at Zoha, who still has her back turned to us. "Being a witch is more than just controlling your powers and speaking spells. A lot of mental work comes into play for you to accept the power and let it pass through your body." I nod, remembering how warm I felt as the current of the water flowed over me.

Letting it take me along its natural courses.

"We'll—" Her eyes flick to Zoha again, "We'll try again tomorrow. See if we could use the connection to scry for her location. The Hala knows you're alive and the Comendeti will gather whatever forces they have to hunt you down. This should allow Valera to find something among the covens."

"She's alive." Zoha breathes out. The tone of her voice is half in disbelief and half hopeful. As if saying that out loud makes it more real to her. Linc takes away the tray and Ava checks my hand for any wounds that remained. It was in perfect condition, at least it appeared so.

I could still feel the pain fluttering beneath the surface. Like the memory of it burned too deep to heal even with magic.

"Yes." I answer. "Well as she could be under captivity and even then, she warned us for *our* safety."

"Our little warrior." Zoha's voice is a whisper, a prayer thrown into the air. I understand the reverence of which we held that title for our beloved little sister.

She looks at me, the ghost of bruises under her eyes darkened them further. Her lips set in a grim line but she was anything but defeated.

At this moment we agree, we will get Zaf back. No matter the cost.

Chapter 17

The ground hums while I lay on it catching my breath. The grass twirls around my fingers as I stroke them. They draw themselves towards my skin as if aching for contact.

For the past two weeks, Ava worked with us daily. Starting with breathing exercises to clear the mind so I can try and use my core. I discovered that I was actually able to feel the strings of energy around us when I space out and didn't *think* my way through the process. Proves to be much harder for an overthinker like me.

I had not changed on another vision of Zafiya yet. We've tried different means of scrying, but we've gotten little to dismal results in that area.

Ava banned me from going back to the brook outside the wards. I'm also not too keen on meeting the Hala again so I didn't protest much. I still feel phantom pains down my arm when my brain wanders back to the memory. It's not safe.

Valera has been sending letters detailing a rise in abductions in witches, most likely in their hopes of trying to find me or Zoha. She's gathered small responses but they've been far from helpful. They've mostly turned the questioning our way, asking for protection or confirming if there was a need to hide or move. I'm starting to see that running away isn't just a trait specific to my mother in this regard.

Zoha has not missed a day of training, but her progress is minimal. Her powers remain undisturbed. She cannot feel vibrations and thread of energies in the elements like I can. She's grown angrier each day at her progress.

Linc was a constant shadow in our training but barely said a word to either of us. He's further curled into himself when he goes into a tirade of training. The attack lit a fire in him. His need to be strong enough to protect me and my sisters became his sole motivation.

I tried seeking him out one night, but Ava waved me away. Telling me to leave him to his keeper training with Valera.

"Let's try tapping into your core again today." Ava stands over me, her arms crossed. I stand up and brush off the dirt and stray grass clinging to my pants. I straighten in front of her and open my palms up to her. With my heart hammering hard in my chest, I'm surprised she doesn't hear it.

"Okay, I'm not sure if—" Ava clicks her tongue to stop me.

"Stop doubting yourself, it's not helping." Her tone is matter-of-fact, not trying to insult me or attack. Simply to teach. How I take that depends on me, so I just nod. "You need your core to center your energy, so you can funnel all of it to your magic."

I close my eyes and I listen to the calm timbre of her voice. To trace the lilts and dips with my mind so I can bring my nerves down. Trying to find my core had needed me to do an uncomfortable amount of *internal* work.

"You need to look through your psyche to remove the emotional blocks and defense mechanisms you have inadvertently established."

"I know. I'm not sure what else is there for me to find." I admit and Ava smiles softly.

"There's always more, always something deeper that affects who you are as the witch you are today. We just need to find that." Sounds easy enough on the surface. Although, one is not normally forced to look at and relive their darkest moments in life. At the same time, amplifying every voice of doubt that ever made its way into your head. It's painful and my gut feels scorched with acid after each attempt.

The one time they tried helping Zoha find her core, she became an unseeing screaming mess for hours. When she calmed down, she refused to talk to me about what she'd seen. Then refused any future attempt at reaching her core.

I look over to where Zoha sits on the ground, sweat still sticking her hair to her forehead. Her eyes shutters, carefully watching us now. Now is not the time for me to rehash our argument over her not trying to do more for her training. I need a clear head. Ava's eyes bear into mine.

Ava's gaze softens a fraction when she sees my hesitation, but her lips are set on a grim line. I know that despite what I'm feeling, we need to force this progress.

Without it, then the longer Zafiya is out of our reach. The longer that she's in harm's way.

I refuse to acknowledge how that would affect the likelihood of finding her as the shell of the person she is. If we can even find her at all.

I hold out my hands and Ava hovers hers over mine. Immediately, phantom hands dig under my skin, warm and steady. Instead of falling into panic, I take deep breaths.

With every exhale, the buzzing in my blood thrums and centers in my chest, pooling there. I'm feeling a bit steady on my feet.

I let myself dig deeper, following Ava's phantom touches as we take a closer look within myself. The ball of warmth in my chest radiates and I think it's working.

My mother's face immediately comes into view. The same hot constriction vices around my heart. The air in my lungs grows sharp as I continue to look at her.

I don't turn away and I continue to watch her, taking this time to account for the features I knew too well. This had been the longest time in my life that I had gone without seeing her with my eyes. Almost like I could reach out to her.

Thinking about her and dreaming about her had not been the same. Both times it always feels like a cloud blurs my vision of her so I cannot see her eyes. Now, when I try to direct the energy flowing inside my body through the core sitting tight in my chest, her face is clear.

If I let myself believe for a second, she almost looks like she's alive. In my vision I step closer, is my mother the key to my core? The key to my powers and my control?

I attempt to reach out to her and as soon as my mind touches her memory something inside me cracks open. Her face transforms and flickers. The hot tears in my eyes spill down my cheeks.

My mind is showing me a million moments in our lives where I often watched her and admired her. The love I felt for her resonated through my body, like golden strings wrapping around me and molding me.

My magic purrs at the feeling and I could feel my fingers spark with warmth.

As more shimmering strings begin to form in front of me, something dark touches them. A black stain smearing the pristine array of silken strings.

I squeeze my eyes tighter, willing away the dark blotches of ink. I only want to see the gold lights that started to form inside me and around me. A vision of my mother flashes in my head. The memory is of her packing up our lives into those boxes. It continues to morph into every moment she refuses to talk about papa after his death, every moment her eyes shutter when I ask her about him or that day of the incident. Every door closed. Every shut down. Each image that flashes through me creates larger black stains on the golden strings inside me.

What was this? The memories continue to rush through me, making my blood drain and sending a chill through me. The image settles on papa's death, the moment that ragged breath came and stopped. That helplessness we all felt in a foreign neighborhood and no one came to help until the paramedics came to take him away.

Finally, the memory stops on that one minute I spent begging mama to use her magic to bring him back. At her anger directed at me and the pain I caused her. My knees buckle and the crack inside my chest grows, as if something deep inside me is being exposed.

This secret, this dirty thing tainting every memory. Every part of me wants to lock it down, and to turn away from this part of myself. All the anger, the resentment. The blame.

Before I could stop it, guards start to come up. Cold metal walls shutting out eyes that may see this ugly seed of distrust.

Sensing my resistance, Ava pulls back and I let myself resurface from the darkness. The last thing I see before I come back to the forest is the image of my father's body in the cold room and I see my mother staring helplessly at him.

It was clear then, why I couldn't use this magic willingly. The realization is bitter on my tongue. I resented my mother and I didn't trust her magic—my magic.

Chapter 18

"Trust is a precious thing. The lack of it hinders your ability to believe in your own reliability, in yourself. In your powers." My vision clears and I find myself looking at the line between Ava's eyebrows. I turn away from her.

Feeling myself sway on my feet I sink to the ground beside Zoha

"I'll leave you to rest." Ava stalks away, leaving me still reeling.

I know that this discovery means that I'm much closer to tapping into my core and releasing any binds I had on my powers.

How would trusting my mother play into this? Regardless of how close I am to the finish line, how sure am I that I can even take the last step towards it?

"What happened?" Zoha's whispers bring me out of my stupor when we start to walk back to the manor. I refused to let her touch me when she tried to pull me into a hug after Ava left.

My hands grip my own arms as I hug them to myself, feeling cold inside. Any attempts I try at to steady myself fails. The more I remember what happened inside my head when I tried to uncover my core, the colder my insides feel. I claim to love my mother truly. We've had our arguments but that doesn't erase the fact that she was caring and loving. She had her lapses, but she was *my* mother. I shouldn't be counting her faults.

When papa died, we found comfort in our shared pains and moved about our lives together. She picked herself up and soldiered on raising us on her own. She didn't break stride, didn't take a moment to grieve the loss of her other half.

She's a formidable force. Finding out that part of me didn't trust her and I blame her for my father's death shakes the very foundation of who I thought I am.

I don't want to think about this anymore. I push it out of my mind until we reach the manor. Linc is waiting for us, pacing by the door. "You didn't come in with Ava, I was about to come looking for you."

Not trusting my voice not to break, I give him a weak shrug and push past him into the house. Something hits me that makes me stop dead in my tracks. Like the ground beneath my feet is speaking to me sensing vibrations from a source I could not recognize. The vibrations flow through my toes intensifying the buzz in my blood.

What was this? I look over at Zoha but she remains cautiously looking at me, not sensing the change. Linc is stalking behind us and I tilt my head in question.

"Is someone here?" At that, he freezes and his eyes quickly dart up toward the stairs. He meets my eyes, his lips pressed into a thin line. "No one of importance, Ava has a guest in her study and she asked us to stay clear for now. We'll have dinner in our own rooms tonight." Ah, this was why he'd been waiting for us then? To act as an escort.

Without wanting it to show, a frown still forms on my face expressing my disappointment. I continue up the flight of stairs up to our room. I close the door before Linc could attempt to come in.

I follow my sister into the bathroom. I'm ready to step out of my skin and wash away any traces of today's session. Zoha is already neck deep in the tub and she watches me walk around the bathroom, I pace.

"If you're going to be restless like this, might as well spit out what's bothering you so I can have my peace." Zoha is offering an olive branch. I know that this is the best she could do in telling me she would hear me out without judgment.

Any attempts to be closer, warmer, have gone awkward at best. This dynamic is throwing us off some. Zoha turns around in the tub and rests her chin on the rim, her back to mine. I lean against the sink and wait for her to continue. A few beats pass and it looks like she's leaving it at that.

"Admitting I have childhood trauma seems like such a farce." Makes me feel like some ingrate discrediting my mother because I doubt her.

I love her, shouldn't I trust her more than anything? We didn't have a bad childhood, that was something I was certain of.

"I know you want to protect her but she has made choices that put us all in this situation." I flinch at that. "She didn't need to beat us for you to have trauma. She forced us to live the life she wanted for us. Iced us out and dictated our very emotions." I frown at Zoha.

"She wasn't a bad mother, Zo." She took away our choice and remade our identities because she wanted to protect us. She had no choice. Hadn't she?

My sister shrugs as if she had come to a different conclusion than I had but chose not to argue. I scrub my hands over my face. I don't want to think about this. What was the point? She was *dead.* She sacrificed herself for me, for us. Whatever decisions she made before is overshadowed by that. Nothing would change that. I turn to leave my sister in her bath.

I need to do something else with my time because so help me god, I've come this far, I would not be stopping now.

Chapter 19

I sneak my way through the halls and back to the study. The vibrations and the disturbance I could feel in the air is much thicker now that I'm closer. It's unlike anything I've felt. I'm certain whoever is behind these doors carries power much greater than anyone I've met. The new high priestess included.

Muffled voices are bleeding through from the other side of the door. It stops when I reach for the door knob. Trepidation makes my heart jump and I reconsider entering unannounced.

I take a tentative step back but the door swings open. My breath seizes up at the young man that stands in front of me. My eyes immediately snap to his, deep blue that grow dark that they are almost black. His gaze trace over my face and they are so deep it threatens to pull me in.

To avoid falling into such arresting eyes, I look at the rest of him. A tall sharp nose and thick brows. Dark hair that falls to his shoulders' frames high cheekbones and sharp jaw. I find myself somewhat taken by his attention.

"I—" I start and his thick lips quirk at one side. A small dimple creases his cheek and I find my eyes drifting towards it.

"You must be Zelle." The timbre of his voice skates over my skin. I force down a shiver that wracks my body.

My physical response pales in comparison to how the magic inside me swells at the sight of him.

The buzz that had always thrummed dimly just beneath my skin blooms and floods my blood. The dull sensation turns sharp. Force polarizes in my hands, warm and prickly.

I want to reach out and brush a hand on the toned arms he has crossed over his chest. But before I make a fool of myself or even realize that this man knows my name, Ava steps around him and forces my eyes to hers.

"You should be upstairs in your room." There's alarm in her voice, a strain.

"I needed to talk to you." Is my pathetic response and I dare another look at the man looming behind her. He's leaning on the doorframe.

Those eyes of deep seas rake over me, watching me. His gaze roams over my face with slow and deliberate movements.

"It couldn't wait." The man smiles at my response then. Almost approving my stubbornness.

"No use hiding her now, high priestess. Might as well hear the girl out while I'm here. Maybe I can do a better job at helping her than you." He turns and goes back inside, his arms still crossed.

He leans against the back of the couch in the middle of the room. Ava and I follow. She finds her own space and settles on the chair across the man.

I sit near the window ledge in front of the man—determined not to turn my back on him.

"I don't understand why we're not making enough progress. I've done all the exercises and we've attempted to find my core but it's not working." I begin without the need for prompting. "We're going around in circles."

"You have to understand that witches train their entire lives even before the gift awakens in them. You've only *just* been introduced to having the idea of powers." She sighs now and leans back, massaging her temples. I fight the memory of what my sister said just earlier. If my mother hadn't hidden our powers and had taught us early on we wouldn't have had this much trouble.

"The…" I look over at the man who has not looked away from me since I came to the room. A moment passes and he raises his brow at me. Challenging me to continue and I revert my gaze to Ava. "The images I see when we try to tap my core, they're memories. Mostly of my mother and events relating to her. What does that have anything to do with being able to wield this gift?"

"You have mental guards in place that grew and developed during those moments where you're trying to protect yourself." The man answers now. "Or rather your inner self. This piece of you who controls your values and your emotions, the one who wields your heart."

He taps his chest with two fingers to emphasize.

"This vulnerable piece of who you are is the one responsible for your core. It holds your magic close and drives your power where you need it to go. Magic does not respond only to your commands and your thoughts. Magic moves on intent. Takes after your emotions, your person." He straightens and starts to pace. "Now from what I understand, and what Ava failed to share with me is that you have issues with your mother, with trust, and ultimately with who you are."

I wince at the way he's picking me apart with such a matter-of-fact tone. His words feel like daggers to my skin.

"This distrust brings about roadblocks that keep you from tapping your powers. You're still protecting yourself from pain but also turning yourself away from magic." He regards me with a look and I sigh. He attempts to ease his statements, only realizing how he sounds. "Unknowingly, of course." My eyes follow him as he paces and Ava remains silent.

"But I feel it." I look down at my hands now, a certain frenetic energy hums below my skin. The power that now feels amplified in his presence. He hums in acknowledgement.

"Ah yes, you feel only a fraction of it. Can you describe to me what it feels like?" I look at Ava, I do not know this man. Is it safe to even disclose such things? Ava inclines her head.

"It's okay, Zelle. The magus is from a cabal that I have worked closely with. We can trust him." His lips twitched, the vote of confidence from the high priestess giving me no other reason to refuse him. I sigh and relent.

"It's in my bones, in my blood. This— magic. Like it's inside me, all over me." He nods at that and stops to turn again and look at me.

"Magic needs to be centered and not free flowing inside you like that." He grimaces as if disgusted, "All messy and unfocused. If you were to access your full power at this stage then you'd have all that energy implode." He flicks his hand in the air and he summons a blob of water in the air. "A conduit is not meant to store that much power, you need to harness it. Mold it to your will so you can release it." With every movement of his hand, the water moves with him forming into shapes and figures following his will.

I have not seen Ava do this before and the show of his control has me taking a step closer before I can stop myself. His smirk widens as he sees me totally seized by his display of magic. He clenches his fist and the water explodes into droplets, soaking the floor and my shoes. I sneer at him and he chuckles lowly.

"If you don't find a way to release it. You will find yourself drowning. In every sense of the way." Ava stands from her seat and joins me near the window. A distant sad look on her face.

"I felt it, when we attempted to tap your core and I tried to bring an ounce of magic to power your core. To let it at least course through you. There's this rejection." She closes her eyes and for a second, I see weariness. "You do not trust magic because for whatever reason this has always been what came between you and your mother, because it's the reason she's lied to you. Your magic wouldn't take because deep down you don't want it to." My back shoots straight up at this statement, and fury comes in potent waves.

"How can you say that? I've been breaking my back training with you so I can wield these powers. It's the only thing left for me to be able to save my sister." To claim that I even have a choice in the matter is an insult. How dare she?

"Your mind brings these images by itself, though." The man has the audacity to use a tone with me. I bite down a sarcastic retort. "In the literal sense, you're hiding behind the memory of your mother so you won't have to let magic inside of you. The question here, little witch, is why?" I grit my teeth at the man who is now standing beside Ava.

He's looking at me with such disappointment. Anger, hot and seizing, boils inside me. I turn to leave the room. When I stalk toward the door and he mutters under his breath. I reach out a hand to open the door but yelp when my skin burns from the doorknob.

"You have no right to hold me in your *wards*!" I spit out the words through my gritted teeth. Instead of bringing it down, he strengthens it. The magic pulses in the air making the hair on my arms stand. I'm feeling cornered and jealous more than I care to admit. I hate his ability to call upon his power with such ease, I turn again to yank on the door.

"Stop running." He orders and I freeze. Not due to any compulsion but because his voice had gone lower, darker and somewhat sinister. "I have no business waiting for a child like you to deal with her mommy issues so you can tap into your magic." I hadn't realized I was crying until the tears drip from my chin and onto my shirt.

Here it is. The truth laid out in front of me. Bare and without sugar-coating. It's my fault. My own damned mindset and pain keeping me here. I cannot bring myself to accept the parts of me that mama hid away like some sin. Magic had failed me, brought me and my family nothing but pain.

I jut my chin in the air, at this stranger who had read me like some distasteful book.

"What does this have anything to do with you?" I'm seething with anger. My hands shake from the emotions threatening to overwhelm me. I'd rather direct all my fury at the man in front of me. His answering smirk tells me he knows exactly what I'm doing.

Magic had been the reason why mama had lived in such fear that she'd lied to us most of our lives. It's the very reason we had to move and why we found ourselves in that lonesome neighborhood and papa–

It's clearly not enough to keep us all together. Who's to say it'd be enough now to save Zafiya? I look at him and I wish my eyes carried all the fury I feel inside me.

"It's *my* sister that's on the line here. *My* parents that died because magic couldn't keep them from dying! I may be a child but I'm the one tearing my own heart out just to save my family. You're nobody." At my outburst, he lunges toward me and I flinch.

He stops close enough that he's towering over me. His face inches from mine, so close that his breath fans my cheeks. His eyes brimming with fire as they bore into mine.

"Flynn." Ava calls him by his name finally. The warning in her voice clear. Her hand grips his shoulder.

I'm trapped under his gaze but I don't balk under its weight. Flynn lets out an exasperated sigh. He shrugs Ava's hands off and he eases back.

It's anything but a retreat. I glare back at him. The poison in his eyes still brimming as he pastes on a deadpan expression on his face.

"Ah yes, a nobody. Then give me back my powers, you leech." At that, I frown at him. Seeing the question on my mind he sneers at me. "You *took* something from me when your mother died. At your untethering, your magic-deprived body latched onto mine."

"Power is finite to a certain degree." Ava explains as she situates herself between Flynn and me. "It doesn't get conjured out of thin air, it is energy and it moves. Yes, we can produce it and call upon elements to replenish what we've spent." She waves her hand in the air and I see what appears to be gold dust build around her palms as her example. "We can call upon nature to harness such energy to power our spells. However, you'd been tethered for years and had no way to act as a conduit because it's likely that you didn't know how. There was no way for you to absorb energy to power your magic naturally."

She inclines her head toward Flynn and his jaw ticks.

"Whatever you needed to cast those spells had to have come from somewhere else—or someone else." I slide to the ground at this. My strength and bravado dissipated.

This is all too much to think about. Not only do my trust issues keep me from actually tapping into the one thing that helps me harness my powers, but I'm a magic thief, too? Can't get any worse than that, I guess.

Flynn takes a loaded step towards me again and growls.

"I'm here to take back what's mine, little witch." He grabs my arms and at the contact white light bursts behind my eyes blinding me. Electricity crackles under my skin and flames burst through me.

Please, oh god no.

It's burning me—no please, not fire. I scream and scream as the heat pulses through me, flaying my skin and exiting my fingers. I'm going to die. I know it.

My chest bows back as more of it pours out of me in spades. It's ripping me apart. There's too much. All of this power everywhere.

As immediate as it came, the pain stops, the memory and the phantom claws of it still ebbing behind my mind.

"What did you do?" My breath is hoarse, but I inject as much venom as I can. Flynn slumps in front of me kneeling. He raises his eyes to me, his anger palpable in the air.

I gasp as blood starts dripping down his nose.

Chapter 20

Linc barges into the room rushing straight to my side just as Flynn shoots out of my reach. My knees wobble and Linc grabs me by the arm, taking my weight on to keep me steady.

I take tentative steps and my limbs feel like lead. Sweat is already working its way on my skin and I grit my teeth against the nausea. Whatever that was, it sapped me of any energy in my body. Making my movements feel stiff and achy.

I look over at Flynn who deposits himself to the nearby sofa. He uses the back of his hand to wipe off the blood coming from his nose. He looks at the blood drops on his shirt and grimaces in disgust. He glares daggers in my direction but I refuse to let him see how uncomfortable that makes me.

Even though I'm shaking like a leaf and my skin is pasty, I jut my chin in the air. Defiance is a tempting mask as any. I keep my gaze away from him—hard as it was to ignore such a huge presence in the room.

"Someone care to explain what the hell happened." I mumble and my voice breaks. All attempts at bravado go out the window. Linc leads me to the chair closest to me.

When I plop down without grace, he steps closer. He places himself between Flynn and I. At the protective action, Flynn smirks—his dimple winking out at me. He leans back. Crossing his fingers over one another. Eyes leveling with Linc.

A challenge, if I ever saw one unspoken. I scoff. *Men*.

"This would explain why you'd been able to make better progress than Zoha." I roll my eyes at this. What progress? Ava waves me off. "You'd also been able to make contact with Zafiya with a vision. But whatever happened now confirms what Flynn is saying. You're siphoning energy from him. Allows for more control so you can use it."

"Wait, what?" I raise my palms up, my head reeling. "You mean I've only been using his magic and not mine?" Ava looks between Flynn and I, her eyes guarded and wary. She shakes her head.

"It's yours, all of it." She assures. Flynn scoffs at that.

"I can argue with that, high priestess. Doesn't feel a whole lot like *hers* when I feel her drain me of what's mine." Ava's face falls flat. Something tells me she doesn't appreciate the tone Flynn is using with her. He notices this too and tilts his head in a subtle bow. A gesture of acquiescence.

"How can it be my magic when you're saying the power comes from him?"

"I've only ever read about this in old texts, although only briefly mentioned." She starts pacing now, recalling what little information she could surmise. "Long ago, when magic and energy had not been so readily available, witches had what they called Sources. They are magical entities that are tethered through a bond. Sources were, as their namesake explains, external wells of power that witches tap into in case their own fails or diminishes."

"A source…" I whisper cementing the idea in my mind with the word. "Like a battery pack?" Flynn makes a disgruntled sound and looks my way.

"I am not a battery pack." His teeth snaps as he bares them to me. His expression wild.

"You can say it like that. Your magic is yours but it needs energy to work. To power spells, enchant objects, or even to mix a potion. Normally, a witch is able to gather their energy from nature. To ask the Mother to give you just enough power as what your magic needs." She shrugs, obviously at a loss. "I can't say for sure if it's a result of the bindings Aria had placed on you and your sisters but…"

"But here we are." Flynn finishes with much less enthusiasm, a flat expression pasted on his face. The heat and the fury now simmering beneath a mask of calm. This feels even more unsettling than his outright anger. I shift in my seat, my body gaining back some strength that I could sit up without wanting to double over. "I never agreed to be anyone's Source." Flynn spits out through gritted teeth. Ava heaves a sigh and her tone is defeated as she speaks.

"You and I both know that bonds are very rarely left to anyone's own choice." I scrub my hands over my arms, trying to rub the warmth back into my skin.

"Can it be broken? This… bond. Whatever caused it, can we break it?"

"Believe me, I tried." Flynn snipes at me. "You, little witch, *cling* rather tightly. It's been an interesting few weeks, to say the least." I wince at his tone, venom-laced and sharp.

"Yeah, my days keep getting better and better." My pathetic grasp on sarcasm slips. My tone comes out much sadder than I intended it to be. Upon hearing it though, Flynn blinks at me.

He releases a long breath and rolls his shoulders. Trying to ease the tension in his neck.

"I admit, I am a bit on edge." His tone is soft, tentative. I only nod at that and I meet his eyes again. "I apologize." I give him a wry smile.

"I just want my sister back." My voice, although steadier than earlier, is little more than a whisper at the admission. I don't care about the magic.

Frankly, I am quite scared of it.

The power is starting to flow back under my skin. I can feel it getting stronger. And now, with Flynn so near me the energy inside me is practically glowing, lighting me from inside.

I would trade it just to get Zafiya back. Linc hears the resignation in my voice and he looks down at me, his brow creased.

"You can take it back, you can have all of it, when I have my sister."

Flynn leans forward then, interest sparking his blue eyes to life. I couldn't help my reaction and lean back, taking as much space away from him as I could.

"First lesson, witch." He angles his head assessing my face, "Bargains are binding. You better be careful about what you're offering while I'm being graceful about it." Ava steps in and her lips curl into a sneer.

"No one is making deals here. We'll train her further within the safety of Meridian grounds so she can expand her own pool of magic. She wouldn't even need to tap into yours once we're done." Flynn stands up then, shoving his hands in his pockets. A mask of casual grace slipping on.

His power surges in the air and my fingers prickle when he draws closer. The hairs on my arms stand on end. He was anything but casual.

"I will take back what's mine." He growls. Ava smiles at him then, white teeth gleaming.

"She is a witch under my coven, Flynn. Lay a hand on her without her permission and break the peace between my coven and your cabal. See how your father would feel about that." At the mention of his father, he visibly pales and he doesn't dare to retort. Ava looks back at Linc. "Take Zelle back to her room to rest and have Valera show Flynn to our guest quarters. I have a feeling he would want to stay around."

Linc grabs me by the arm without needing more prompt to take me out of the room. He doesn't relent until we're outside my bedroom. I brush my fingers over his and he jumps back as if not realizing he'd still been holding me. The crease that had formed between his brow deepens.

"I'm fine." I know he wants to probe more. The concern in his eyes is obvious enough. Yet he can't bring himself to say anything. The hesitation is salt to my wounds. We used to share everything with each other and we rarely had to ask.

Now that I'm retracting into myself, I see him at a loss for what to do. An abyss between us is gaping and it grows wider

He's my keeper, my supernatural protector, and he can't seem to speak up in my presence. This grates me. He knows me better than anyone in this manor, including my sister. He can't even bring himself to comfort me with a familiar joke.

He knows I need a friend now more than ever.

Instead of voicing this out though, I turn around and leave him by the door with the same concerned look in his eyes.

Let him brood over it, I'm pretty sure he wouldn't do anything about it, anyway.

When I enter the room, Zoha is on the floor with a map spread out in front of her. She's holding a pointed white crystal tied to a leather strap circling it. Ava taught her how to scry, but she was even less successful than I am. She doesn't look up and merely inclines her head in my direction.

Yes, even with my closest friend and my sister living under the same roof as I am, I have never felt more alone.

Chapter 21

I wake up with most of the chill out of my system, but something feels awfully empty inside me. The hum under my skin is quiet, almost undetectable unless I look for it.

I peek inside me to find the bundle of warmth and vibrations that always seem to rummage through my system. I only come upon a black awning void. I must have drained myself more than I thought.

Before retreating out of my mind, I look closer and I stop short.

There, burrowed deep inside the dark is a golden thread. It looks thin and weak but golden and glinting either way. I picture myself reaching out to it and wrapping it around my fingers and wrists. It snaps on tight.

I yelp and retreat. When my mind clears and I'm fully back in the room I could feel that thread inside me, still. Like a phantom limb, not bothersome, per se. Though, strange.

I sit up in bed and look around me. Zoha's side of the bed is all made up. She must have left early this morning to train without me. I'm surprised they let me sleep in.

The warm light of the mid-noon sun peeps behind the curtains. I know they're finishing their lessons soon. I wonder how it went today.

I make a mental note to ask Linc instead.

Zoha and I have talked little about her own progress with magic. She's got her breathing exercises down but any attempt at bringing her powers out fails.

Ava says it's because I had been more open to the idea of magic that my body didn't reject it as much. Although I had emotional blocks, part of me still believed in it. Zoha, on the other hand, is a cynic.

Nothing harder to train than someone who doesn't believe in it. Due to this, her triggers and training are much more different than mine. They are slower in progress, too. Which annoys me more than I care to admit.

Not to mention, I apparently have a magus forced into this Source bond with me. A wave of shame comes over me and I grimace. Part of me wants Zoha to make leaps and bounds in progress. If she's better and stronger than me then the responsibility wouldn't fall on my shoulders. I wouldn't have to be the one who fails.

I rub my hands over my face to clear my head. It's such a disgusting train of thought so early in the morning. I refuse to travel down that road.

I wipe away any remnants of sleep from my eyes and head out of the room. When I do, the thread inside me unspools further and glows, casting a dim light inside my chest. I tug at it and something tugs back in response. The sensation makes my stomach dip.

Strange.

I pad my way down the stairs to hunt down some food but I stop short on the landing. The thread inside me tugs harder. Unable to resist the call, I follow where it tries to lead me.

I walk up the stairs. A feeling tickles at the back of my head and I have a pretty solid guess at who's waiting at the other side of the thread. The tugs are impatient and an image of Flynn tugging on a leash makes me grimace.

I'm led through the hallway and find the room at the farthest end. This must be the high priestess' way of making sure he and I remain far away from each other. The threads inside me says that wouldn't have made a difference.

I cross my arms over my chest. I refuse to open the door. The least he could do is get off his ass and open the door to greet me.

Sure enough, it opens and Flynn stands in front of me. The easy quirk on his lips and the dimple creasing his cheek grates me so.

I raise my eyebrow as I look him over. He looks like he's just rolled out of bed like I did. Crumpled cotton shirt and ruffled hair that falls over his forehead.

"Had a nice nap, witch?" His refusal to use my given name annoys me even more but I refuse to let my flat expression falter. I'm sure he'll take it as a win if he riles my temper enough.

"You called?" His grin was anything but friendly.

"I didn't call for you. I was trying to pull my magic back in, you see. The power you stole." Without breaking my stare, I reach inside and grab that thread I feel so strongly now and give it a hard pull.

Flynn gasps loudly and he sneers at me. The pull grants me warmth and the gaping void inside me fills a little.

"Don't you dare." He warns me under his breath.

Interesting.

I give it another hard tug and he grunts. The warmth filling me makes me shudder in relief. The murderous gleam in his eyes is back. He doesn't bother to mask his fury with the indifference he seems to be so fond of.

Now that I know what the thread is for, I caress it with phantom hands. The bond to my Source. It's obvious from the way he grits his teeth that if I pull on it, he cannot fight the request to give me the energy my magic needs.

"Not so fun when I do it, huh?" I say with a smirk. When he does it, I only ever feel a tug, an awareness of his presence. I run my hands against the thread again. Gently now, providing him some reprieve. It vibrates as if bowing to my touch and Flynn lets out another grunt, not pained this time but of something else. My cheeks heat as I see him release a shuddering breath.

"Careful with that, witch." The bite in his tone is gone, his voice now near guttural. I clear my throat, my smirk immediately falling, and I let go of the thread.

"I'm sorry." I mumble and clear my throat. "I came because I wanted to ask for your help." Flynn crosses his arms now and leans on the doorframe. The space between us lessens further and at this distance his scent grows stronger.

It wafts through me, warmly. He smells of pine and smoke, strong and distinctly male. I tamp down the instinct to take a deep breath lest I appear like a madwoman.

"As if stealing from me and assaulting me isn't enough." I stiffen to bite back.

"Assault?" My hackles rise. "I never—oh." His answering grin stops me short. I take a second to recover. His smile grows wider with amusement. "Oh, you're actually making jokes now."

"I am. I've been known to do that every so often." He tilts his head again, watching me. This is more disarming than his anger.

"You're in a chipper mood." He simply shrugs. He turns to leave but I stop him, tugging on his shirt sleeve. Careful not to make contact with his skin. His eyes lower toward my fingers and I let him go. "Look, I don't know how much you know about me." I clear my throat again, hearing the breathiness and refusing to let him hear the effect of one smile does to me.

"You don't need to do this. You know," He uses his hands to gesture toward me. "Go through the pathetic excuses you have planned for stealing from me." His brows furrow and his face falls flat—*that face*. The sharp angles of his jaw, the eyes deep as the ocean, and the occasional boyish dimple that sets me off. It's too good for someone with such a rotten attitude.

"Like I said." I interrupt him, my tone firmer. He stops arguing and crosses his arms in front of me. "I'm pretty sure you know nothing." I raise my brow, waiting for a retort. When he doesn't, I relax a little. "This wasn't my choice. A few weeks ago, I didn't know I was a witch." I throw my hands up in exasperation. "A few weeks ago, my mother was alive, Flynn." My voice breaks and I look away until the burn in my eyes calm. "Magic was nothing but a fantasy to me and my life was the boring painful truth I wanted to escape from with it. Now…" I clutch my hands to my chest. "Now everything is upside down."

Through this, he remains quiet, the sarcasm and biting comments gone. I start pacing in the hallway, feeling restless on my feet.

"I didn't want to make you my Source. I didn't want anyone to get hurt. I just wanted to protect my family. I didn't even get to make a choice." Tears now hot on my cheeks flow freely. Why I was bearing my thoughts to this stranger was a wonder to me.

At that, recognition flits through his expression. A recognition of pain and his eyes soften. From this, I know that the lack of choice aggravates him, too.

"I know and I'm sorry for being too hard on you last night." He runs a hand through his hair and looks up at the sky, damning or begging the fates. "I'll help you train as much as I can, but I want this bond gone."

"Help me find my sister and we can break it, just tell me how to do it." He angles his head again. A gesture he seems to default into when he looks at me with those assessing eyes.

The predatory gleam no longer there, instead there is guarded sympathy. His eyes flick between mine as if attempting to read into me.

"Let's make a deal then. When you get your sister back, we will sever this thread and I will no longer be your Source." *When.* Part of me is relieved at this stranger's boost of confidence. It was not a matter of if I'd get her back, just when.

He sticks out his hand for me to shake and I hesitate, remembering the last time our skins touched. He realizes a heartbeat later and draws his hand back.

"Right, best we don't do that."

He tugs the thread between us and I could only describe the feeling as if he ran the tip of his finger down my back. I suppress a shudder and reach out to grab the thread from my end. When I do, it thrums with power and the thread grows heavier—thicker in my hands as if standing closer to each other and our phantom touch fortifies it.

We both let go and stand there as the golden light inside our chests dissipates but it remains looming.

Chapter 22

"You mean to tell me that all you've been doing this time are breathing exercises?" Flynn and I snuck out of the manor and out to the fields opposite our usual training site. We're standing face to face now, both in sweats.

He plants his feet to the ground and crosses his arms in front of me. Never mind that he looks like he's a foot taller than me, his question was enough to make me feel so much smaller than the magus. Before I can embarrass myself with an excuse, he stops me with a hand in the air.

"Don't answer that. I forgot you're basically a toddler."

"Can you be any less patronizing?" I say through gritted teeth.

"No." He deadpans. He starts walking around me in a circle, inspecting me like some item on display. "Do you have an affinity?" I give him a weak shrug. He stops in front of me again and points to the ground. "Wait for me here." Ignoring the fact that he talks to me like a dog, I sit, and he leaves me for a few minutes.

He comes back with a bag and a couple of wooden ritual bowls in his hand. He sets all four bowls in front of me and takes out the items in his bag.

He pours water from a container in the first bowl. Scoops up dirt into the second. Places a candle and lights it with a match for the third. The last one, he puts a paper airplane. At that, I give him a look and I see him bite down his smile.

"Hey, I make-do with what we have right now." He dusts off his hands and sits back on his heels. "This is the affinity ceremony." He gestures to each bowl in front of us. "Witches have what we call affinities, a certain inclination towards one specific element. As I'm sure Ava has explained, you are a conduit of nature—of energy. You can harness energy from any and all elements available to you so you can channel that into your magic.

"There are elements, or one, that would be much easier for you. One where you will be most drawn to and thus wielding that specific element has the most effect." He hovers his hand over the first bowl and the water vibrates under and ripples.

It stirs inside the bowl. An invisible force creating a current, casting waves into the water. The liquid moves higher and higher from the bowl as if reaching towards the hand he holds above it.

"Mine is water." He retrieves his hand and the contents of the bowl stills. "Knowing your affinity gives you knowledge of your strength and your weakness."

"Why hasn't Ava done this with us, if it's so important?" He crosses his arms and hums under his breath.

"Simply because you're not ready for it." He shrugs before I could protest. "The witch needs to be attuned to their core as a means of grounding themselves before the ceremony." I deflate at this. Even now, being unable to access my core proves to be a hindrance.

Images of my mother pop in my head again and I feel myself shut down further. This is hopeless. I make a move stand, but Flynn shakes his head to stop me.

"Wipe that defeated look off your face."

"I don't have a look." I argue but Flynn's deadpan expression tells me that I, in fact, have a look.

"Let's try something different today." His lips curl a little, "Something we would not be telling your high priestess about."

I blink at him and he only stares. He's waiting for me to agree. I look around, nervous about getting caught.

He doesn't push and waits for me to come to my own conclusions. I could refuse and let myself take a much more natural path, albeit the slower path. Or I can skip ahead with my Source's help so I can finally get even footing and find the power to take my sister back.

I take deep breaths and steel myself against my doubts. It's my choice. I nod and Flynn smiles then.

He closes his eyes and shakes his arms to relax his limbs. The movement causes his hair to sway from his forehead and it makes them look too silky not to be touched.

Again, with such thoughts. I reprimand myself and bite the inside of my cheek to keep myself from reaching over. His hands hover over the bowls in front of us.

"*I call upon the ancient quarters, hear me.*

Let air breathe life, and fire break bonds to free.
As earth takes root, and water brings the key.
Heed my prayer, so let it be.
Show this witch her affinity."

When nothing happens, I blink at Flynn who remains unmoving. He continues to chant the same five rhymes. On his third run, unbridled anger surges inside of me.

The thought of failing even at this simple ceremony kindles fury deep inside me. I clutch my hands into a fist and attempt to slap Flynn's hands away.

When our skin touches, the ground starts to rumble.

His eyes snap open and the stark blue pins me in place. I pull my hand back from him. He looks up at the sky as the birds around us caw and flutter away. The wind begins to whirl, whipping my hair in its wake.

The flame on the lone candle in front of me shoots up in the air. The bright light from the flame lighting up the sky and bringing tears to my eyes. The water grows and sloshes out of its bowl soaking the ground. The bond grows inside me, tugging my gut restlessly. I kick back, toppling the bowls and they spill over each other, mixing in front of me.

"What's—" My question cuts off when I feel my chest crack open and my magic builds inside. It starts off warm, pleasant. In one short breath it starts to overwhelm me.

My blood boils and sharp pain sears through my body. I scream, the pain blinding me. My back bends and my chest lifts toward the sky, like something trying to get out.

I try to breathe against the internal flaying, but I'm suffocated.

I hear Flynn curse loudly and he tackles me wrapping his arms around me, trapping my arms between our bodies. His weight pins me and his voice calls to me. His desperation scratching his throat as he calls to me over and over.

I could barely hear him over the ringing in my ears and my screams.

Then that tug, that strong incessant tug at the bottom of my belly brings me back from the blinding pain and I follow it. I grasp it, tightly wrapping the thread around both my arms and yank.

Flynn screams and I scream with him as fire fills my blood again and then darkness envelopes us.

Chapter 23

Flynn is still on top of me when I crack my eyes open, his breath fanning over my cheek. I shake him and he stirs. He blinks at me and his blue eyes are glassy.

"Are you okay?" I ask him as he peels himself off of me. He grunts and curses under his breath. It was dark and I push my hands in front of me only to be met by a rough wall—no, not a wall. I glide my hands through the enclosure, feeling the roughness bite through my skin. Tree bark.

Flynn feels around us as well and shoves his shoulder through one side of the enclosure and it gives way. He falls forward and groans when he lands on his arm. I peek through the hole and find him dusting himself off. He turns to reach his hand to me so he can help me down.

"We shouldn't touch." I say, reluctant. Feeling the scratch in my throat from the screams caused by one single contact with his hand after his affinity spell.

"It doesn't matter now. You can pull at that bond as much as you want and I wouldn't be able to give you an ounce of power. I'm running empty." His voice strains. I lean towards his outstretched hands and he grabs me by the waist and helps me to the ground. I turn around to look at where we were and a gasp leaves my lips.

"A tree!" I jump almost losing my footing when I land. Flynn anchors me to the ground with his palm on my the small of my back. Undeterred, I squeal. "We were inside a tree!" I whip my head back to Flynn. "I did that." I whisper and he nods.

"You did." I raise my eyebrow at him, I detect a tinge of pride in his tone. "Calm down, witch." He deadpans and looks up at the tree. At *my* tree. Assessing it. "Earth, it is then." He says with a hum before he turns to walk away but I take a second to look at the tree.

It broke through the once flat terrain, the roots weaving through the ground and bursting out. The trunk is thick and unnaturally wide. It had to make space for it to hollow out and encase Flynn and me.

The branches are spread out, sprouting bright green leaves. My jaw drops a little as my eyes trail its height. It doesn't look like any other tree I've seen before. It bends and twirls in ways I don't think were naturally possible. Like in its rush to grow it broke over and over just to accommodate its size. It's beautiful, in a grotesque unnatural way.

I made that. Sure, I may not exactly know how but still. Pride swells in my heart and somehow, looking at this gnarled tree part of me settles. I had power and maybe it's uncontrolled now.

Maybe I can't get it to follow me yet but it's magic, nonetheless. I might just have enough to bring my sister back. I'm smiling like an idiot and Flynn stands next to me, watching me with side glances.

"I don't think I've taken a moment these past weeks to just let it sink in. I have *magic*." I look down at my hands. "Here. In these hands. Whether I want it to or not." They were shaking from the exhaustion that is bone deep. I couldn't complain. I see the white scars on my palms and my smile falters.

"What's wrong?" He looks at my hands and I tuck them to my sides.

"I think... I think part of it woke up when my dad was dying." His breath catches in his throat and I keep my eyes down. "I prayed so hard. I prayed for something to hear me and save him. Something answered back. I felt something stir."

"Intent is a potent trigger." He surmises. Acknowledging my thoughts and listening. There was comfort in that. Comfort in being listened. It brings for me is so strong that I wouldn't be able to stop myself from telling him everything. The truth barrels out of me despite my inhibitions trying to stop it. I couldn't even bring myself to tell Zoha when my suspicions came.

"I remember, I wanted so badly for him to be okay and I saw threads of energy inside me. I wanted them all to go to him. To keep him alive but—" I shake my head to fight off the thickness in my throat.

"You wouldn't have been able to." Flynn says, his tone soft. He's not being mean, just telling me what I already know. "That kind of magic would have demanded more than what you could provide. If anything, you would have died with him."

"I was so angry at mama, I thought I wasn't able to do it because I wasn't powerful enough but she would have been." My eyes burn now as I remember the expression on her face. She'd just learned her husband had died and her daughter was lashing out at her blaming her for his death.

"We're magic, little witch. Not gods. Death is part of nature, even if we will it not to be." I release a shaky breath. I shouldn't be comforted by this fact but I am. Hearing him say it like that confirms the fact that no magic in the world would have kept my dad alive.

I don't have anything to say about this, not wanting to dig into it deeper than I already am. So, I take one last look at that tree and I turn to leave. When I take a step though, my strength gives out and I land on my knees with a curse.

"Give me a minute." I laugh a little at myself. My limbs ached and I couldn't move. I try to lift myself up but my back groans in protest. I give up on trying to stand and slide to the ground. I curl into myself. "You can go back, I'll follow you later." He scoffs at my dismissal.

I hear clothes rustle and he comes into view as he lies down next to me. His eyes to the sky. We lie there in silence and it allows me to gather my thoughts.

He turns to face me, mirroring my fetal position on the ground. This feels too close but I don't think I could move even if I wanted to.

I watch his eyes dart between my features. Cataloging the details of my face and I pray that the heat I feel in my cheeks aren't too visible for him to observe. A frown creases his brows.

"Spit it out." I prompt and he laughs at my crassness. The smile slides off as quickly as it came and he sighs. He brushes the fiery strands of hair that fell over my eyes. The contact makes me jump. Not because a flash of power surges through me but because his gentle fingers were warm against my skin.

"That was irresponsible of me." He starts and before I can protest, he shakes his head to stop me. He needs to say whatever he's thinking. "You didn't have full control over your magic. The energy almost burned you from the inside."

"It was my choice, anyway." I swallow against the sudden dryness in my throat.

"I knew better." He sighs, his breath fans over my lashes and I close my eyes, a pathetic shield from the vulnerable intimacy. "I shouldn't have tried to rush you through the process." He brushes his fingers against my face again, as if he couldn't stop himself. "I'll be a proper teacher next time and you'll be safe."

I don't say anything else after that. Neither does he.

I don't move. Neither does he.

Maybe he also finds this silence as comforting as I do.

Chapter 24

"Follow me." Flynn uses his arm to brush away leaves and branches in his way, holding them as I pass. He's leading us further and further into the forest outside Meridian.

We found our way home yesterday. It had already grown dark and Ava had gotten so furious about the spell Flynn crafted in place of an affinity ceremony. It wasn't proper or safe, she admonishes. I could swear her brown hair stood on end and her eyes were glowing.

Flynn took responsibility for it and had taken on most of the verbal lashing. He had groveled endlessly so Ava wouldn't tell his father about his transgressions. When we told Ava about my affinity to earth though, her anger lessened, and she let us go with a warning.

Today, Flynn had woken me up before the sun even started to rise. He conjured up little water butterflies in my room and splashed them in my face. I was less than pleased to see him grinning when I opened my door still soaked.

"Where are we going?" I finally ask as a thin coating of sweat gleams on my skin.

"Just follow me and you'll see." He's pulling me along with him, his fingers gripping my sleeve like I'm some errant child that needs to be held lest I get lost. I don't argue, I have less than stellar record in these woods.

"I can't go out of the wards, Flynn." He doesn't break stride and doesn't even look at me when he answers.

"Someday, you would have to." He makes a sharp turn and I almost stumble into his back. I hiss at him under my breath. "Not today, though."

"Just tell me where we're going or I'll scream for help." This time he looks at me over his shoulder, amusement clear on his smirking lips.

"I'll leave you here if you don't shut up." I roll my eyes at him and pretend to zip up my lips. Satisfied, he starts pulling me along again. Not even fifty paces after, he stops. "In here!" He exclaims and pulls me through a wall of tall grass. Before I can curse him again and tug my sleeve free from his hold I stop in my tracks. A soft gasp leaves me before I can stop it.

The stream is cradled in greenery. Thick trees almost bending out of its way to keep the sparkling water hidden. Smooth stones covered with moss and life protrude from the water to act as steps that lead to a wooden pathway that winds up the rocky side of a hill.

The planks that made for a makeshift stairway up to the jutting and overhanging rock ledge of the hill are barely visible. The ledge ends with a steady stream that disturbs the surface of the water below. It sparkles under the sunlight and into cascades of loud roaring currents to a lake so clear I could still see the green, moss-covered rocks below.

The crashing and rippling of water constantly fills the air with a pulse. It is almost eerie, how the place looked so untouched and yet pristine—like it's been cared for and yet only by the select few.

Charmed—that's the only way to explain such a sight. Like a hole had been punched in the thickest part of the forest only for an oasis to materialize and call out to wandering souls.

I look at Flynn and he's watching my reaction. When I find myself at a loss for words, he nods satisfied at leaving me dumbstruck. His blue eyes glittering along with the reflection of the lake.

"I used to come up here when my dad visited Meridian for business." He lets go of my sleeve and walks ahead of me. I ignore the immediate coldness in the absence of his proximity. He takes steady steps on the smooth stones. His familiarity with them is obvious.

He waves me over as he sits on one of them and he lets his feet dip through the water. I mirror his position and look at him over my shoulder.

He looks totally in his element. My eyes stay on his legs as they make languid motions, creating ripples across the surface.

"My father is the high priest of our cabal—" He leans back on his arms and tilts his head up to the sky. "He and Ava often had dealings before, so we went here a lot. There weren't a lot of witches my age so I often find myself wandering around Meridian Manor on my own."

"This coven and your cabal are allies?" He inclines his head and his dark hair falls over his shoulders.

"Allies? I wouldn't say that. It's more of a... breeding arrangement." I cringe then and he laughs. "Crass, I know. It's all so archaic, but our families have long since offered each other's unknowing young witches and magus to wed." This piques my interest.

"Should I assume that you are already betrothed?" He shrugs and smirks.

"Curious, eh?" I scoff at his expression and he kicks up his leg to splash water my way, and I squeal from the cold. Before I can retaliate, he slides down from the rock and dips into the water. He swims toward the deeper end of the lake, ending our conversation.

I slip down, much more reluctant than Flynn's careless abandon with the water. As soon as my body is submerged, I let out a sigh, it's a bit cold but refreshing nonetheless.

I dip my head and let it soak my hair. The chill makes my scalp prickle. When I resurface, Flynn is swimming back to me. His eyes almost glowing. A strong tug below my belly makes me yelp and he smirks.

Scoundrel.

"Today's lesson." The smirk never leaves and my eyes are stuck on his dimple. "There are different ways to replenish your magic." He swims around me and I follow the sight of him. His comfort and ease in the water is a sight to behold. He has his hair pushed back in and it reveals thick slightly-arched brows. They make him look sly—dangerously so. Not noticing my sudden interest in his face, he continues.

"Nature grounds us, reminds us that our power, grand as they may be, comes from the Mother. By allowing ourselves to be one with these elements, energy courses through your body. Absorbed through your skin, your senses," His eyes flick down my neck. "Through... your body. That energy powers your magic."

"I don't feel anything." I say, the tone sounding more defeated than I intend it to be. Flynn floats on his back.

"Again with that look." He flips his hand and a splash of water soaks my hair.

"There is no look." I mumble under my breath.

"You are not letting it in." I watch him as he continues to float around me in a circle, the very image of calm and collected. "Dig your toes in the sand. Feel the earth beneath you and see how much magic is around you." And I do, let my toes burrow through the smoothened rocks.

Soft and undisturbed sand lay beneath. I dig further until most of the wet earth covers my feet. Solid, it makes me feel solid being barely buried and yet connected with the ground.

"Breathe." I take a deep breath. The crisp scent of cedar mixed with the damp moss. "Ask nothing of it, only for it to make its presence known." I furrow my brow.

"Easier said than done." I mutter under my breath. I don't need to look at him to know he just rolled his eyes at me.

"Just try. Clear your mind and just *feel.*"

"I *am*." He laughs at my impatience. The timbre of his voice sparkling just as brightly as the water around us.

"Don't think about finding your sister or of having to tap your core." He stands in front of me. Eyes boring into mine. His voice is a bit deeper when he says, "Revel in the feeling of being one with the earth. Let it relax you." When he sees me start to form an argument, he silences me with a look. "Close your eyes."

"You better not be pulling a prank on me." I groan and he laughs. I hate that the sound of his laughter feels like fireworks on my skin.

"Feel the current of the water, sway with the motions." He whispers—almost croons it to my ear. I shudder as the water around me grows colder but it was not uncomfortable. Rather, the cold took away some weariness in my bones.

Then I feel it before I see it in my mind. Pulsing threads of magic surrounding me, touching me. Waiting for me to let it pass through. They're in the water, wading and directing the current.

In another breath, I grab the green thread of the earth that's already winding their way up my legs. Once I reach out to them, it responds willingly. The thread pulses with energy and it rushes through me like a steady heartbeat. I let out a laugh of delight and Flynn watches me.

"I can feel it!" He grins then and a lightness in his eyes shines. I lean my head back and feel the heat of the sun on my cheeks as it starts to rise. The warmth, as if in this too, fine threads of energy seep into me.

Connection to the earth, to nature. This feeling of being embraced by the world—it was unlike anything I've ever felt in my life. Everything now feels brighter, more vivid. The elements are speaking to me, giving me energy.

It's nothing like I could have imagined it to be. The senses that I would have used to seeing these pulses of energy everywhere had grown dull. My mother's bindings had cut me off.

I know mama was only trying to protect me and my sisters. I understand why she wanted to protect us as witches, but part of me hates that she did. The black stains on the golden threads of her memory bubbles up. A bitter taste coats my tongue.

It makes me feel guilty for wanting magic, for feeling a yearning inside me despite how much it failed me. How much it caused my mother to lie to me. Wanting it after it had killed her feels like a betrayal. This thought breaks my connection and I'm back to feeling detached—so apart.

"Where did you go?" Flynn breaks through my thoughts and I frown.

"It was wonderful. Truly." A tinge of disappointment betrays my voice. "I hate that it makes me feel like I've been so utterly *deprived*." I don't want to feel this way. Flynn is quiet then, letting me stew in my thoughts. "I just wish she'd given me a choice."

I clear my throat to change the topic. The conversation turning too somber for comfort. Before I can say anything else, he interjects.

"I've forgotten..." I look at him then and find him mirroring my position, face towards the sky. Arms floating in the water, fingers lazily raking through the surface. "That this is supposed to feel like a gift." I wait a beat for him to continue, but he continues to make languid strokes.

"What do you mean?" I prompt. He hesitates but lets out a breath before looking at me.

"Some of us, witch—" The nickname he uses offers little to no bite this time. "Were trained in this craft so early in life that the first memory we have are of magic."

"Is that so bad?" He offers me a tight smile.

"When your life is made of nothing but the craft, it's hard not to want a sense of normalcy every once in a while. When your measure of worth relies so heavily on your magic, it's hard not to start wishing you didn't have it." He lifts a hand and water flows through his fingers into balls of shining liquid.

"Love. Family. A home." Every flick of his hands, the water flows with him, into different shapes as he wills them to. "These things, you've been given... so openly. So freely and without conditions. Some of us never had that." A distant look has now painted his face, he looks younger now, soft around the edges. Sad. He looks so defeated and sad.

"You have a family. Your cabal."

"Not in the ways that count." He relaxes his hands and the water droplets circling the air drops with it. "Magic can be burdensome sometimes." The urge to comfort this man flares in me. I muster up enough bravado to feign a smirk.

"Well, lucky for you, the Mother happened to just drop a thieving witch on your lap to take some of that magic off your shoulders." I make a dramatic bow. "Glad to be of service." He turns all his attention to me and the air almost crackles.

I feel Flynn grip the bond. Strong enough that I couldn't control the startled sound from my lips. I look at my hands, feeling him there as if he touched me physically. I look over at him. His eyes darker and boring into mine, a flush on his neck—evidence of a heat I can feel creeping on my skin, too.

He takes a step and the Source bond flares to life, my knees almost buckling at the surge of power. His lips part when he releases a shaky breath. Another step.

We were so, so close.

I could see the dark wisps of his eyelashes framing such seizing blue eyes. The space between us electric and taut. If he takes another step—

"Zelle." The timbre of Linc's voice shoots me out of my stupor. I whirl around and find him standing over us, his arms crossed. My eyes widen. How long has he been standing there while Flynn and I—what? Hovered around each other? What exactly were we doing?

The muscle in his jaw ticks as he crouches down to reach for me. I look over my shoulder at Flynn, who's smirking at Linc.

"Ah, keeper. I don't believe she called *you*." Linc's lips peel back into a sneer.

"You keep your hands to yourself, magus." Flynn raises his hands from the water in a noncommittal gesture and shrugs. This seems to irk Linc even more.

I pull my feet from its buried state and swim towards the edge near his feet. Only then did he dare take his eyes off of Flynn to look at me.

"Let's go, your training with Ava is about to start." Linc reaches for me and as soon as his hands hold mine, we turn to smoke and disappear into the air.

I gasp, he's finally learned how to shadow jump? Since when? I don't ask these questions. Even as shadows I can tell Linc is in another mood. Instead, I direct my attention back to Flynn who is still looking up at us watching us go with his hold still firm on our bond.

Chapter 25

My hand twirls around the stem of the forget-me-nots spurting from the vase at the center of the dining table. The light blue petals seem to push themselves open as I brush my fingers through them. The small stems swaying along as I will it, they look like they're dancing.

A small smile forms on my lips at the sight. Ever since Flynn and I did the makeshift affinity ceremony a week ago I'd find it easier to tap into the green threads of the earth.

I don't just draw energy from them but now I'm able to make small movements in plants. More and more I've become aware of their energy. It's as if identifying my affinity allowed an innate sense of knowing in me. Knowing where to look and how, a natural sixth sense.

Spells and focusing that energy to funnel into my magic though... That's a different thing. These days I've been training with Ava and Flynn have helped me improve some. Yet both have told me my unstable handle on my core limits my ability to let my magic follow my intent.

What sense does this power bear when I cannot wield it to follow my intentions? It all boils down to what's stopping me from fully accepting it, not resenting this unstable magic in me.

It comes with me trusting that my mother did what she had to do. Lie to her children to protect us and yet when I try to visualize her face, all I see is her death. If we knew how to wield magic, we could have avoided her death entirely. We could have fought the Comendeti with her that day.

All this internal work with Ava had led me to finally admit that a part of me hates my mother. This magic, because it's the very reason she's dead and my sister is gone. How ironic that it's the only thing I need now, to accept it, forgive it and *her* so we can actually make progress.

Zoha kicks me from under the table to draw my attention to her.

"Where's your head at?" Her eyes are on my hands, watching its movements. I shake myself from my thoughts.

"Sorry." I mumble as I brush off my hands. I hadn't realized that I've been crushing the forget-me-nots in a death grip. Flynn tugs at the bond between us and I shift in my seat.

Another thing that changed is the fact that this Source bond between us grew stronger. Like this phantom limb grew and now bears a significant weight between us. Easier to reach and much harder to ignore. I blame it on the fact that he likes to tug on it just to catch my attention or to annoy me.

With the Source bond being so prominent, I sometimes siphon too much of Flynn's magic. Happened on more than one occasion. Each time it leaves him weak and glaring. I had as much control on that as I have with accessing my core. So, he tugs and tugs to annoy me, his own flavor of petty revenge.

Ava's watchful gaze doesn't leave the flowers that have now visibly stilled once I drew my hand away from it. She takes a spoonful of her vegetables and she chews contemplatively.

"I'm glad we're making leaps and bounds of process for your magic." She says after a while. She's being generous.

"I can make plants sway and trees to bend branches in my direction but that's it. Leaps and bounds is stretching it." I give her a weak shrug and I push around my food. Losing any of the appetite that would have come up at the sight of such a small feast. Flynn clears his throat and speaks.

"High priestess, I appreciate your hospitality for this past week but I am needed back home." I sit straighter then and shoot him a look. He doesn't even spare me a glance. Why hasn't he said anything?

His presence had been the key to my said progress, miniscule as they are. Although we have not attempted a touch since the blast of energy, having him around made me feel powerful. More capable.

Would I make any more progress without him here?

I dare not voice this out. I know he's only here for our deal which was for him to get all his magic back. To cut the Source bond, I shouldn't be so dependent on him. I lower my chin and slump to my seat.

I would be lying if I said having him around hadn't become a comfort. A safety net. Feeling the bond grow tight between us during these training sessions anchors me. As if telling me, *yes there is power inside of you.*

Ava leans back and purses her lips.

"Your presence here has been helpful, to say the least, Flynn. Why don't you stay at least until Zelle could build her strength more?" Heat flushes my cheeks. Everyone in the room knows that I need Flynn for my training and it puts my ability to shame.

So much for independence.

Another tug on the bond, stronger this time. I couldn't help but to look at him. This time his eyes meet mine, softer now as if reading my mood.

"I know, and I have been more than happy to assist her." He admits, his brow creasing a little as if surprised to admit this himself. "But cabal business requires me to leave the soonest. Zelle should still be able to siphon my magic over planes in case she needs it." He angles his head and nods it my way. Permission and encouragement.

"If you must." The high priestess flourishes her arm, politely waving him on. "But," Her eyes dart between him and I. "If you can spare the time, I would like to invite you to Esbat for the new moon in a few days." His brows shoot up to disappear under the silken tumble of his raven hair on his forehead. Valera's head whips toward Ava.

"Esbat is private and only those within our inner courts are allowed to participate." Ava takes a sip of the wine and she whirls it once. Twice. Before looking back at Valera.

"Flynn is the Source for one of the Triune witches in our coven, Val. It's the least we can do as thanks." She bristles at Ava's tone but nods.

"Esbat?" Zoha asks, wary and guarded eyes darting between the keeper and the high priestess.

"A celebration done under the light of the full moon. We will perform rituals within a sacred space when the moon is at its most powerful." Ava leans back on her chair, swirling the wine still. "Witches from our coven will come home to Meridian on this night. We will perform rites of cleansing, recharging—healing."

"It's also a time for prayer and offering one's heartfelt desires." Valera supplies. "It is only done by our inner court because it is an intimate celebration." She glances at Ava sideways, "Power can…" She trails off, "awaken urges. One can get drunk in all that energy so impulses are stronger."

Without meaning to, I look at Flynn. Remembering what happened at the lake before Linc stepped in. As if thinking of the same thing, his eyes glint and his lips curl into a smirk.

"It would be an honor, high priestess."

"Is that a pout I'm seeing?" Flynn's voice makes me jump and I whirl to find him stalking his way towards me.

"I don't pout." I counter weakly, knowing full well I *was* pouting. After dinner, I had been feeling restless so I made my way to my tree—the one I had conjured during the affinity ceremony with Flynn. I had just taken a seat just below it when Flynn showed up.

"What are you doing here?" I wrap my hands around myself and I frown at him. Not that his presence is unwelcome. He shrugs as he sidles up next to me, careful not to touch me.

"It's not hard to figure out you've been sneaking your way here every night after training." My cheeks heat at that. I had thought I'd been smart with my actions and that no one would notice me missing from the manor.

"This..." I raise my eyes to the tree in front of us. To look at the roots and the branches that bent and grew in unnatural angles. "This tree reminds me that I'm not a complete failure." This is tangible proof that magic is inside me. That part of me is powerful somehow.

Despite how most of my training ended, I could always come here to remind myself that things aren't hopeless. That somehow, if things are done right, then I'd be able to wield my powers. Will it to follow my intentions and finally be *mine*?

"Oh, stop with the self-deprecating talk." Flynn grumbles and I look over at him with a sneer. "What? I mean it. You're a witch, bound or not. Your mother couldn't really take that away from you."

I bring my knees up to my chest and I rest my chin on them.

"I can't stop thinking how different it would have been if she'd just let us *be*. I wish she'd trusted me enough with the truth and let me in. If she did, maybe she wouldn't be dead today. Maybe, my dad would have lived, too." Flynn leans back on his hands and stares up into the darkening sky. His dark hair swaying with the wind.

"Was it so bad?"

"What do you mean?"

"Your life. Was it so bad that your mother had chosen to give you a normal life for as long as she could? Dead parents out of the equation, of course." His face darkens and he frowns. "Dead parents are horrible, regardless." I let the question hang between us, his tone showing me enough that he, too, knows what it's like to lose a parent.

"It wasn't." Far from it. We had been such a happy family, content in our togetherness. It was only after papa died that we had started to fall apart as a family, but even then, mama took care of us. Ran herself ragged to feed us and to send Zoha to the university of her choosing. "I just wish she'd trusted me enough to let me decide for myself so she didn't have to do all of this alone." It would have helped me understand her choices. I bury my face in my arms crossed over my knees. "I sound like such an ingrate."

"Wanting a life different from the one you lead is not you being ingrateful of what you've been given, witch. Especially if all you've hoped for it to be given more control over your life than what was granted to you." His voice is soft and I hide my quickly heating face further into my arms. He understood, somehow. The shame and the ache for demanding more from a parent. "Come." He beckons and I look up at him. Flynn turns to me, crossing his legs. His clothed knee bump into my shin and he jostles me. He raises his palm to the air, his face pensive, waiting for me.

"I want to show you something." I mirror his position and I hover my hands over his. "Close your eyes and breathe." His eyes pierce mine, deep blues sparkling in the night. I let out a long breath and close my eyes.

Then I feel him pull me in. Unlike how Ava would usually use phantom hands to find my core, Flynn tugs me through our bond and I fall into him. Into his psyche. At first, I see nothing but smoke, but I know it's him. The smoke starts to take form.

I see a man, one with dark hair cut close to the skin, his blue eyes filled with anger. He looks like Flynn, but so different. He has frown lines, angry imprints on his skin that shows how much he detested life. His eyes crinkled and narrowed. Without a word he raises his hand and brings it to my cheek.

The impact makes my ears ring and my teeth slams into my inner cheek filling my mouth with the taste of copper. I see black spots in my vision but I look back at him. At the angry man who looked at me with nothing but distaste.

"This is a simple spell. Your cousins could do it in their sleep at your age!" He bares his teeth to me and leans in close. I shrink into myself but I don't talk back. He shoves me by the shoulders, his fingers digging deeply into my thin shoulder. "Again!" His voice booms and it makes my knees quake. "You are the heir of this cabal, it is shameful how average you are at this!"

The man in front of me disappears and the vision changes. Now I'm faced with the image of a woman, sickly and weak. Her brown hair ragged and damp with her sweat. Her brown eyes, unfocused and unseeing as she lays in her bed staring at the ceiling. Her thin arms searching, reaching for something—someone that isn't in the room with us.

I sit by her and watch the life drain out of her. Watch as her magic blinks out and it takes all the light from the room. I stay even in the darkness, holding her hand in mine as she starts to grow cold to the touch. I don't want to blink. I don't want to take my eyes away from her. I think she's going to disappear if I do.

I only move when I hear his voice from the doorway.

"Enough of that. Your training will not wait." He doesn't even spare her a glance. Anger burns my throat, burning away the grief in my heart but I don't say anything and follow him out.

There's nothing but anger and punishment in these moments.

Each flash, each new image it was of magic. Of power growing and growing. New heights and new spells. New skills.

Yet, there is always anger, disappointment. Of needing more than what I can provide.

Until it stops.

I gasp and I scramble away from Flynn. He is pale and his breathing is ragged but he doesn't take his eyes off me. They were his memories. His internal battle that he'd won over. The memories that protect him and his core, self-preservation and the need to excel.

I know why he's showing them to me. Why he's letting me into his past to show me a reality different from mine, one that I had thought I'd wanted.

He leans back on his elbows and stares up at the sky. His breathing shallow and shaky.

"Your mother was beautiful." He doesn't respond for a moment and he gulps down.

"You have the same eyes. Not just in color but… Kind and soft." His admission creates a lump in my throat.

"I'm sorry." I whisper. I want to reach over. To hold his hand and to squeeze until his pain simmers out. Instead, I lie beside him, curled up and staring at his profile. He doesn't look at me when he speaks.

"For what it's worth, witch, your mother had her reasons and I doubt it's because she didn't trust *you* with your powers. Magic is currency in this world and greed is a sin that drives everyone that's in it."

We don't say anything else and wait until the stars succumb to dawn and sunlight washes over us.

Chapter 26

The library within the Meridian Manor carried books from different ages and languages. The leather and edges from the books scratched and worn from so much usage. It's only been a few days since Flynn had left and already, I feel restless. I had asked Ava for time in the library, to allow me to pour myself in the books.

What I was looking for, I was uncertain. My focus is going everywhere. I feel myself getting farther and farther away from what truly matters. Because it's been more than three weeks since my vision with Zafiya. More and more I feel less of her.

Feel less certain if we can find her or find her in any retrievable state. If she's even—

I shake my head against the dark thoughts forming in my head. I have a stack of books in front of me. Most of them summoning spells. Location spells that I have tried reciting into the echoing halls of the library. All are fruitless.

Ava had said these spells have limitations, if one's target is too far or protected with wards then it wouldn't work. Magic is finite, she reminds me, limited and vulnerable against countermeasures.

I pry open another book, the scent of the weathered pages bringing little comfort. There has to be something here. Anything.

A plate of sliced fruits slides on the table I was occupying and Linc sits on the chair beside me. I give him a nod of thanks and pop a slice of orange in my mouth.

"I can't find a spell I can use to find her, Linc." I thumb through the pages of the book open before me, "There has to be something else I can do."

"You're doing the best you can by training your magic so you can use it when the time comes. You need it to protect your sisters." Linc slides his hands through mine in a gesture of comfort and I tighten my fingers through his.

"Did you hear anything from Valera?" He shakes his head, a grim no.

"She's traveled to the farthest sister covens possible. Most covens are pacifists, the very mention of the Comendeti scares them even more. None have come forward with any information that we can use to even begin the search for their lands." He grits his teeth but the hand around mine remains gentle. "Trying to go against the Comendeti is unheard of for them. Any encounters are only ever brought on by defensive measure and never…"

He trails off. From the books and spells I've read, there's rarely a spell that brings harm so this makes sense. Protection, healing, and blessings. These things take precedent.

Witches live peaceful lives, at most. In fact, they aim to do so. There were attempts to retaliate against the Comendeti but most of it led to failure or death. Their hired monsters often kill witches before they even get the chance to get close. Monsters like the *Hala*.

I shiver at the memory of the fog demon. If they had things like that in their arsenal, I don't blame the witches for steering clear. After so many deaths and their need to preserve blood lines, the witches have stopped fighting against the Comendeti. Although I resent whoever decided that a few kidnapped witches are better than trying to vanquish such evils.

I'm getting a headache just turning these thoughts in my head. How long have I been here anyway? I let out a sigh and I pop another orange slice in my mouth. I've holed up in the library for a few days since Flynn left. My tree now feels a bit lonely if I go there on my own after training.

I shake the thought away. Loneliness is poison that makes me thirsty for any antidote, I see. I rub my face with my hands and I speak to drown my thoughts.

"Do you think the wards around Meridian are dulling my abilities to locate her?" Linc purses his lips and narrows his eyes at me.

"Valera has been outside the wards. Ava has scried for Zafiya outside the wards too, so I doubt that would make a difference." Of course, he would be quick to deny the theories but he looks out the window of the library. It has a clear view of the path leading to the forest clearing we frequent for training in the distance.

"The only time I had seen Zafiya was when I went outside the wards, by the brook. What if I'm the only one that can reach out to her but I can't do it when in hiding?" He shakes his head and stands then.

"It's too dangerous, Zelle."

"Not if you come with me! You can shadow jump us out of there at the first sign of danger." I plead but now he refuses to look at me.

"No, I'm not as strong as Valera. I can't risk it." He shakes his head again, his lips set in a thin line which told me there would be no convincing him otherwise. I cross my arms and huff out a breath knowing full well that conversation is over. "I came to tell you that Ava had asked for you, preparation for Esbat will soon be underway."

I wave him off and he begins to stalk out the room. He looks at me from over his shoulder.

"Whatever you're planning to do. Don't." He didn't wait for an answer before closing the door behind him. I stare at the wooden door and I open another book.

Good. I don't think he'd like the answer I had for him anyway.

Chapter 27

I'm in the middle of shoving candles and ritual tools into my pack when Zoha walks in our room. She spares a glance at the contents and then looks at me.

"Linc has already told me not to." I shove the notebook filled with spells I copied off of the countless grimoires I can get my hands on in the library. "I will still do it. I need to."

"And you will." Her tone had been anything but encouraging. I turn to face her.

"What do you mean by that?" She shrugs.

"This is magic, Zelle. You wanted this, didn't you? We're *magic.*" Her tone drips with sarcasm and I frown at her. How could she even begin to think that is what I wanted?

"I never wanted any of this." I raise my hands to the room and I clutch them into fists when they shake with the effort. My books, my interests, they could have all burned in hell just so I can get our lives back.

It's unfair for her to bring this up now. Part of me thinks it's mostly because she probably had another fruitless session today and she's lashing out. I didn't want to take it today, not when I'm anxious about my plans for tonight.

Am I being reckless? Maybe. But I need to try and I don't need her bearing down on me now. So I hit her where I know it'll land, that gaping hole between our relationship.

"You don't know what I want now, Zo. Not after papa died." She grabs me by the arm, her eyes ablaze with anger.

"You don't get to throw that around." Her voice is low and carried all the venom she could muster.

"Throw what around? The fact that you left? The way you're shutting down now and leaving all of this to me just like the last time?" Her sharp inhale fills echoes in the room. I had no chance to see her hand raised in the air, a slap waiting to happen. I meet her eyes and I dare her to do it.

She catches herself and her anger melts away. Her eyes line with silver and her shoulder sags when she drops her hand.

"This... this is not like that at all." I know that. I know that I'm being unfair but so is she. "I had to leave."

"You were never there. I was forced to fend for myself. I was forced to become the big sister. I was forced to follow mama's insistence to brush papa's death under the rug. You left *me*, Zo."

"I couldn't breathe in that house. I couldn't stand in that kitchen without seeing him on the floor. I left the house because I couldn't bear lying to myself." Zoha wraps her arms around herself.

"What are you talking about? We were all dealing with grief and you left. Mama had to do her best to keep us all fed."

"I know you would protect her. You understood her more than I could. I just couldn't stand pretending that there isn't a big gaping hole at home. One she refused to acknowledge." She takes a deep breath and she closes her eyes to fight her tears. "Papa took all of the air with him when he died. Mama didn't even talk about him anymore." Her eyes line with silver but she fights the tears from falling.

I didn't want to hear it. To hear her blame our mother for why she left. I turn my back to her and resume packing. She walks to me and wraps me in a hug.

"You keep telling me mama was bad for not talking about him, for not letting us heal our grief properly but at least she stayed." I swipe the tear that escape but not before Zoha saw it and she sighs.

"I'm sorry, Zelle. I never wanted to leave you. I never meant to. I left the house but never you. Never Zafiya." I lean into her, all my anger feeding a deep-seated pain.

"I never wanted this to happen, Zo."

"I know, I was wrong to say that. I just—I'm jealous that you're able to do something with this cursed thing and I can't." She tightens her arms around me. "I'm sorry."

I don't say anything. She sniffles and takes a step back. She straightens herself out, removing any trace of the vulnerability we just shared. She marches to our closet and throws the doors open. She grabs a thick jacket and shoves it into my bag as well.

"Someone has to stay behind in case they come looking for you." She swallows and keeps her eyes on her hands. I look up at her. "Besides, I would be more help here covering for your stubborn ass than attempting to grasp at magic I barely feel inside me." She zips up the bag and tests it for weight, satisfied as she hands it to me. The coven performs rituals for Esbat outside under the moonlight.

It would be easier for me to slip in and out without getting caught. I only need to cast a spell without the confines of the wards that could be blocking me in an attempt to protect me.

Zoha comes back to the closet and pulls out a black velvet dress and drapes it on the bed. I run my fingers through the material. It's beautiful.

The neckline dips low with a straight V that would meet on top of the center of my chest. There are silver stars embroidered around the edge of the flared sleeves. The material is soft against my skin and it glimmers when the light hits it a certain way. It reminds me of the surface of the water at night. Where silver strands ripple and reflect the moonlight. It's perfect for Esbat.

"Got to dress the part." She quips and nudges me with her elbow.

"Where did you get this?" I whisper as I let my fingers glide over the smooth material of the garment. I hear her shift on her feet and I look over my shoulder.

"I..." She trails off and clears her throat. "Ava still had a trunk of mama's old stuff." I frown at her. Not out of anger but confusion.

"Why didn't you tell me?" She shrugs weakly.

"I wanted to—Really, I did but I guess I just wanted to look around on my own before sharing this part of her with you." I smile at her and I pull her into a hug. That lapse, that argument already forgotten. My intentions were wrong for starting that up but I feel lighter. *We* feel lighter.

She lays out her own outfit—A blue silk chemise dress. It had nothing but thin straps to hold it up over her body. The neckline would pool above the swell of her breasts. My dress looks modest compared to this one.

I'm certain Zoha would look like sin incarnate wearing this. The distracting vixen of the night. She holds my gaze then; a gleam of unshed tears coats her eyes. Brown eyes that are severe and so like mine.

"Find her and bring her home to us." My throat is thick so I could only nod.

I had no expectations on what Esbat would be about. It definitely wasn't a feast under the stars. There were torches speared to the ground every few feet. The flames burning bright.

It illuminates the silverware on the long expansive table. Food, wine, and more food overflowed on every discernable surface. It was a party. A party of witches.

An absolute revelry.

Down a few feet from the table is an altar filled with flickering candles already melting through and half-filled vials. A large metal bowl takes up most of the space where piles of smooth crystals of varying colors and patterns are placed.

The altar signifies the middle of the magic circle. It is surrounded by symbols of nature, pots of plants are scattered, large jugs of water and earth line the ground everywhere. A line of salt is heaped on the ground to form a circle around the entire perimeter. It is large enough to accommodate all the witches present for the ritual. Meant to be both protection and a way to contain energy. The sacred space.

Ava steps out of the crowd and up to the altar. Barefoot and dressed in a white flowing robe. Her chest barely contained by the fabric and her hair bound in warm brown waves cascading down her back. This— this is the high priestess. A circlet sat atop her forehead and a clear crystal gleamed under the moonlight. Her emerald eyes glimmer brightly.

"Sisters, I thank thee for your presence on this holy night." She opens her arms and raises her palms to the sky, imploring. "Tonight, as the new moon is at its highest, the Mother shall bless us with strength. Give back the power for that holds this coven to its highest state."

Zoha and I stand shoulder to shoulder. A little intimidated by the formalities. We glance at each other sideways. This was the first ritual we were to witness.

The hair on my arms stands on end at the sensation. It feels like champagne bubbles over my skin. There's no denying that the air crackles with energy, it calls to something inside me. As if the wind is whispering, beckoning for us to join its flight.

Zoha is wide-eyed and gulping. She feels it too, at least some part of it. Already, I see her try to rationalize it in her mind. Deny the energy. Deny the magic so vast in the air. I squeeze her hand until she looks at me. I take her hand in mine.

"Breathe." Remembering how Flynn had asked the very same thing from me back at the lake when my mind raced. "Let it in." I tell her and she breathes in. Deep and holds the cool air in her breath for a beat. She does it again.

She takes big gulps of air. She holds it inside her lungs as if there's an essence in the air she could absorb before she lets it back out into the night. When her eyes open, I could see silver lining her eyes.

Finally.

I can see her face relax into a contented smile as something inside her shifts. I know she could feel it then, the small kernel at the center of her chest drinking in the electricity. Her magic is awake.

"Revel, dear sisters! It is a night of celebration and healing." Ava calls again and the witches break out into a cheer. Instruments start playing. Everyone is singing, dancing around the fire in the middle of the sacred space.

Each jump and cheer shake the ground. It quivers and shakes as if it, too, was dancing along—celebrating with the witches. My bare feet absorb the energy it's giving. Strong and potent in my blood.

I thank the earth for its gift, and I pray that it keeps me hidden. I have not learned to glamor yet, but I hope this overflowing energy fuels my magic enough for it to follow my intentions tonight. I edge my way out of the clearing.

My back hits the trees hiding me from sight when that familiar tug in my gut makes my skin prickle—Flynn! I peek and I see him materialize from smoke, Valera holding his arm rather stiffly. I can see his dimple all the way from here. His smile shows no discomfort despite Valera's death grip.

Some of the younger witches in the bunch hoots and celebrates upon seeing the man. Excitement and curiosity palpable. The steady beat of ritual drums now grows louder.

Flynn's eyes search through the crowd. Perhaps in search of me? The tug in the bond makes my belly dip again. I shiver against the sensation. I'm tempted to step up to him and touch his skin so that our bond can purr from the contact.

A selfish part of me also wishes for the other witches to see he's my Source. I groan, I had no right to feel possessive over him. I don't even notice how I found my way out of my hiding spot and into his view. My breath catches in my throat when his eyes meet mine. Our bond flaring to life on the connection.

He smirks and slips out. Not so subtly ignoring that gaggle of women around him. I walk towards him and fight off the sudden weakness in my knees upon seeing his eyes rake over me.

"You clean up well, witch." He says lightly and I shrug off his compliment. He's wearing a dark blue shirt under a thick jacket, it makes his eyes look severely darker. The loose cotton pants and lightly ruffled tumbling hair do nothing to relax his aura.

"You look good too, Flynn." His blue eyes soften and he shoves his clenched hands in his pockets.

"I would ask you to dance with me but–" He tugs on our bond to emphasize his point. I almost stumble into him at the force of his pull. I glare at him as I take a few steps back, keeping our distance. "Now, see." His smile grows wider. "That's a look I recognize."

"Don't tease." I fuss over the dress and brush off imaginary lint off my sleeve. "This was my mother's." When he stays silent, I peek a look from under my lashes and he's perusing me with such intensity that I quickly look away again. He clears his throat.

"I have something for you since I cannot offer such a lady like you a dance." He pulls out a satchel from his pocket and deposits its contents on his open palm. Chocolate in glistening wrapping paper tumbles out and my eyes widen. I reach for them before I even begin to speak.

"How do you know I like these?" He rolls his eyes as he smiles and his dimple winks on his cheek again.

"It's not hard to notice, you're the only one to ever reach for dessert every time after dinner. I'm sure Ava only ever has them out for you at this point." I unwrap one and pop it in my mouth just as Zoha comes up beside me, effectively popping our bubble.

"Hey, *sis*." She almost hisses. "I think you're forgetting something?" She nudges me with her shoulder and lifts her eyes to the moon which is now glowing brightly in the sky.

Ah, right. Focus.

I berate myself and I can't believe I allowed myself this distraction. I send a small smile towards Flynn.

"I have to go." He tilts his head to the side, studying me.

"Well, whatever you're about to do—" I cringe, was I too obvious? "I trust that you will keep yourself safe. Tug on the bond if you need me." He bows his head and leaves me looking at his retreating figure.

"For the record, I absolutely did not want to break up that party of yours." Zoha teases, her tone filled with mirth. Her eyes zeroing in on the wrapped chocolates still in my hand. "You looked awfully cozy." She murmurs and I give her a playful shove as I feel my cheeks heat at her insinuation.

My smile slips off and I look back up the moon.

No more distractions, it was time to find my sister.

Chapter 28

Thankfully the crowd is well immersed in revelry that it had been way too easy for me to slip out without notice. It takes me only a couple of minutes and a few tumbles to find the pool at the bottom where I had once submerged myself. Back to where I first connected with Zafiya. I pull out the contents of my bag, a bag of salt, candles and bowls. I lay out the jacket that Zoha had packed and kneel.

I flip my notebook open and find the different spells. I sit by the sand near the water and enclose myself in a circle of salt—protection.

Then I begin.

Chant after chant, all the words are foreign and strange on my tongue. These are spells from the different witches from varying eras. Every time I finish a spell to call for my sister, the wind only howls. Empty.

None of them are working. Why are they not working? I was sure. If the moon is at its highest tonight, shouldn't my magic be brimming with enough energy to power these spells? Tears burn my eyes, why can't I make it work?

I read through the spells again. They were all calling forth forces to locate lost loved ones, to find what the heart desires. None of which have made me feel anything other than feel like a fool.

I toss the notebook into the water and watch it flow with the current.

I look up at the sky. The moon is cresting. It sits right above me looking over me and shining so brightly.

"Please." I plead. I clutch my hands together and kneel, eyes toward the moon. "Please, dear Mother." I choke back a sob and I try to scry again.

I wait for the crystal to react to the map to point me towards my sister but nothing happens. Again, I look up at the moon, tears blurring my vision. Desperation gripping my throat tight.

Wind blows again, gentle and caressing my tear-stained cheeks. Instead of cool air, it was warm and hot like a soft breath. My eyes widen.

Maybe calling on *the* Mother was not working because I had to call on mine.

I take deep steadying breaths. It barely calmed my hammering heart and ringing ears but it filled my lungs with the same warm air. I wrap my hands around myself, looking deep down. And finding those dark stains in my magic. The ones festering like a sore wound.

"Mama?" I call out, my voice weak and shaking. "If you're there. I need your help." The wind around me howls and it grows warmer. Taking away my chill.

"I don't know what else to do. I'm sorry." I call to the wind. I picture her in my mind. I hug myself tighter, needing the pressure to calm my roaring heartbeat. I'm looking so deep into the darkness inside me and I'm scared I would fall down without a chance of getting back up.

Then a glow, an ember blinks, slow as if eyes waking from such sweet dreams. The images of my mother flash in my mind again, the lies, the times she had pushed me away from magic. All the times she had hidden a part of herself from me.

I think of the fear she must have felt losing her coven. Of the uncertainty in the days she had with papa out in a world she barely recognized. Unguarded and shunned.

I think of how she must have felt when she got pregnant with Zafiya. How she must have been so happy and yet so scared that she had *three* daughters. What should have been impossible to her as a witch and yet here we were.

"Mama, I need you." My voice is barely a whisper, watered down by my tears.

"Zelle."

Her voice rings in the air and my eyes snap open. There she was, as vibrant as the sun. She brings light with her. She stands a few feet in front of me, over by the surface of the water. I let out a sob at the sight of her and she smiles at me with such sadness. I rush to my feet but stop when she raises her hand to me.

"Don't break the protection circle."

"Mama." I call to her again because I didn't know what else to do. I didn't think I'd have been given the chance to do it again.

"I'm here, sweetheart. We don't have much time; the moon is cresting."

"I need to find Zafiya, they have her and I can't—" I lift my hands as if to show her the emptiness. Their uselessness. She comes a bit closer, but never enough for me to be able to reach her. "My core, I can't access it because..." I trail off.

"Because it failed you. Because I failed you."

I shake my head to deny it but she simply smiles at me. There's no use lying to my own mother.

"I know you were only protecting us."

"Knowing why doesn't mean you have to agree with my choices, Zelle, and disagreeing with them does not mean you love me any less. It just means you have a mind of your own and you recognize that your mother is human. One who had made many mistakes in her life."

She looks at the forest behind me, at the path that will eventually lead her to the manor. Her face falls into such sadness that my heart hurts to see her like this.

"I let my fears dictate your future. I took away your choices because I wanted so badly to protect you. I stifled your gifts and took away your chance to get to know this part of you because I was scared that they would take you away from me. I made you feel guilty for even wanting it in the first place."

Her face falls and the lightness in her face dims. The need to cross over to comfort her is like a punch to the gut.

"When I saw how your eyes sparkled when this small part of you recognized the magic you've seen in me, I had to shut it down. I

wanted to pull you far away from it and I had lied to you just to keep you in the dark longer."

She looks back at me now and tears shone in her eyes. They reflect mine and it washes over me. I wish to run to her, to touch her but I can't.

"You did your best, mama. I know that." Even hearing the words from her was painful. To hear her openly admit the very thoughts I tried to bury deep inside me is too much to bear.

"I don't own you, Zelle."

Silver flecks of tears rim her eyes.

"I failed to see how you have all grown into such powerful young women and had hidden my fears and my grief. It was all I ever knew to do. To hide. To pretend things will be okay. I didn't see how much I hurt you and your sisters when I did that. It wasn't magic that failed, Zelle. It was me."

"No, that's not—" I start but she shakes her head.

"It's okay to think so, too. It's okay to admit that I wasn't the mother that you needed me to be at times."

I fall to my knees. My strength leaching out of me. She had her reasons but she was wrong to dictate how we were supposed to lead our life.

"You were still my mama. I wouldn't have traded that for anything else." She needs to know—she has to know that I wouldn't have asked for anyone else but her as my mother. She smiles at that and she crouches in front of me, to meet my eyes.

"You are twice the woman I am—was. I know you have all the strength you need to save your sister. Let it in. Trust this beautiful part of you. I was wrong to make you feel like it was something that you had to turn away from for me. I don't think I can ever properly ask for forgiveness for forcing you into a corner. I have so many regrets and my biggest one is that I wouldn't be able to teach you how to wield your magic."

I do not let the hurt win because now I know that her fear was only as strong as her love. That her need to protect came from her knowledge of this world and its nightmares. She wanted none of it for us. It was wrong but it was love.

"I love you." My breath catches in my throat. "I forgive you." I say in earnest. As tears flow down my cheeks. I reach out my hands toward her but my hands pass through her image. My skin tingles, warm as the times she's held them.

"I love you, sweetheart. I only wish to be better to you in the next life."

Then she disappears and gently becomes one with the wind around me. Through the blur of my tears, I see the moon. It shines with intensity. It reminds me of her eyes, as bright as the last time she looked at me. When she smiled at me with such longing and regret before she forfeited her life.

I shudder as the stains inside me dissipate in the brightness of my forgiveness of *her*. All that is left is the golden threads of magic, the strong steady thrum of my core. In a blink, my mind goes quiet.

Empty—no, not empty. Peaceful. Calm.

Chapter 29

I dig my hands into the soil and let the energy wrap seep into me. I let it flow through me and into my core. The energy pools there, I hold it, let it build. I feed it all to my magic.

And then the words come out of me.

"Bound by blood,

I call to thee.

I seek thy path,

Show unto me."

The power flows from me. From my center, out into my tongue, weaving itself into the spell. Into the words. Bringing with it my desire, my intention. Then a blast casts out of me. The light blinding, I was looking at white.

A vision, I am seeing and I am not. My sister is curled onto herself, too thin. She is so painfully thin, her cheeks hollowed out. Her eyes sunken. She looks at nothing, her eyes glazed. Her dry lips look like she had not had a drink in days.

Tears burned anew, my sweet, sweet sister. Now a shell of herself. I scream for her but she doesn't hear me. The vision wavers and fades.

No! I need more!

I dig deeper. I clutch the soil tighter in my fingers and take in as much energy as I can. It continues to waver. I scream for her again, over and over. Begging for her to look. To feel me.

In desperation I plunge into myself and see the Source bond, strong and pulsing inside me. I just need enough to keep the vision alive. With urgency, I pull, pull, pull. The energy from the bond courses through me in waves.

Flynn's powers flood my core like blue spring water.

The vision goes steady. It's so clear that it looks like she's right in front of me. When I call to her again, my voice tinged and laced with magic, I see Zafiya react. She can hear me.

"Zelle?" Her voice cracks.

"Zaf, it's me. I'm here." I plead for her to hear me, for her to know I am coming. Then she nods, closing her eyes sliding down the floor. I could feel my limbs shaking, from the strain, from the cold. All my warmth is seeping out of me, hollowing me out. "Where are you? Do you have windows that you can peek out of to see what's outside?" She shakes her head weakly.

"N-no windows. I'm in a cell underground. It's cold." Cold. Is it up north? It's the middle of the year which areas are still cold this time?

"Did they hurt you?" I see her hesitate, her bony hands hiding the marks on her arms.

"Yes. They come and feed from me more often than before. Something broke inside me and now they're taking my... magic by force." Her eyes fill with tears and curls inward, making herself look even smaller. I make a mental note, she is aware of her magic now. I was hoping it had somehow awakened to protect her instinctively but it had only drawn the Comendeti to feed more often. "What are they, Zelle? Why won't they just kill me?" The wind knocks out from my lungs and I grip my own shaking hands.

"I'm coming for you." An earnest vow. It seals our connection with the remnants of magic I pull from the Source bond. It's the last thing I could tell her before the vision breaks.

Then I am alone, under the moonlight, the only sound in the air is the trickling of the water. I collapse to the ground and groan.

"Shit, little witch." I almost jump out of my skin and turn to find Flynn stumbling towards me. "The least you could do is ask." He wheezes, his hand clutching his stomach.

He looks pale, a sheen of sweat shining on his forehead. I utter a silent thank you to my mother before making a move to breaking the sacred circle. I crawl towards Flynn who fell to knees on the sand.

As soon as I break the circle, violent winds burst from behind me. I almost topple forward from the force. Flynn catches me by the arms.

He curses and attempts to pull me behind him. I turn around to look at what he's seeing, only to find my nightmare walking in a predatory pace towards me.

The two Comendeti who had stalked us. The damned magic eaters are here

A feral grin spread on both their lifeless, grey faces. Rows of teeth glinting in the night. They must have found me when I created the connection with Zafiya. The magic flowing both ways and leading them straight to me.

Flynn attempts to stand but the trickle of blood down his nose is the sign of our damnation. I took too much too fast and had weakened not only his magic but also his physical body. I was worse for wear.

I look behind us now, from where Flynn had appeared. If he had found me so quickly from the bond, the witches for Esbat are not far from here. We cannot run back and lead these magic eaters to a feast made for them. To lead them to where Zoha could still be.

Flynn glances at me from the side of his eye and nods slightly. Understanding that we cannot put the rest of the witches at risk.

"We come for you, witch." The woman speaks. Her voice was of many, of those from here and before. It makes my scalp prickle at the sound.

"Run, Flynn." I say under my breath. "It wants me, not you." He sneers at me

"Like hell I'm leaving you here." Ignoring the fact that both of us could barely stand.

They take another step towards us, taking their time. Knowing full well we have very little to no fight left in us.

"Call to your other sister. I can smell her on you." The male one smirks at me, teeth promising nothing but the worst death imaginable. I couldn't bear to ask *how* the

Comendeti consumed magic but if the teeth were any clue... I shudder at the image.

"Screw you!" I spit at their direction and both hiss at me. Flynn sends me a sideways glance as if to say.

Way to plead your case.

I didn't have time to react because in a blink they lunge towards us, and I scream. Flynn clutches me to his chest, his own scream swallowed behind a grunt.

Then the Comendeti's piercing hiss stops in a grunt. They've hit a wall—no, a shield and bounced off from the impact.

"Linc!" I call out and he materializes in front of me. His eyes brimming with the promise of murder. He grabs me and Flynn. Then we turn into smoke before the Comendeti breaks through the shield. And they lunge at where we were just sitting.

We materialize a few feet away from them, behind a boulder. Linc curses.

"We need to get out of here." We press our backs to the cold stone, breathing hard. "I can... I can mask you, shield you but only for a few minutes." He gulps and risks a glance toward the Comendeti. "Not enough that they would not follow the trail."

"We can't go back to the manor. It'll expose the coven." I tell him in hushed words. Linc nods, agreeing, albeit with difficulty.

"I know a place." Flynn speaks up. His eyes meet Linc's. The animosity between them temporarily forgotten in the midst of certain death. "We have a safehouse not far from here, we can go there, mislead them. It has a portal directly linked to our cabal. Runes and wards protect it. It only opens with my blood." Flynn rolls his head loosening the tension clinging there. "They can't chase us down a portal." He glances at me then and gives me a weak smirk, an attempt to lighten the terror vising my heart. "Old man wanted to make sure his line didn't die with me."

I tuck that information away. He had safehouses for Flynn not because of paternal concern. He wanted to make sure his heir lived enough to bear his own, ensuring that their bloodline continues.

"It could work." Linc says after a beat. Contemplative.

"It will." Flynn insists.

"We need to lead them away from the ritual. Away from Zoha." I add on and Linc's eyes shine with the moonlight.

"Are you up for it, keeper?" The challenge in Flynn's voice seems to rile up my friend and his lips press into a thin line.

"Just tell me where it is." Linc grabs us both. Visible effort showing on the veins throbbing just above his temple. We are fully hidden once we turn to smoke once again, flying through the sky and reappearing. When Linc loses his breath, we land on the ground. Each landing hit harder and harder as his strength drains away.

I pray he has enough in him to bring us all to safety.

Chapter 30

It takes close to an hour to lose the Comendeti, Linc had to make different stops to mislead it. On the last jump, Linc drops both Flynn and I to the damp ground.

Spent and covered in sweat, his blonde hair sticks to his forehead, breath heaving. I lay a hand on his back as I peruse the area. We were in the thick of the forest, the moonlight could only peek through the trees.

Safehouse is an exaggeration. The house is barely as big as a shed. Green vines cover the walls. The windows are so dirty it's impossible to peer inside to see anything. The wood panels on the door worn but sturdy. I give Flynn a sideways glance and I hear the rustle of his clothes more than I could see his shoulder shrug.

"Inconspicuous was the goal, not comfort." He stalks toward the steps toward the door and a sensation wafts through me. The wards make my stomach turn. I know it's part of the spell to make everyone turn away from it. Still, it's hard to ignore that part of me urging me to leave.

Before I can move, Flynn utters a spell under his breath. His eyes locked to the door, most likely seeing the runes he needs to unlock before we can come in. "Hand me your knife."

Linc staggers towards him to hand him a small dagger from the holster on his thigh. I slip my hands around

Linc's waist to take on his weight and he rests his hand on my shoulder.

Flynn runs the blade down his palm and I wince at the well of blood that builds there. Before any of it dripped down, he uses that same hand on the doorknob and it creaks open.

He lets out a shaky breath and gestures for us to come in. Flynn shuts the floor behind us. He takes the small gas lamp and matches that were set on a small table near the door and lights it, illuminating the room.

Pushed at the farthest corner of the room is a small bed. On it are blankets stacked on top of the pillows. The leftmost wall is a kitchenette, where a small wood burning stove that could warm the entire room sits beside a cupboard.

Pans, mugs, and an assortment of jarred preserves line the wall. To the right, by the bed, is the sink. Tucked underneath are rugs and a wooden bucket.

A small chair was pushed to the last corner of free space in the area. Quaint. Clearly, this is meant to house only one person. Having all three of us here, with Linc and Flynn being both towering men, made the entire room cramped.

"We would have to stay the night." Flynn ushers Linc to the lone chair, and he slides down to the floor beside him. His back to the wall. I remained standing by the door, hands clasped together behind my back not wanting to take up any more space.

"We can't. It's not safe, despite your runes." Linc is breathless and he could barely lift his head to peer over at Flynn.

"I—" Flynn clears his throat and scrubs his palms over his face, "I'm empty, absolutely spent." He doesn't look at me but I still feel a pang of guilt at that. "I almost couldn't open the door through the runes." His pallor from when he first found me in the brook hasn't improved. His skin is pale and his eyes are dull.

I attempt to grasp at any remnant of magic within our Source bond, but it stays silent.

"Can't we recharge outside?" I ask. Flynn shakes his head shrugging off his jacket. It reveals the dark blue shirt stretching over his chest and I school my face in cool disinterest.

He hands me his jacket then and I realize I still wore the velvet dress Zoha picked for Esbat. The hem is torn and muddied. I wrap Flynn's jacket around me. His smoky scent of pine warms me further as I take in a deep breath.

"Too risky. We don't know how far along we lost the Comendeti. Any attempt at magic outside this safehouse would be like lighting a beacon for them to follow." He juts his chin toward the bed. "You can take the bed, witch. Your keeper and I should be fine here."

Linc grunts in agreement. His eyes scanning me closely as I moved to take a seat on the corner of the bed.

"What were you doing out that brook, Z?" I clutch Flynn's jacket and tug it around me tighter. The fabric, still warm from his body, chases away the cold that rattle my bones. I refuse to look at him. That tone in his voice signals his anger.

I don't need to be reprimanded like a child.

"Doing what I can to find my sister." I almost hiss at him. "Not sitting on my ass praying to the moon like nothing is wrong in the world." Linc's eyebrows shot up in surprise at the sharpness of my words.

The surge of anger may have been uncalled for, but it worked. Damn the consequences, *it worked.* I finally reached Zafiya after weeks of silence and I found her.

Not Ava, not Valera. *I did*—outside those wards that were said to only protect us. The same wards that hide us away from my sister while she suffers in captivity.

"She needs me, Linc and I found her." Linc sits a little straighter then, he takes a deep breath and looks away from me. His brows bunch together.

"Why didn't you tell me? I could've been with you, shielded you while you did what you had to." I took a moment to just look at him. The tension in his shoulders and the way he flexes his hands on his laps.

This was more than anger. It was hurt and disappointment. Not only in my choices for the night, but my refusal to trust him as my keeper.

"I did tell you, remember? And you told me you wouldn't risk it. That you wouldn't let me!" He winces at this. He cannot deny that. His silence is enough of an admission.

"No one should *let* you do what you want. It's your magic. Your sister, at stake." Flynn interjects and he sends a look of distaste towards the other man. "Would you mind getting some wood for the fire, keeper?" Linc stiffens further, his ears reddening now in fury.

I hold my breath, the space within the house is cramped enough with the three of us here. Surely male egos would need more room than what we have now. Thankfully, Linc leaves without so much as a retort.

I let out a breath and slump further into the bed. Tension leaking out me. I'm utterly so tired. I look at Flynn who's watching me, his eyes curious. His eyes almost look black in the dark and it makes him look even more severe.

"Thank you." I whisper and he smiles, a weak tug at his lips.

"Get some rest." He says gruffly under his breath and he leans his head back. Heat creeps up my cheeks then. Guilt coming on strong and plentiful as I see the sight of the disheveled magus.

"I'm sorry for pulling too hard. I—I needed more time."

He shrugs and draws up one leg to his chest. He rests his outstretched arm on it.

"Glad to be of service, little witch." I almost smile back at him, but he speaks further. "If it helps you find your sister sooner."

Right. The bargain. Once I find Zafiya, we'll sever our Source bond and he'll be rid of me. I don't speak then and I lay down. I turn my back to him then, refusing to let him see the evidence of my disappointment.

Teeth.

Rows and rows of teeth are right in front of me. Blood dribbling from them and slicking my cheeks with red stains.

No.

I want to scream but I can't move. Couldn't take my eyes away from the teeth—the mouth that sneers at me. The owner of them step away from me to reveal the face of the magic eater. Eyes of darkness, now alight with mischief.

"Your sister tasted like sweet berries, child." He takes a deep breath, his nostrils flaring. His tongue spears out—a serpent's tongue—as if it could taste her from the air.

I try to free my arms to shove him away but feel weight pinning them down, my hands full. I look down and find myself holding my sister, clutching Zafiya to my chest.

Her face looks clean and serene. Her cheeks are as plump as the day of her birthday. Instead of the older version of my sister, I see her as a child, her red hair in those high pigtails. She looks like she's sleeping, as if I shook her hard enough, she would open her eyes. To look at me with the same muddy eyes as mine.

But her yellow jacket falls open to reveal her body.

Her gaping open chest. Her flesh flayed. Her heart was gone, ripped out from her body. I know. I just know sharp teeth took them in one big bite.

I still couldn't scream. I couldn't look away. My eyes locked on her empty chest until the image burned my eyes. Searing itself there to ensure whenever I closed them, I'd see this. See her death.

Someone grabs my chin, forcing me to look away from the gore. I'm met with eyes that remind me of the ocean. So vast like the deep blue sea.

"Flynn." I whisper, somehow finding my voice as he looks at me. His hands come up to my cheeks and I lean into the warmth. He rubs away the tears that dampen them.

It's okay. Everything's going to be okay. His mouth doesn't move, but his voice echoes inside my mind. There's a sad smile on his lips instead.

"She—" I try to look down again at my lap, where I could still feel the weight of my sister's body. But he grips my head preventing me from doing so. He keeps the languid pace of his thumb brushing my cheek.

Eyes on me. Just on me. Again, his voice echoes. Such tenderness in them. I nod and I stay there looking at him.

I keep staring into his eyes, drowning in all that blue, even as the dream starts to crumble.

The safehouse is dark with the gas lamp's fire dimmed. The fire too low to chase the shadows away. The cool air makes me shiver despite the thin blanket wrapped around me with Flynn's jacket on top.

I look toward the arm that I had draped over the side of the bed, like I moved in my dream trying to reach out to him. My hand grazes warm skin. Slowly, I pull my hand back but Flynn stops me. His fingers lace with mine.

I move just until my cheek hits the ends of the mattress, enough for our eyes to find one another in the dark. A churning in his—there was concern, an awareness. Whatever had happened, he had found his way into my mind to pull me out of my nightmare.

We lay there. No words spoken, cloaked in the night, looking *into* each other until I fall back into a dreamless sleep.

✳✳✳

The next morning, Flynn drags his hands over the door frame, eyes closed. He's casting a spell and drawing more runes, thankfully not with his blood.

When he steps back, completing his ritual. The door frame glows bright. He turns to look at me, a slight smirk on his lips as he opens it with a bit of flourish.

What was a door that once led to the forest outside, now opens to an antechamber. My eyes widens and I gasp, a portal. My reaction makes him smug.

"Unbelievable." In awe, I take a step inside. Unlike the damp coolness of the safehouse, the antechamber we enter is cozy. The walls are lined with a printed ivory wallpaper and gold molding. The fireplace fills an entire side of the room, bathing the atmosphere in warmth and the smell of burning wood.

A bright red settee is angled right in front of it, such a contrast to the otherwise neutral room. As if someone had taken a bucket of red paint and spilled it into the painting drawing the eyes to its morbid color. Lush pillows in different shades of cream overflow the settee as if to hide the color.

"Welcome to the Vandevyre estate." Flynn closes the door after Linc steps in behind me. I whirl on him.

"Can't you do this spell for us to portal to where Zaf is being held prisoner." His lips tighten and he shakes his head.

"No, we can't. These doors were built with the intention of being used as portal doors." He walks toward the table where a pitcher of water sat. "The doors are only able to connect to each other, like two sides of the same coin." He pours water in two glasses of water, handing me one and the other to Linc.

I dart my eyes between the two of them. Neither of them spoke to each other this morning, even as we all stirred awake and Linc saw our still joined hands.

Flynn leads us onto a foyer where a sweeping staircase goes up to one wide corridor. Much like the antechamber, the walls are the same color of creamy ivory. Gold trimmings and fixtures spread throughout the room. It makes me feel so accurately aware of the dirt still clinging to my skin and clothes, I wrap my arms around myself.

"You look fine." Flynn says under his breath and I don't deign to answer. My cheeks heating is answer enough for the both of us.

Across from us is a hallway that leads straight into an outdoor patio. I could see a glimpse of a lush garden from the glass doors. I make a mental note to ask Flynn to let me see the garden so that I can recharge some of my energy.

Right below the arching staircase is an open doorway. Which I could only assume leads to the kitchen, judging from the smell wafting from it. My stomach growls at the scent and my cheeks heat. Both men deign not to address the sound of my hunger.

"You will find empty rooms upstairs where you can wash up. Spare clothes are available for each of you. We'll discuss our plans over food." Flynn moves aside to allow us to pass him toward the stairs. Without looking back, he heads down the hallway leading to the garden.

"We need to get back to Meridian." Linc says as we climb up the stairs. I'm certain he's been waiting until Flynn is out of earshot. I shoot him a look over my shoulder.

"Not yet. I'll ask Flynn for a map so I can try scrying again." I look down my hands and a small shimmer of energy thrums there, still recuperating. "I can't lose the connection with Zaf. I know it's there. I can feel it." I continue up the stairs and Linc tries to block my way with his body.

"You can do that from Meridian. With Ava." I look at him square in his steel eyes. They churn like storm clouds.

"What if the wards break my connection with her? What if I lose it again?"

"That connection may very well lead the Comendeti straight to you if they detect it on her."

"All the more reason for me to stay away from Meridian, where Zoha would remain safe while she trains her magic." I push past him and walk up the corridor to find various doors leading to empty bedrooms. Before I make a move to open the door, I send a glare his way. "You didn't even ask about her." He stops on his tracks then. A flash of guilt clear on his face before he schools it into an empty expression. "Never once asked me how she's doing or if she's okay."

When he doesn't answer, I choose a room at random. I push open the oak wood door and it creaks. I step inside and frown at Linc when he tries to follow me in.

"I'm pretty sure I won't need company while I relieve myself, thank you." Linc huffs a breath despite the blush that blossoms on his cheek. He stalks toward the room directly adjacent to mine. He stands there by the doorway looking at me.

I could understand his concern, but I'd be damned if I would run back with my tail between my legs. Not when I feel my connection with Zafiya pulse to life as my powers slowly recoup. I shut the door behind me and head to the bathroom, weary of my keeper's stifling need to keep me away from harm.

I think I just lost my friend in place of a protector I didn't ask for.

Chapter 31

I would have wanted to stay in the room away from Linc. Without shame, part of me also wants to avoid the rest of the monsters waiting to devour me outside my door. My growling stomach doesn't agree with me though, so I'm forced to sneak out into the hallway.

Linc's door is shut. I utter a small prayer of thanks. I opted out of shoes and pad my way through the hall barefoot in an attempt to make as little sound as possible.

I let my nose guide me towards the dining room. A huge table occupies the middle of the room. Every surface of the table is covered with food and I gape at the copious amount of it.

Flynn sits at the chair farthest from the door, he flicks his gaze my way the moment I walk in. I raise my eyebrow at him and gesture towards the food in question. Even Ava had not served us this much food at Meridian.

"The kitchen staff got a bit carried away. We don't get a lot of guests here." He looks toward the door behind me expecting Linc to walk in behind me. When he doesn't, Flynn brows quirk up. I give him a weak shrug.

"Let him sulk in his room." I mumble under my breath. He clears his throat and juts his chin toward the chair in front of him.

"Eat, you're swaying on your feet."

Without saying another word, I take a seat in front of him and pile meat on my plate. He slides a plate of chocolate tortes and I grin. He smirks at my reaction.

"I knew you needed your fix, sweet tooth." I melt at that. That not only had he notice my inclination towards chocolate but feeds into it. Flynn pops open a bottle of wine and pours it in a glass.

"Here. For the nerves." He nudges the glass to me and I nod in thanks.

He watches me over the rim of his own glass as I eat and drink. The food is spiced differently than Meridian. This is more flavorful and robust. It suited my taste and I cleaned off my plate before I even realized it.

Flynn proceeds to shovel more food in front of me and I look at him through my lashes. A small smile tugs at his lips.

"I will leave soon to find my sister." I was the first to break the silence. Flynn blinks and hums his head in consideration.

"I expected no less." He leans back on his chair and finishes off the wine he'd been nursing.

"I need a map. I know I can scry for her now." Flynn nods and he waves his hand over the table. Our table clears out in a blink and a map appeared out of thin air. "What—"

"Maguses have better use of powers without spells, while witches are stronger conduits for the elements." He stands up to walk behind me so we can both look at the map in front of me. "We can perform tiny tricks like conjuring up objects with the right thought and intent. Nice little trick." He leans over the table and points to the map.

"It wouldn't give you her exact location since it relies on her energy trail. Although, that could give us plenty of information to where we can begin our search."

Our. He's intent to come with me to find my sister. I know it's only because he wants to break the Source bond as soon as possible. Even so, knowing that I wouldn't be alone in my search is comforting enough.

"I couldn't very well let you go alone, siphoning my magic without restraint. Now that you have full access to your core, you can run us both to the ground with your antics." He says lightly and I bite down a chuckle. "We can create a portal once we have a plan in place."

"It has to be soon." Planning—all this planning takes away all the time I have to save Zafiya. I try to stand so I can start pacing but Flynn holds me by the shoulders. The warmth of his skin sends small jolts through the cotton shirt I found in my room.

My eyes widen at the contact. Magic no longer bursts out of me, uncontrolled. He smiles as if understanding the shock on my face.

"Since your core can help ground yourself and to control your powers. This…" He slides his hands down my arms and I fight back a shiver, "is no longer an issue." I look up at him and our eyes meet. He clears his throat and steps away flexing his hands before he uses them to rake through his hair.

"Finding her now would be the easy part, Zelle." The softness in his voice disarms me but not as much as his usage of my name. We both let the moment hang between us for a heartbeat more then he continues. "You may be forgetting that we would very well be breaching a Comendeti base. We need to be ready for a battle."

"You can do that, can't you?" I'm no warrior. The spells I utter work only half the time, I am in no way capable of handling a Comendeti with that. I deflate further. "My training and research are a far cry from battle prep. I wish witches didn't live out to be such pacifists. We don't even have spells we can use to attack."

"Wipe that look off your face." The familiar banter makes me smile and I see him relax upon seeing it. "The simplest of spells, when used right, is a better offense than anything. I promise I will protect you and your sister the best I can but you are more powerful than you give yourself credit for." He offers me a smirk. "I should know, some of your power comes from me." I scoff at that, but I smile, anyway. "You still need to arm yourself to the teeth in case something bad happens."

I sigh then, knowing full well what he isn't saying.

If we were to face the Comendeti then something bad is bound to happen.

A plume of purple smoke puffs and fills the air. I attempt to clear it out by waving both hands over it.

"Careful with that." Flynn hisses, he's standing over his own—cliché as it is—*cauldron*. The room is lined with a variety of glass vials and jars. All filled with a mixture of herbs and liquids of varying shades and colors.

The floor has rows and rows of pots with live plants that make the air feel damp and full of life. Their energy weaves gently with the atmosphere.

I give Flynn an amused grin and he sends me a deadpan look. I grab another vial and shake it slightly to watch the blue liquid slosh about inside.

I try to suppress the giddy excitement that makes me want to make little, tiny jumps where I stand. Back when I had read up on books about witches, the topic that excited me most was potion making. The alchemy. The art of mixing ingredients to create something magical always fascinated me.

"What are we making again?" Flynn had taken me to this room and had positioned me right in front of the cauldron after our discussion. He had pointed one finger at me and told me not to move under any circumstance.

He then proceeded to dump different labeled bottles in front of me. He had listed each of them down on a piece of paper and had given me another stern look.

"Follow this to the exact measurement and order." He had said with a grim expression. Now, I happily follow the list and let my eyes wander around the room. It takes Flynn a minute to answer me, his face bunched in seriousness.

"A smoke screen of sorts." I give him a wry look and he shrugs.

"...of sorts?" He chuckles then and shakes his head turning his attention back to his own mixture. The slight upturn at the corner of his lips shows me he's enjoying this as much as I am.

I had not seen Ava or any of the witches in Meridian make potions much less use one. Too embarrassed to even ask about it, I never brought it up during my training. I peer over Flynn who threw a sprig of rosemary in his mixture before it starts bubbling.

"Why do you think Ava didn't teach us about potion making?" He doesn't stop stirring but pauses to blink at me.

"I would think she'd feel you aren't ready for it." I frown at that. Had I been that bad during our training sessions? "Don't pout." Flynn counters without looking back at me. "Potion making requires a certain finesse. I'm guessing due to your situation and time constraints she had to prioritize. It's hard to pick and choose which lessons would have been more useful for you."

"All that core work and I could have been doing this instead." I mumble as I pour all the blue liquid down my mixture. Another—much larger—puff of smoke gurgles from my cauldron.

It covers my face with a thick coating of purple dust and I cough. Through the smoke I hear Flynn let out a mocking laughter which I knew just meant he was waiting for that to happen.

"I told you to be careful with it." He snickers at my measly attempt at retaliation by throwing a piece of crumpled paper towards him.

Yes, he's really enjoying this as much as I am.

Chapter 32

Flynn lays out a map in front of me—one that I am not familiar with. No, it wasn't the map of Earth or the world that I know of. The language written on it is also something I have not seen before. Linc takes a step towards the table and leans over it, he lets out a startled gasp.

"How are you in possession of an enchanted map?" Flynn smirks at Linc and crosses his arms over his puffed chest. I almost roll my eyes at the audacious show of male ego.

"The Vandevyre cabal has connections with the Elven camps, it was a gift. This—" I furrow my brows and continue looking at the weathered map.

"Wait." I raise my hand in the air cutting him off. "Elven? As in elves?"

"Yes." His simple answer rings in my silence. He waves his hand in a dismissive gesture. "You're missing the point." I don't tell him that he's the one failing to understand why I'm confounded. "This was the business I had to attend to a few days ago. I figured it was something we could use." He shrugs but I don't fail to notice that he'd put in this much thought at saving my sister.

My heart warms at the fact that the magus had not doubted for a second that I would find my way to my sister one way or another. His constant vote of confidence is touching. I make it a point to hide the smile that I couldn't bite down.

"What's so special about the map?" I squint at it and rub my eyes. The lines are wavering and moving, shimmering in and out of the paper—each time it creates a different form. "Tell me I'm not the only one seeing it move." I grumble and Flynn chuckles.

"This map allows the wielder to temporarily open portals. To make doorways to traverse in an alternate—albeit unstable dimension." Linc answers me then, he captures his own chin in his hand, deep in thought. "Think of it as slices of space in the atmosphere that you can squeeze into. When you're inside that space—you're present but *not*. In the same plane but at a different frequency."

"The figures you see on the map are the ripples and distortion in the air." Flynn explains further. "These slices, as the keeper calls them, can be used for traveling large distances while remaining undetected." Linc straightens then, sneering at Flynn.

"Absolutely not."

"Wait—why not? This is perfect! We can get to Zafiya and avoid the Comendeti altogether." Hope blooms in my chest. If we had something so powerful within our grasp then rescuing her wouldn't be as difficult as I dreaded. I quickly wrap my mind around the bridge between Zafiya and I. It pulses at my attention.

"What the magus isn't saying is that these slices are constantly changing. If you're caught midway and the pocket of space collapses within itself then you're trapped."

"You don't have to come with us, you know." Flynn taunts, his eyebrows cocked. His eyes gleam with mischief. Linc bares his teeth at him.

"Like hell I'd let you take her alone." Before I could attempt to cut between the two of them, Linc lunges over the table and grabs Flynn by the collar of his gray shirt.

"If you have a better alternative, by all means…" Flynn looks almost bored.

"It's the best shot we have, Linc." I touch his arm and both sets of eyes, blue and steel flick to my fingers. Linc tenses but lets go, he stalks toward the far end of the room. A grimace on his face.

"Who invited the grouch?" Flynn quips and sends me a wink that makes me roll my eyes. I look down at the map and fail to bite down a smile spreading on my lips. I peer at the connection again within me and my sister—it brightens. Beckoning me.

I'm coming, Zafiya.

Flynn links his fingers through mine and the thread between our magic flares to life. My blood roars at the sudden rush and I fight to keep it down, I could almost feel my hair lifting.

Ever since I had managed to open up and reach my core, magic flows through me so freely. It feels like it's always on the tips of my fingertips so easily reachable.

The threads of energy are now drawing into me as if curious by the conduit in their midst. I must learn how to shut it out so power wouldn't surge out of me in lack of control.

The other day during my bath, the water rippled until they were floating out of the tub and into the air around me. When I managed to tamper my magic it all came down. Raining down on me and almost flooding the bathroom floor.

Linc takes my other hand and gives me a tight smile. He had not agreed to any of the plans Flynn and I laid out, but he didn't try to stop me.

At some point during the night, when we had planned out our escape route he had given up. Left the room and told me he'd follow my lead and will stand behind me for protection.

"I don't need a bodyguard." I protested. My voice shrill and my fists white-knuckled at my sides. Linc had only given me a blank expression, his grey eyes hard.

"I can shield you better when I'm near you. We're not trying to negotiate like we're going out on some excursion. We're jumping straight into the maws of magic eaters." He leaned in, jaw ticking in restrained anger. "I will guard you whether you like it or not." Before I could protest Flynn agreed with Linc, to my surprise.

That was probably the first time the two of them stood on the same side of an argument and I couldn't help but relent.

Through hours of planning with Flynn, we had managed to work on a few spells and potion mixes that would be useful in case we face a Comendeti head-on. The vials of those potions secure within a satchel in my pocket.

"Now or never, Flynn." I mumble under my breath. Trepidation is thick in the air but he still manages to chuckle at my tone.

"Give me a moment here." He holds the enchanted map in his free hand and mumbles an incantation. It starts to glow bright and my eyes widen at the sight.

Right in front of us, a sliver of black void appears in the blink of an eye. It was like someone took a great sword and slashed the air. It ripples, its movements similar to that of thick liquid.

"Remind me again how this works." I urge, my nerves are singing in my bones and I grit my teeth to ensure my voice doesn't shake. Tendrils of green vines burst out of the wooden floor. Their small bodies start wrapping itself around the soles of my shoes. My magic no doubt feeling my fear of taking the step towards the opening.

It's rooting me down where I stand.

I could have sworn I can hear the earth speak to me through those vines. Telling me to stay if I was so afraid. I chose to ignore it and focus on blocking out the flow of its energy.

Neither Flynn nor Linc comments on the vines. Good—I don't think I had enough in me to even pretend to be brave at this point.

"With the use of the map, we should have two openings in the atmosphere as we speak. This one." Linc juts his chin towards the void in front of us. "The other, near the area your crystal landed on last night. Think of it like Flynn's spell is a tube. He stabs through the atmosphere to rip open through the veil between each dimension.

"Through that tube, we can go in through one end and come out of the other." Linc points toward the map Flynn has in his hand. I don't think he needs to be looking at the map to know what it was showing, it seems to be speaking to Flynn. I could feel magic coming from it, one too strong for me to wield. He curses under his breath when the black void blinks out.

"Won't open long enough." Flynn grumbles and goes back to uttering another incantation. A crease between his eyebrows.

"Like I've said, it's unstable. The tube collapses upon itself." Linc glances at Flynn. "Have you ever used one before?" Linc asks when another portal appears in front of us. Though I realize we should have asked this question earlier.

I look over at the magus. A smirk pulls at the side of his mouth, but his eyes remain on the portal in front of us. His bravado is carefully in place, but I see a hint of uncertainty playing behind his expression.

"Only to ever transport objects and letters." His throat bobs in a swallow. My eyes widen at his admission.

"What do you mean…" I trail off then. "Wait—"

Before I can finish my protest, he jumps into the void tugging me along and we fall. The sliver in the atmosphere closes just as soon as Linc jumps in with us and the world is nothing but darkness.

Chapter 33

I land with an audible *oof* on top of someone and I attempt to push myself off. Flynn groans and he uses my shoulders to lift me off his chest. Linc is on his back a few feet away already cursing as he gets up.

"I can't believe that worked." Flynn grins at me and I shoot him an incredulous look. I hit him with my fist and he laughs.

"You mean, you weren't sure?" Flynn shakes his head and laughs harder. With me still sprawled on top of him, his laughter shakes through me and I end up laughing with him.

"I guess luck is also a form of magic." I muse and I move to get off him. He lifts me easily just in time for Linc to walk towards us. We landed in a back alley where the cobblestones are muddy and scuffed. The damp wind clings to my skin making me shudder and I grimace at the scent that permeates the air. The acrid scent of vomit and what I deduce as beer is so strong that it burns my nose.

"We need to move. I hear a couple of voices through there." Linc points toward one end of the alley. He waves a hand over my face and Flynn's. My skin tingles with traces of magic, a glamor. I know that even if I see both familiar faces now, they are much different if anyone or anything perceives them.

We huddle close, pulling on cloaks over our heads. With a steady pace, we make it out of the alley and onto a street decked with the same cobblestones. Houses line the cobbled street, each more inconspicuous than the next.

If I didn't know any better, I would have assumed this was a regular charming town in Europe. I stumble over my feet when my eyes land on the people—if I can even call them that—walking the street. Most creatures stand on two feet but their skins vary in color and texture. Some of them have elongated ears and horns. Some have fangs for teeth. Eyes of predators everywhere.

The very human part of me jolts at the sight and I immediately want to run. Flynn grips my arm and leans close.

"Calm down. You look like a deer in headlights." I swallow against my drying throat. I don't tell him that I feel very much like one. Like one wrong move and they'd see the infiltrator in their midst and they'd be out to kill me within one breath. My heart hammers in my chest at the reality of my own mortality.

I don't think it's ever sunk in that I might be way in over my head until this moment. Until I'm faced with creatures I never knew existed. Never dared dreaming of.

"Hey, hey. Look at me." Flynn grabs my chin and forces me to look at him. It reminds me of that time he had done the same thing during my nightmare. "No turning back now. Remember why we're here."

He pulls me closer to him and we begin to walk. He keeps his hand on the small of my back. His warmth seeps into my skin grounding me. I take another deep breath and Linc looks at me and Flynn over his shoulder.

"Up there. Looks like it's a tavern." I slide my eyes toward the establishment he's motioning towards. I make it a point to ignore the creatures. The tavern door is open, laughter and merriment boom out of it.

A female with green skin comes out with a bucket tucked on the side of her hip. I know well enough about lore to know that she is an ogre. Her arms are thick and bulky and her hands are about the size of my head. She had tusks protruding from her bottom teeth. She looks built to kill. Flynn rubs circles on my back. I'm shaking at the sight of the ogre.

"We're not going in there." I breathe.

"No better way to get information than a tavern full of drunk creatures. If they're anything like humans, alcohol is our friend right now." Flynn says under his breath. I look at him, eyes wide and I shake my head. His brows are set and his lips are downturned.

He's doing it and I can't convince him otherwise. He nudges me toward Linc like a child and he gives me a reassuring smile.

"I'll be okay." His smile slips off when he looks at Linc. "Stay here. If I don't come out in an hour..." He trails off and I close my eyes to banish the images that flood my head.

"Try to look for mercenaries." Linc wraps his arms around me, resuming the rhythm of Flynn's comforting touches. I hate that I don't feel as reassured. I hate that I can even notice that now. "From what I know,

Comendeti often hires mercenaries to handle hunting witches."

"Well... who can better fill those demands for magic than those born to consume it." Flynn's tone is contemplative and he gives the tavern a long look. He pulls his cloak tighter around himself. When he walks, he fakes a limp and he bends over like his back is no good. He's effectively shed off his normal swagger.

Flynn passes the ogre who now, I observe, is a barmaid. The telltale sign of an apron tied around her waist is a giveaway. She shoots him a no-nonsense look and follows him inside.

I have nothing else to do but to watch as he disappears from my view. I'm left clutching our bond willing him to be safe and come back to me in one piece.

I'm pacing.

Linc follows me with his eyes while I leave trail marks over the cobbled steps. He's given up trying to calm me down. I look up at the sky, periwinkle and sunset orange bleed is already bleeding through the blue. I would have loved to stop to appreciate such a sight if not for the nerves jangling my bones.

"He'll be okay. If he's not, you would have felt the Source bond respond." That's not reassuring in any way shape or form. I throw my hands in the air and groan but keep my voice low to avoid being discovered.

Linc and I have settled behind a few crates beside one of the houses across the bar. I slump down next to him and sigh.

"I don't feel right letting him take such risks for me." I admit. The moment Flynn went into that cavern, things didn't feel right with me. I'm unsettled and antsy. If only I hadn't been so shocked to see those things, I probably would have tried harder to stop him.

"Something tells me he's not the type to do things he doesn't want to." His tone is anything but sharp. It had a resignation to it, though I couldn't quite understand why. I pull my knees up to my chest and rest my cheek on them, I keep my eyes on Linc. His hair is longer now, the blonde curling over his neck slightly. There was a time that I would have tunneled my fingers through his hair without thinking about it. Now, I keep my hands tucked around me.

The abyss is still growing between us. Before I can help myself, I ask.

"Was any of it real, Linc?" He stiffens at the sudden detour of my thoughts. It takes him a beat before he says.

"You're my best friend, Z. Keeper or not, nothing would have changed that." He leans his head back and stares up at the darkening sky. "Sometimes, I wish I wasn't. Then this wouldn't be so complicated. *We* wouldn't be so complicated. God, Z. I know I've been nothing but a pain but the need to protect you is so overwhelming and it's not just because I'm a keeper." He pauses, taking a second to swallow against his dry throat. "I lost my mom in this, too." My eyes mist.

I'm a bad friend.

A horrible, good-for-nothing friend. It had not even crossed my mind again until he said it. Dianne was in the car with us. Dianne who—the image of her face down inside the car flashes in my head—burned alongside mama.

"You're all I have left." Tears well up in my eyes and I swallow against the thickness in my throat. Oh, I've been so caught up in my own grief and rage, I didn't even think about him. I've antagonized him in my head because I've let my fury take reign.

The incessant need to keep me hidden and his attitude towards Flynn all makes sense now. He'd been grieving and I've let myself get tangled up with Flynn because of this Source bond. I grimace, remembering the times I've ended up conferring to Flynn over Linc.

With nothing to say for myself, I reach over to lace my fingers with his. He looks at me. The silver brimming his stormy eyes breaks my heart. I lean into him and he rests his forehead on mine. His breath fans over my cheeks and it cools the hot tears that trail them.

"I'm sorry, Linc." I hug him. Crushing him to my chest and he hugs me just as hard. All our frustration with each other, all our love. We pour it out in that embrace. We don't relent until we're both steady. He leans back and brushes my hair away from my face.

A familiar lightness is back on his face. The tightness in my chest loosens and I smile up at him. He straightens and pulls me up with him. He glances back toward the tavern.

"Hour's up. Let's go." We walk close, shoulder to shoulder.

Even though we're walking into a den of creatures unknown to man out of our own volition, I feel steady on my feet.

Chapter 34

We slip in through the front doors and I thank the Mother no one looks our way. Creatures of varying sizes and colors fill the area. The horned and winged beings jeer at each other. Their drinks splash over the rim of their mugs. I sniff and cringe—beer. Stale beer apparently is a drink not exclusive to human enjoyment.

A trickle of fear goes through my system and I dig my heels to the ground, refusing to try and get closer to any of them. Linc presses his chest to my back and pushes me to the closest empty table. We have to squeeze through different bodies and I fight back my own tremors.

"Stay here." Linc says under his breath and he guides me to sit. He disappears into the crowd leaving me to the task of calming down nerves. I pray to all that is good that none of these creatures can smell my fear.

Breathe. You're a witch with magic. You can fight back when you need to.

A lie. Blatant but effective at keeping me sitting. I take a moment to scan the tavern to look for Flynn and I tug on the Source bond lightly. He tugs back and I could sense him somewhere behind me. He's most likely engaged in conversation with whatever creature he could trick into one.

"Yeah, bosses are so caught up in finding the rest of the sisters they won't bother paying for any other contracts." A male voice sounds from the table next to ours and I lean a bit closer to hear more. "They refused any other witch I bought for them this week." I peer over my shoulder, letting my hair fall a bit over my face for cover.

The male is blue-skinned. He has the head of a lizard and it's attached to a body similar to a human, two limbs and his build was that of a thin young man. Human-*ish*, yes. Except for the tail that hangs limply twirling around his boots. A forked tongue slithers out his mouth every few seconds.

"I've seen the one they had in the holding cell, just a lass, that one. I doubt it had the amount of power they were talking about." The male across the humanoid lizard retorts.

This one reeked of death, his grey skin hanging loosely over bones. His eyes are hollow but he didn't strike me as blind as he turns his head to look at other patrons here and there. I have no doubt they were talking about Zafiya, about me and my sisters.

I take more even breaths now, not out of fear but to calm the fury that iced my skin. Magic tickles my fingertips begging to be released. I reel it back lest I end up burning down this building before we get the information we need.

Linc comes back from the bar and places two mugs of beer on our table and I grip the front of his shirt. He frowns at me and I motion to the other table with my eyes. He leans over the table then, an ear toward the two males beside us.

"Shite. I've heard any attempts at finding the sisters failed, all tucked away in their coven and refusing to come out. The Hala had almost gotten one of them a few weeks ago but nothing else." The lizard added, I fight back a shiver. They already knew about my attack, how widespread is this network of monsters?

Before I realize what he's doing, Linc turns toward their table and leans.

"That's bullshit about those witches. If I knew any better, the bosses just don't want to give up more magic." He's adopted a heavily slur and his words barely came out clear. He hiccups and jabs a finger toward the lizard. "They're stocking up their own supply just 'cause the other covens are getting better at hiding." The lizard hisses at that.

"Selfish pricks, that's what they are." The bone creature says. Linc leans in even closer, his body almost draping over the chair. The two males follow suit, they huddle over the table.

"I bet they're going to bleed us dry and leave us with no magic to fend for ourselves." Linc's voice drops two octaves, only loud enough for me to hear. I don't dare move or turn my head. I know Linc is trying to instill doubt to build conspiracies with the folk. "I don't know about you both but I'm running low." I'm hoping one of them would be dumb enough to lead us right into the Comendeti doorstep. Afterall, fear is a great motivator for the truth.

With that, an idea pops in my head.

I close my eyes and mumble under my breath. A spell spilling from my tongue—as if by memory or recognition, the words form before I could even think about it.

"Darkness and death,

bring unrest in blood and breath.

Let nightmares become real,

Come forth now and let terror reveal."

I say the spell three times, sweat building and rolling down my back from the strain. It's a huge spell, my magic roars at the release. As I finish, dark smoke creeps through every crevice and crack.

My eyes grow wide and I observe the creatures' reactions. None of them seem to break pace even as the smoke begins to thicken. The patrons do not see this. Their merriment continues even as the smoke wraps itself around all of them. It enters their mouths flooding their bodies. It will fill them with fear. Scare them beyond reason.

The lizard is now enveloped in the smoke. He inhales it without knowing and he turns three shades paler. He blinks against the potent emotion flooding him.

I need to wield his fear and point it towards the right direction. I turn to them and pin my eyes on the male.

"I heard the Comendeti are being hunted down." I keep my voice grim and my eyes wide. Let him see the storms I conjure. "The witches are using their keepers to communicate between covens. They're building an alliance. I heard one keeper in particular has been to almost every coven to gather fighters." I hope word of Valera's exploits around the covens trying to find the Comendeti would have reached them. The way the lizard's eyes widen proves enough that they have.

I stand up slowly, I raise my voice louder but keep my eyes on the lizard. His tongue dashing out tasting the air now filled with true terror due to my spell.

"The witches are done with being hunted and they are planning to retaliate."

"That's crazy talk." The female ogre from outside steps in. She's giving me a stare that would have made me up and run under any other circumstance. I smirk at her and watch the fear spell go into her body in the form of the smoke. Once it does, her eyes dart across the room as if she was no longer sure how crazy such talk was.

"Oh, but it's not. Why do you think those magic eaters have been holding back on their payments lately?" A few mumbled agreement ripples through the room. "The witches are hunting them and who do you think they're going to track down first?" I turn slowly, meeting every wide eyed being, "Who would be caught in wards and traps set up by those witches? Who have they *seen* take their folk? Who would have left their scent at the places of all of the witches' disappearances?" Each question I raise in volume as loud as I could.

The air is electric. Their fear is pounding through me now. Their own powers suddenly spiking in an attempt to shield and protect themselves. This thickens the energy around me and I see threads of them pulse. I reach out to them and invite them to the closest conduit—me. I use it to continue feeding the fear spell. My knees buckle at the impact and my magic purrs at the power building in my core.

"Us! They're going to hunt us first!" It's Flynn who answers from the back. Anger splitting his handsome face into a deep sneer. At this, the crowd gasps and some stand so quickly that chairs and tables topple over. I put my hand in my satchel and take out the smoke potion. I throw two of them to the ground.

A huge plume of purple smoke erupts from the broken potion. Chaos ensues and every creature lets out a sound that could make ears bleed. Their screams of terror echoing. Some of them run out the tavern, breaking windows. All of them tumble to run out of the fabricated danger. Some of them fly off straight out of the roof and creating holes in the ceiling in the process.

Before the lizard and the boney creature could move, Linc grabs them by the collar of their cloaks. He shoves his face close enough that both creatures wince. They whimper as if this human man is the scariest thing they have ever seen.

"The witches are here!" His grey eyes are wide. Looking a bit crazed, he stares at them both and they cry out.

"No, no, no!" The bone creature screams, shaking his head.

"We need to lead them to the magic eaters, they're the ones they're after. Not us!" Linc supplies. At this, both males nod.

"Let's do it." And so, we run out of the burning tavern and into the street where it had cleared out. Soon the creatures who ran out would fall out of the spell and would no longer feel the terror. The irrational fear would disappear. They would most likely come back and look for the one responsible for the spell.

I would be long gone by then, by death or by escape, I still don't know.

Chapter 35

We run through the streets, my legs burning as I struggle to keep up with the creatures. The lizard is slinking away at such speed that I'm lagging behind. Flynn grabs me by the arm to pull me along.

He reaches through my satchel and grabs a vial. He throws it toward the two male creatures and he sends a sharp shot of water toward it. It creates a small explosion of smoke and water that makes the creatures shriek. I look at Flynn, a question hanging off my tongue.

"To keep the illusion of danger longer." He explains and we continue to follow the two males. In a matter of minutes, we reach another nondescript house. I would not have known this was any different than the rest of the houses around it until we were a few steps away from it and the image ripples. It briefly shows me an image of a much more weathered building. Taller and more sinister. The walls are made of scratched rock. Dark and cracked.

It flickers back to the image of the small house, quaint and sweet. A glamor—of course. With wards strong enough to discourage anyone from stepping close to see through it. I could already feel it working through my system, my gut telling me to run far away.

"Here, they're here. The witches—" Before the lizard could finish his sentence Linc sends a wall of his shield toward him. He flies a few feet from where he stood and lands on his head. Knocking him out right away.

When the boney male witnesses this, he screams, his voice cracking as he lunges for me. I will vines to shoot out of the ground and he stumbles before he could reach me. He falls to the ground and more vines wrap around his limbs.

Flynn curses under his breath and conjures water around the male's head, drowning him in the process. I steer my eyes away from the scene. I could hear the creature choking. Such a horrible sound and I couldn't bear another second of it. We were not here for death— at least not yet.

"Flynn, stop."

I grip Flynn's arm and the water falls away as his eyes loses focus as realization hits him. The creature slumps to the ground and Linc is on him right away. He uses his shield to push him down. I grab another vial from my satchel, one filled with purple liquid. It had a lot of lavender, I remember. A sleep potion and I tip it down his throat, this should ensure he wouldn't be getting up soon.

Killing these creatures would probably be the best thing to do. If they were to regain consciousness while we were inside still looking for my sister, Mother knows what they could do to harm us. Yet, I don't want to bring Flynn or Linc over that edge.

It's one they won't be able to come back to. Regardless who they kill and what for, the memory would haunt them. I guess now I realize why witches are such pacifists. To wield such power and yet vow never to harm with it.

Linc busies himself hiding the bodies from sight. I look over at Flynn. He's staring at his shaking hands. I take them in mine and pull him closer.

"I almost..." He trails off and his voice shakes. I rub his hands a little, willing some warmth back into them. No, witches are not violent. Magus are no different and his reaction is evident. The guilt at making him do such vile things wedges inside my chest. I caress our bond as well and he closes his eyes tightly at the feeling.

"But you didn't." He looks at me, his eyes the very image of churning deep-sea waters. I cup his cheek and give him a shaky smile. "You were just trying to protect us."

He leans over me and rests his forehead on my shoulder. He's shaking. I wrap my arms around him and he sighs.

"I think that terror spell got to me, too. That's all." He buries his face in my neck and hugs me tighter. I pat his back as he takes steadying breaths. His arms snake around my waist and he pulls me in.

I hear Linc clear his throat and Flynn stiffens. "If you say one word..." He grumbles in a whisper only I could hear. He pries himself out of my hold. He clears his throat.

"Sorry to interrupt." Linc deadpans and he motions toward the looming house behind us. We immediately fall into action and sneak around the house.

We find no other way in but the front door. We settle ourselves behind the house, out of view. The dark completely blankets our forms.

As I look over at the house, my heart thrums in my chest. My connection with Zafiya is preening. I know she's inside. I can feel it so stark in my bones.

Flynn takes one calming breath before he uses water to push through the locks of the front door and breaking through. It opens without a sound and I let out the breath I've been holding.

Before we step in, I peer at the dark sky, the moon peeks behind the clouds. The moon that now reminds me so much of my mother and her presence. I utter a silent beseeching.

Be with me in the dark, so that when I am lost, you may lead me with your light.

There are no lights here and the dark is thicker. We step into an empty room. The shadows inside seem to swallow all the light peeking through the windows. Flynn, who is behind me, takes a closer step. A protective stance that has him almost curling his entire body over mine.

"Stay close. We go in and out." He murmurs as we sneak further into the back wall where a door was left ajar. Linc takes point and pushes the door open. It creaks so loudly I couldn't stop myself from cringing. I couldn't ask Linc to shadow jump without knowing the traps they have in place against it.

We can only hope that the Comendeti is distracted enough by whatever chaos that transpired in the tavern that they left the house. Beyond the door is a set of stairs that lead to a deep basement.

The connection with Zafiya flares to life inside my chest, I choke down a whimper. Sensing my need to bolt down the stairs Flynn grabs me by the arm.

"She's down there." I whisper. Flynn nods, knowing as much. Linc peers down the stairs and looks back at us.

"We don't fight them, Z. We grab Zaf and we run. If we see one of them, we run."

"No heroics." I promise. I know we couldn't afford to go on the offensive. None of us point out the obvious, though.

That running from the magic eaters is close to impossible. I start to break into a sweat.

On mostly silent feet, we make it to the damp room. There are no movements here. No sign of life that could otherwise indicate there's anyone else with us. My eyes scan the room and it looks utterly empty. I shake my head refusing to believe that we've found nothing.

"This is impossible." The fluttering in my chest is telling me that my sister's here. Linc takes a step forward and inspects the rest of the room.

"Close your eyes." Flynn whispers and I do. He tugs the bond and directs it where he wants it to go. Then I feel it. Magic is thick in the air, the energy buzzing around it to supply the illusion.

"There's a glamor." I deduce. Linc hums under his breath and agrees.

"Glamors are nothing but masks. Visual parlor tricks. Use the connection with your sister to lead us to her, trust your magic to lead us to her." I take a deep breath and clear my mind.

I reach into myself and my core glows. The core that I have not had enough time to know but now I trust with my life. It's what has led me so close to Zafiya now. This was a gift, passed on from mama and our ancestors before her.

Now, it'll be our salvation.

I close my eyes and my magic roars inside me. I hear Flynn's sharp gasp as he feels me take some of his energy from the Source bond. There's gold dust in the air around me.

My eyes remain closed but all-seeing. I follow the flow of the magic. It runs deeper into the house. I follow it through and it leads to tunnels that likely weave under the entire town.

Flynn's hands tighten on my shoulders and his sharp intake of breath tells me he's watching. Linc's footsteps follow not far behind. Whatever they're seeing and whatever I'm walking through is enough to make them jump.

"Visual parlor tricks." Linc murmurs, more to himself. An assurance that the horror that they're seeing is not real. From the shake in his voice, I know it is definitely spelled to ensure no one would wander deep into these tunnels.

I keep my eyes closed and follow where my magic points me to, my steps sure and echoing. After what seems like forever, the hair on my skin rises and the gold dust bursts in front of me. Here, she was here!

I open my eyes and am met with a cold and mossy wall. I look around me, this part of the wall looks the same as the rest of them. Undeterred, I place my hands on the wall and am met with the cool damp stone.

I let my hands roam the slick surface until my hand falls through an opening. The image of the wall remains undisturbed but I go through it. An illusion.

We find ourselves in another room, damp and dark. Flynn flicks a hand and little floating flames light the area. There was barely any space for both men to stand and the air here is colder. Flynn holds my hand as we continue along the dark room. Our footsteps echoing in the dark.

Then we see it. Steel metal bars jutting from the ceiling to the floor. A small decrepit cage with my sister inside it.

I whimper and run into it, slamming on the bars. Zafiya barely flinches at the sound. She's curled on the floor with her back against the wall and her arms wrapped around her legs.

"Zafiya, it's me. I'm here." At the sound of my voice, my sister covers her ears with her hands and she shakes her head.

"You're not real. You're not real." The rasp in her voice is enough to bring me to my knees, sliding down the bars. She'd been screaming so much that her voice had turned to gravel. Tortured with tricks and subjected to horrors I can't even imagine.

"Can't you get to her?" I whirl to Linc and see his body burst into smoke. He flies to the bars but as soon as he makes contact, he flies back. Deterred. His body reforms and he's instantly winded. He can't get in.

"Zaf." I call to her again, "Look at me. I'm right here." I'm reaching to her, squeezing myself through the bars so I can reach as far as my body would allow me. "I promised you, right? I said I was coming." She opens her eyes and looks at me. They were glassy and unfocused.

She curls further into herself and I cry for her. Flynn conjures up more flames and she flinches as each one of them appears out of thin air. The room illuminates and I finally see the entire state of her.

Her ragged yellow dress. Her bleeding arms and torn nails. She had lost so much weight that her cheeks were sunken. Her eyes bruised.

"Zaf, oh God. It's me. It's me." I beg for her to recognize me. "It's me, little warrior, it's me." At the endearment her head snaps up and the blank look on her face changes. She breaks into a sob and she crawls to me.

She reaches me and the moment I could I pull her to me and I hug her, the bars still between us. Zaf wraps her arms around my waist and clutches me. Her fingers dig into me as if she could hug me tight enough and she'd dissolve through the bars.

"Get her out of here." I beg them both. "Please, get her out!"

"Flynn, start the spell." Linc instructs and I hear Flynn start the chant with the enchanted map in his hands. Linc falls to his knees beside me. "Use your magic, pry the bars open." I call to my magic then, rage wrapping so tightly around it that my body shakes at the violent surge inside me. I don't even need to tap into Flynn for it to come to life—my anger is fuel enough.

Plants burst out of the floor and it stretches, as if it had been stuck there waiting to finally be able to pop out. It grows and grows until thick vines wrap around the steel bars attempting to pry it open. Linc takes one of the bars and pulls, he conjures up shields and wedges it in between to help with the push.

Not enough.

I growl and let the same plants wrap around me. I let the magic flow through me, freely consuming all last vestiges of energy it needed from me. I am only a vessel.

I let the power course through me and flow out of me unabated. With my arms wrapped in earth and life I pull the bars open and it cracks under my strength. I hear Zafiya gasp at the sight of me and my magic.

The bars snap and a small opening allows Zafiya to squeeze through. She pushes herself through, caring very little about scratching herself on the bars. She leaps out through the gap and into my still open arms. I whip my head to Flynn and scream.

"Take us home, Flynn!" A sweat breaks out on his forehead. I knew I siphoned only a little of his energy into me earlier on the way here but by the looks of it he needed far more to wield the enchanted map.

Zafiya whimpers in my arms and buries herself into me as if hiding. Linc curses and he stands projecting his shield to the entrance of the room. I stiffen, I don't need to guess what's causing such a reaction because footsteps echo and the wind starts howling.

They're here, we're running out of time.

Flynn hurries his incantation, his brows furrowed in concentration. His hands are shaking, I feel the air ripple around us. His labored breathing is testament enough to the strain.

I reach over the plants that have now settled in the cracks and I pull on all their remaining energy. They start to wither as their energy fills me. I push all of that through the Source bond, praying that the bridge wasn't one-way.

Flynn's eyes widen as he feels it course through him. I chant the unfamiliar words, picking the words from his lips. I let our bond open so freely that his words were mine. Our voices echo and meld into one another.

The Comendeti steps through the illusion and both of them stand in front of us, sneering. They stop right in front of the shield Linc has set up.

"Hurry!" He urges. A howl of wind fills the room and Zafiya starts screaming, her eyes aglow. Her skin grows hot to the touch and the wind hardens around us. The Comendeti hisses as they take a step back from the wind—from Zafiya's magic.

"Flynn!" I scream his name and my words are swallowed by the storm inside the small room. It's getting harder to breathe, Zafiya is pulling all the air. Her magic is wild, uncontrolled and stronger. It's feeding on her fear.

Linc falls to his knees gasping for air. My vision wavers. But only enough for me to see a portal open in front of us. Swaying like a black flag in the wind.

Flynn grabs me by the wrist and pulls me towards the slice in space. I scream for Linc and he makes it in time.

It's already starting to collapse when we start running inside the darkness.

I almost heave a sigh of relief until I see that the Comendeti step through and the portal closes in.

Sealing us in the darkness with them.

Chapter 36

"Run—run now!" Linc screams as he takes Zafiya from my arms and he runs. Flynn doesn't let go of my wrist, almost dragging me along. Their strides are longer than mine and I'm lagging behind.

The Comendeti are stalking closer.

Flynn shoots walls of water behind us in an attempt to slow them down. He barely has any energy left to sustain his magic. His power wavers and he's two shades too pale. His lips set in a grim line.

The Comendeti summons their own wind, it feels sharp on my skin. They're feeding off of the spells Flynn has cast out. They're grins growing wider with every inch they advance toward us.

"Go faster." Zafiya urges from Linc's arms. I almost couldn't hear her over the blood roaring in my ears. Moonlight peers through the end of the portal signaling our freedom.

Flynn curses again and I know what he's realizing too. These magic eaters are coming out with us whether we like it or not.

"We'll figure it out." His hand tightens around me and he pulls harder.

Linc disappears through the end of the portal and we shortly slip through. We are back in the brook where the

Hala attacked me. Flynn pulls me out of the void and turns around to face the opening.

"Linc, go get help. Now!" I scream at him. He looks at me, torn. I give him a firm nod. We both know he cannot shadow jump all three of us at the same time. He's too weak to even get far enough with Zafiya in tow.

"I'll come back as soon as I can." He says before they turn into shadow and the wind takes them. Part of me is relieved at that, even knowing that he might not make it back to us. At least they have put distance between themselves and impending demise. I scramble to my feet and pull Flynn with me.

"Flynn, they're coming!" I attempt to run but he pulls away and faces the open portal. He grabs the enchanted map strapped to his waist. It starts glowing as he chants.

The opening starts to waver even more than usual. My eyes widen.

He's trying to close it.

He's trying to break the opening with his power. I peer through the portal and see that we don't have long. They're slipping through. I touch our bond and I funnel the rest of my energy into him. He roars as I feel the magic cleave out of him too fast, draining him in seconds.

But it works, the slice in the atmosphere starts closing.

There's no relief in his eyes. He turns to me and we run from the portal. We take a few steps away when one of them slips through before the opening completely collapses trapping the other in the void. The female magic eater screams, her haunted voice echoing in the forest. The devastation rings in the night.

Her pain shakes the very air around us. I stumble and Flynn barely catches me, my knee slamming to the ground.

He grunts as he falls with me. When I get up, he doesn't.

"Flynn!" He tries to push himself up but fails. I feel for the bond and find that he's empty, not even a flutter of energy in his reservoir. I shove my hands under his arms and pull him, dragging him through the dirt. "You have to get up."

We're almost at the edge of the forest, we'd at least be hidden from the Comendeti there. I attempt another pull but I almost fall over him. My arms weak and shaking.

"Leave me." Flynn croaks. I frown at him and continue dragging him, huffing a breath. Every inch I can drag him over is an inch away from danger.

I am not going to leave him here. The screaming of the remaining Comendeti echoes through the forest again. It makes my teeth jitter with the sound. It's not getting closer to us yet. Distracted by its grief but I'm sure it would soon hunt us down.

"No. We need to get out of here." I ignore his request and continue dragging him along.

"Like I said—"

"Shut up, I need better ideas." I snap at him and he has the nerve to chuckle. We cannot wait for Linc to come back with help. I look around us.

We make it behind the thick trees just by the end of the brook. The moon is high, bringing silver glints on the surface of the water. I take a second to look up, a niggling feeling starts in my chest. It's trying to tell me something.

The blue threads of the water flare to life as the moon peeks through the clouds and bears all its light on its stream. I gasp.

A sign. I look up at the moon and utter a small prayer of thanks.

"Flynn." I point towards the brook and he looks back at me.

"As much as I want to go for a dip, little witch. I don't think now's the right time." He quips, despite his voice going breathy with the strain of keeping himself upright. I duck under his arm and pull him up with me.

He limps alongside me as we make it towards the water. He hisses at the cold and I hold him tighter around the waist. Threads of energy are flowing with the current going passing through us.

I look up at the moon again and it glows at my attention.

"Let the water take us downstream." Flynn shoots me an incredulous look.

"What?"

"Just do it." I risk a glance toward the grieving magic eater's direction and my heart thuds in my chest. She's seen us. She lets out a bloodcurdling scream and I feel it reverberate through my bones. She points at me and snarls. I didn't have to hear her speak.

I know a promise of vengeance when I see one.

Flynn grips me by the waist and I wrap my hands around his neck. He quickly sinks his entire body under water taking me with him. The water glows as magic spurs to life welcoming him in his element. It wraps around us and I feel weightless as it takes us in its arms and drags us along the rapid current.

It takes us down, down, and down the stream.

Chapter 37

I take a lungful of air when we reach land. I cough when I accidentally swallow water along with it. I look around me, I don't recognize where we are but we just banked near the opening of a river. One that I know for sure would lead to rougher and deeper waters.

I stretch my hands and let my fingers find Flynn in the dark. My hands brushes against skin and I know it's him. I crawl towards him. He's on rocky ground. Face half-submerged in the water. I pull him as best as I can but strength eludes me.

I raise his head and use my lap to keep it elevated. I brush away his dark hair and I tap his cold cheek.

"Flynn." He doesn't so much as stir at my voice. I keep tapping his cheek. "Flynn, wake up." He doesn't move. My heart lurches in my chest. He can't be—

I lean over him and I hold my breath as I try to listen for an intake of air. When he does, I let out a cry. It's weak and far apart but he's breathing. I rest my forehead on his and take a moment to calm down. To tell myself he's okay. I press my hand over his chest and the small rattling of his heart soothes me even more.

I open my ears to the night and I hear nothing but nature's music. The chirping of insects and the hoots of an owl. The stream is a constant sound filling the air and the rustling of trees accompany it. I breathe a small sigh of relief.

The Comendeti is not here, at least not yet. We can't afford to stay here long. Flynn is already shivering from the cold and my fingers are losing feeling in them. I try to pull Flynn out of the water again and I manage to get his upper body on solid ground. He wouldn't drown if I put him down.

I close my eyes and concentrate on finding any remaining drop of magic in me. There must be something left in order to conjure up fire but I'm met with an empty and slumbering core.

"Just hold on a little more." I urge him and I brush my knuckles over his frozen cheek. I shuck off my wet coat and at the movement it frees my moonstone pendant from its usual place underneath my shirt. It gleams under the night sky and I hold it in my hand. It's vibrating.

Oh, Linc. This is my connection to him, my friend, my keeper all rolled into one. I press it harder into my palm until it warms from the remaining heat in my body.

"Linc, come find us." I whisper to the stone. Nothing happens.

Fatigue washes over me and I succumb to it. I lie beside Flynn, throwing an arm and a leg over him to keep us both warm. The contact also comforts me as much as his presence.

"Linc." I whisper again. "Come find me." My body hurts and I whimper as cold wind blows our way. I call for my friend over and over as I watch the moon beam down on the two of us. As if to say, they're here. *Right here.*

When my hands could no longer hold the stone in such a tight grip, I let it fall and I close my eyes. The fight leeching out of me as shivers start wracking through me.

My sisters are safe and are with each other now. I picture Zafiya being ushered into those healing baths by Ava and Valera. Zoha would hover over her so closely and she will not let our little warrior out of her sight. A smile breaks out of my numbing lips at the image.

"Hey Flynn, if this is the last time I can tell you anything, I'm really glad you were my Source." He doesn't answer. I lift my head and I hover over his face. Still handsome even in its pale pallor. I brush my fingertips over his eyebrows, tracing his features. Is it so selfish that I'm glad I somehow dragged this unknowing magus into this mission and risked his life with mine?

I think part of me had been so scared of the fact that if Zafiya were to die, she would do it alone. If I were to lose this battle tonight, at least I have this man next to me. I lightly brush the skin on his lips and I blush at how soft they feel.

Peace settles into me, a bone-deep warmth that I had not felt for so long.

In the face of imminent death, knowing my sisters are safe somehow brings me relief. My eyes burn from unshed tears. Had my mother felt this way when she chose death in order to give us the chance to save ourselves?

"If I were to die tonight, I'd have you." When his eyelashes do not flutter and there is no semblance of a response, I sigh. I rest my head on his chest, pressing my ear against his heartbeat, the steady rhythm washing over me.

So selfish. So, so, selfish but only the night is here to witness my sin.

I interlace my numb hands with his and I let my eyes drift as sleep welcomes me.

Linc eventually finds us with Valera shadow jumping with him. I couldn't tell how long Flynn and I had been on that bank when their shadows burst in, disturbing the air.

The sound of their rushed footsteps wake me and I crack my eyes open to see Linc's face hover above mine. He wraps his arms around me, tightly securing me to his chest before he starts shadow jumping to make our way back to Meridian. He is shaking but he smiles when I reach up to touch him on the cheek.

"You came." I say under my breath and he nods.

"I heard you call for me. I just couldn't get there fast enough. We made it back to where I left you and had an encounter with the Comendeti." I stiffen at this. "We're all okay. Ava managed to use her wards to deter the magic eater from coming close to the manor." He looks down at me and a crease forms between his brows. "I was worried."

"Thank you for taking Zafiya to safety first." He nods and then looks up to Valera who has Flynn thrown over her small shoulder. It would have astounded me to see such a sight, Valera is a petite woman and Flynn is a full-grown man. Yet she doesn't break her stride even as Flynn's limp body swings with the motion. He's still unconscious but before I can ask, she touches Linc on his shoulder and we turn into smoke one last time.

When we materialize in front of the manor, I see Zoha pacing in front of the open doors. Her eyes are sunken and bruised. A tinge of guilt creeps up at the sight of her. I barely made any attempts at contacting her to ease any of her worries after I disappeared on the night of Esbat.

A whimper escapes her as she runs to me.

She wraps her hands around my neck and tugs me close, pulling me away from Linc's arms. She sobs into my shoulder and at her touch, all remaining energy saps out of me and I cry with her. We crumple to the ground.

"Don't you ever disappear on me again." She whispers to me.

In a daze of tears, Valera leads us to our bedroom with Linc taking Flynn to his room to rest. My legs wobble at every step and Zoha keeps an arm around my waist to keep me from losing my footing.

In our room, I find Zafiya on the bed. Still covered in the dirt we found her in. When she sees us, her wary brown eyes grow wide and she takes careful steps toward us. I open my arms to her and she melts into my chest.

Feeling her frail body against mine breaks me inside and I crumple. Tears burn my throat. I have my sister in my arms. It's been too long since the last time I've seen her.

"You're here." I mumble against her hair and hold her tighter. The relief is coupled by such a strong sense of fear. Of this being a dream, of this being temporary. I let out a sob, my emotions are choking me.

I never want to let her go, to let the world touch her again. She cries with me, clutching my still damp shirt. Zoha inches closer and she wraps her hands around the both of us. We stay there holding each other until my cries are nothing but hiccups.

"Let's get you cleaned up." I murmur softly and Zafiya only nuzzles closer in response. My heart stammers in my chest at the contact.

We lead her to the bath and Zoha helps her lift the clothes she had on. They are the same ones that I had last seen her in, the yellow sundress for her birthday. It's barely recognizable now that it's stained with dirt and blood. I share a look with Zoha and her lips are quivering in her effort to stop her sobs.

When she's out of the dress, I couldn't help the soft gasp from escaping me. Zafiya's skin is pale and bruised, mottled and bleeding. The sure evidence of the abuse and pain they must have bestowed on her. Her ribs peek through, they had starved her. She has bite marks down her back and arms, they are still blood-crusted.

A knife to the gut would have been better than seeing her like this.

"They... took small amounts of magic through feeding." Zafiya hovers her palms over the bite marks on her arms, as if hiding them from us. "They feed enough to keep me down and enough to keep them sated." Zafiya lowers herself to the bathtub, submerging herself in the warm water.

A sigh escapes her and she wraps her arms around herself again. The tears burn hot on my cheeks.

"There were times where I hoped that they'd drain me just enough so magic would not come back and so they can be done with me." Zoha takes a washcloth with shaking hands and starts scrubbing the dirt away from Zafiya's skin. "But it stayed inside me and kept growing and each time they'd come back and *drink*."

"I'm sorry, Zaf. I wish— I wish we could have gotten you sooner." I'm clutching the edge of the bathtub to keep myself from doubling over. My stomach feels like I swallowed rocks, heavy and sharp inside me. She shakes her head. The fiery hair that we all share, dull with dirt.

"None of it was your fault." Zafiya mumbles when she closes her eyes as we both gently wash her. We don't speak anymore after that. Relishing the ritual that is taking away the dirt that sullied her and she lets us cry the tears she didn't shed.

It takes us a couple of water changes to ensure she *feels* clean. Her skin had grown pink from scrubbing but the wounds are already looking much less grim.

"Mama's dead, isn't she?" I take a sharp intake of breath and meet Zoha's wide eyes. Zafiya shakes her head and grits her teeth. "They told me how she died. Used the details to torment me for weeks." Her eyes are dry of tears but her face is ghosted. My mouth opens to speak but I close it when words fail to come up. "I don't want to talk about it anymore." She completely shuts down and I don't have enough courage to try to convince her otherwise.

She stands from the bath, still covering her body with her arms as best she could. I move to her and wrap her in a huge towel and dry her off.

"I'll get you some clothes to change into." Zoha leaves the bath and Zafiya follows her shortly. Her expression blank, still.

I fight the urge to follow them when I look down on myself. My clothes were muddy and torn from the river. So, I take a quick bath myself. Moving through the motions of washing my aching limbs. I don't avoid the cuts, the sharp stings of them centers me and keeps me from drifting.

Part of me is thankful I didn't come out unscathed. The cuts were reminders of what could happen if we ever find ourselves in harm's way again. They are battle scars.

Once the cold inside my bones had dulled into a distant ache, I step out of the batch and into our bedroom. I find my sisters squeezed together in bed. Limbs tangled and clutching each other. I make my way to them and sit by the edge of the best where I can stay up listening to both of their breathing.

In this quiet, the fear spikes in my system, strong and potent. Mama was right to keep us far, far away. Part of me wants to do the same now. How easy had it been for them to take my sister. How easy it was for these monsters to tear us apart.

I wish I had some magic remaining in me to utter a stronger protection just so I can keep them safe.

I keep watching them even as the sun rises, breaking the night. Still, I don't sleep a wink.

When our room is lit with the gentle light of daybreak and the shadows cannot hide in the corners anymore, I allow myself to slip out of the bed and out on to the hallway. My body protests through every move but my mind is too wired. The manor is silent and my feet make no sound as I make my way through the halls.

The sun shines so brightly through the windows and I take a second to just bask in its light. The warmth caresses my skin. Some of its energy seeps through my skin and a flutter of magic comes alive inside of me, easing some of the pain in my body.

I continue to walk through the house until I find myself in the adjacent wing where I once found Flynn's room. I'm certain that he's sleeping here somewhere. The Source bond, dull and weak as it is at the moment, starts to grow taut as I make my way to his room.

When I find myself standing in front of his door, I hesitate. I have no intention of waking him, some small part of me wants to make sure he's fine, though. I couldn't even see him off properly before Linc led him away.

It hadn't been long since I found myself in front of his bedroom door to ask him for a deal to help get my sister back and yet so much had changed. I caress the weakened bond inside me. I know that I have to part with it soon and I feel guilty for the longing that is already awning inside of me at that thought.

His door opens and I jump back. Flynn is leaning on the door frame and I know it's due to the fact that he could barely stand and not his usual display of swagger. His pale lips quiver a little when he takes a deep breath.

"Hi." I murmur and he tilts his head as he studies me with his eyes. "I came to—" He reaches out to me and slides his hand around the back of my neck to tug me to his chest. The contact immediately makes my skin feel electric. Even depleted, a touch from my Source sparks power in me.

I wrap my arms around his waist. Bury my nose into his chest and let the smoky sweet scent of pine envelope me. I remember how I was able to funnel some of my energy into him. So, I give him what little I was able to take from the sun and he groans.

"You don't have to do that." He mumbles into my hair as he hugs me tighter. I shake my head and tilt my head up to look at him.

"I don't even know how to thank you." His eyes soften and he rests his forehead on mine. His breath fans over my skin and I bite my lip to keep from whimpering.

"The fact you didn't leave me when I told you to is thanks enough." His other hand cups my cheek and I lean into his touch.

We are too close. My heart is hammering in my chest. With his hand still resting at the back of my neck, I hope he could not feel my hammering pulse through my goose-fleshed skin.

The coldness that was threatening to break me from inside eases in Flynn's proximity.

"What did you mean when you said it was okay to die as long as you had me with you?" I stiffen a little. I glare at him and weakly punch his chest. Flynn laughs softly.

"You weren't supposed to hear that." I mumble and he hums as he continues to brush his thumb over my cheek.

"No dying anytime soon, little witch." I smile and I press my cheek into his warm palm. We are sharing a breath and it makes my pulse stutter even harder. There's nothing else on my mind but his skin on mine.

Is it simply just because he's my Source? That having him hold me this way makes me feel steadier than I had any right to be. Is it only because of that?

"Shut up. You're thinking too loud." He complains and I laugh.

"Glad to see some of your sass is back, that should mean you're recovering enough." I say lightly, masking the turmoil in my head before I step away from him. Not wanting to lose contact, I lace my fingers through the hand that was cupping my cheek. He smiles at me with such softness that my throat tightens.

His eyes roam my face, studying me and I see the moment they land on my lips. They grow stormy dark.

It's too easy, to take and to keep taking from him. One move and the space between us where our breaths mingle would be gone. He is temptation in the flesh, my magic beckons to him and I swear I could feel our bond purr between us. The contact of our skin charging it with a different kind of energy, it makes me heady.

"Do you feel it, too?" I reach deep inside and find that our bond is burning hot. The magic beaming bright with the emotions churning inside my chest. "I think it's the bond..." The longing to hold him and hug him so tight that he'd be crawling under my skin threatens to drown me.

My thoughts come to a screeching halt as he drops my hand.

He takes a step back and gives me a wink. I frown up at him and stiffen as his eyes shutter. Immediately, I knew I said something wrong.

"Thanks for checking in, witch. My body is all fine and well unless you want to see for yourself." He smirks again, flirtatious but guarded. He's putting up walls. All the softness from earlier replaced by his cocky façade. I take a moment to stare into his eyes and all I see is his cold mask, the one he wore on the first few nights when we met.

"Flynn—" I start but he shakes his head to cut me off.

"We're even." He straightens and runs his hand through his raven hair. It falls limp almost covering one eye. I clutch my fingers to keep them from reaching out to brush it away.

The burn of rejection grows hot on my skin and my cheeks heat from a starkly different emotion than earlier. I give him a curt nod, not trusting my voice to waver if I answer him. I turn and start walking.

The quiet snick of his door rings loud and clear even after I've reached our bedroom.

Chapter 38

"That female Comendeti is still lurking outside our wards." Valera says over dinner. Ava sighs and rubs her temples at the news. It's been only a few days since we've gotten back. Each day we're greeted with more reports and sightings of the magic eater.

"I'll go out to recast some wards as a precaution." We all know full well that she is here for us. She would not stop until she sinks her teeth into me or one of my sisters. Gone was her need for strategy. Now, she's waiting us out. She's using brute force to get her way.

I would be lying if I said I wasn't worried.

Linc has taken it upon himself to go on rounds. He assures me that we are far from danger, but it does nothing to ease the anxiety clawing its way through my stomach. I look over at Zafiya, she had gotten so much better with the healing from Ava and her cheeks no longer looked sunken.

She refuses to sleep with the lights turned off. Zoha and I often have to coax her back to sleep when she wakes up in the middle of the night with her nightmares.

"She wouldn't stop, you know." Zafiya says as she pushes around the food on her plate. Her appetite lost at the mere mention of the Comendeti still hunting us. She contorts her face in disgust.

Zoha leans a bit closer to her, angling her body as if ready to throw herself in front of Zafiya at the first sign of danger.

"That's for us to worry about now." Linc assures her and I hear Flynn scoff. I look over at him. He swirls a wine glass around attempting to look like his old casual self. Although, I have not seen him take a sip from it since we sat here. The scowl on his face is proof enough of his foul mood which was far from casual.

We haven't talked about the morning I came to his room. I don't see the need to hash it out, letting my pride dictate my decisions on the matter. It was clear that I misunderstood the meaning of our affections somehow.

He meets my gaze and his eyes, the color of the ocean, harden a little. I bristle.

I shift in my seat and direct my attention towards Ava and Valera who share a look between them. There's nothing but concern mixed with fear in the high priestess' eyes. I know she's been reinforcing the wards to protect the coven. Trying to mislead the magic eater away from the manor but it had not worked.

The tension in her shoulders and the bruises under her eyes are evidence enough that things are not doing good. I don't think I've ever seen her this weary even after she learned the news of my mother's death.

"What is it?" I ask and Ava reluctantly meets my gaze.

"Your sister is right." Valera answers me. Her face grim. She has her fisted hands laid on top of the table, visibly restraining herself. "The magic eater will not stop until she finds herself right in front of the manor's doors."

"Valera." Ava cuts in, a warning clear in her tone.

"We never attempted any offensive attacks on the Comendeti before. Nothing in our history books says that they can be destroyed." Valera leans forward on the table and juts her chin towards Flynn. "But he just proved that they could be incapacitated to some degree." At that, he raises his glass and smirks.

"You're welcome, glad I could help rewrite history." He shoots another dark look my way and I purposely do not turn his way. "You know, as one of the Triune's *Source* and all that." The bitterness in his tone makes me flinch but I don't step up to his bait.

"What are you saying? Can we actually kill it?" I ask Valera and she nods. Ava shoots her a sharp look and cuts in.

"That's the theory, yes." Ava clears her throat and tucks her hands below the table. "When they held you in that cage," she addresses my sister, "you said they had to... feed off of you until they only had enough." Zafiya, to her absolute credit, looks at the high priestess in the eye and nods.

"Yes, they always stop until they're drunk off of my magic and they come back a few days later and take a bit more." I cringe at the image that flashes in my head.

"Did they ever drain you?" Valera asks the question now, her eyes determined and set on my sister. I know she already knows the answer but needs confirmation.

"No, never. They always leave a little bit each time."

"Our theory is that they are much more similar to us than we thought. Much like how witches are conduits, we have limitations to how much magic we can wield before we burn out and our power would always demand to be released." Ava taps her fingers on the wood, restless energy radiating off of her. "We cannot store copious amounts of energy at a time or we'd be like walking timebombs." Valera points to Flynn and then me.

"Pretty much like what happened when the two of you would make contact when you had no control over your core." Linc, who has mostly been silent, makes a small noise in his throat as he processes the information then he speaks.

"It couldn't be as simple as that. They killed many witches in their time." Ava nods agreeing with Linc, a haunted look dimming her eyes just a little.

"We know that, but…" She trails off and looks toward Valera. Another silent conversation between them. Ava releases another breath before speaking again. "But we've never had witches that had enough magic to do it. As the Triune, you three amplify each other's magic greatly." Ava looks at Flynn, "One of you is also Sourcing from an heir magus. These are odds we've never seen before."

It's a gamble. I can see why Ava is reluctant to even discuss this.

Most of what they're aiming to tell us is based on half-guesses and lack of records. If what they are saying is true though, then we have a way out of this.

We just have to find enough magic to burn them from the inside.

I spare a glance toward Flynn and remember how my magic felt when we first met. The surge of energy between us caused my magic to explode out of me in waves. It was painful and searing, there was too much of it.

No, I doubt I would have been able to contain that much energy inside me without consequence.

It seems we've reached a plan, then. One none of us would care to admit is our only choice. If magic was what the Comendeti was after, we'll give it all to her.

She'll be drowning in so much of it that we can only hope she would not find her way back to the surface.

Chapter 39

"Break the bond." I grab Flynn's arm before he finds the chance to slink back to his room after dinner. He turns to me with a scowl and so much of me hates seeing him direct such animosity to me.

I miss him more than I care to admit. Breaking the only connection we have right now is the last thing I want. Despite that though, I know it's the right thing to do.

I've taken so much from him. I've put his life in danger when he didn't have as much stake in this game as I do. I'd tugged him along in my missions. Forced him to train me. On top of that, he is my Source. His magic cannot resist me when I ask it to yield. Even without his approval, I have the ability to take his energy to power my own magic.

I've also taken a few liberties with my affection so I cannot blame him for his attitude with me now. He has every right to resent me.

"What are you talking about?" He yanks his arm out of my grip and starts walking up the stairs that would lead to the hallway to his room. I side-step around him and block his path. I won't scurry along and let him mope now.

Not when we're heading into another dangerous mission. Not when he hasn't asked for his part of the bargain which is to sever our ties. I have debts to pay.

"You heard what Ava said, I'm a factor in this. We're Source bonded and that should help you vanquish that magic eater." He snarls and I grip his arm.

"No. I can't go in there, still connected to you." Hurt flashes in his face and his jaw ticks at his restraint to snap at me. He tries to maneuver around me but I hold him by his arms, my magic preening at the contact. I pull my hands back, careful of my boundaries. "I know you would not want to risk your magic now, not after we've already rescued my sister."

"You think *that's* what I'm angry about right now? You assume I'm even thinking about my magic?" He hisses at me as he steps up to me. His chest brushing up against mine and I fight the urge to take a step back.

"How in the world would I know what's going on in your head, Flynn?" I grit my teeth when I start to feel the burning behind my eyes. "You shut me out, *you* did that. I know that the bond can be tiresome. That being my Source was never your choice." His eyes bore into mine and he steps away, chuckling under his breath.

"I don't have the energy to deal with you." He waves his hand dismissively. "All you ever think about is this damned bond."

"Then what else is there to think about?" I raise my voice. Shrill and breathy. He whips his head my way and he sneers at me. His eyes have gone dark with his anger.

Then I feel him reach toward that connection gripping it in a tight vise. I gasp at the pressure inside my chest. The bond struggles against his hold.

"Flynn—" My breath catches in my throat and he tightens his grip even more. I grimace at the sensation. It feels like he's plunged his hands into my chest and squeezed the air out of my lungs.

"This is nothing but an open channel between energies, Zelle." He stutters when he says my name, as if it was an unfamiliar word that he needs to reform on his tongue so he can say it right. "It cannot make you *feel* things the way you think it's making you." He loosens his grip on the bond. I only had a moment to take a breath before funnels a surge of energy through me. He's flooding me with enough power that my hands start to shake with the need to expel it.

I want to protest but I close my eyes as I feel the energy filling my core. My magic stretches in this abundance of power. Some of it tumble out of me and the air around us starts to hum. Gold flecks flare in the air around us enveloping us in shimmering dust.

My magic knows the energy came from him and the sense of familiarity feels like a soft kiss on the cheek. But his energy doesn't make my heart somersault inside my chest.

I reach out to him, my fingertips brushing along his arm. My skin heats at the contact and my blood roars. It's *him*.

It's him that tightens my chest until my heart hammers in my throat. That elicits such strong physical reactions from me that I cannot help but just let my body succumb. That every time he touches me all I want to do is sink into his warmth.

It's him that makes my mind go silent. Where my worries, doubts, and anxiety evaporate at his proximity. Him that had been my constant source of confidence—not magic—because he never doubted me.

He'd pushed me to the edge until I learned. He had believed in my abilities and he was willing to risk himself to save my sister without question.

I take a sharp breath and my eyes widen at the realization. I look up at him and his eyes, the color of churning seas and awakening skies. He's watching me, a crease forms between his brows. He cups my cheek in his palm and I sink into his touch.

"It's not the bond." I whisper to him and his eyes soften. It's you. It's us. His thumb brushes over my cheek and a sigh falls from my lips.

He steps closer and rests his forehead on mine. His nose casually brushes my cheek as he dips a little lower. He takes my hand and rests it on his chest. His warmth spreads over my palms. His heart is hammering so fast it rivals my own.

"Do you know how frustrating it is for me to know you feel the same way, only to have you blame it on the bond as if these feelings were *forced* on you?" I didn't know his voice could be this gentle, this tender, this laced with pain. It hits me like a strike to the gut. His admission cleaves apart my resolve and I take what I should have taken long ago.

I raise myself on the tip of my toes and press my lips to his. The kiss is soft, chaste, and it takes my breath away. His lips against mine break apart any reason, any thought. My heart stutters.

I lean away and he chases after me like a man starved. I welcome his touch with my own. He leaves tentative fluttering kisses at the corners of my lips and I melt into him.

He hums appreciatively at my reaction and tilts my head back so can slide his lips harder over mine. I would happily die here if I could.

Flynn wraps his arms around my waist as he leans back so he can look down at me. His breath skates over my heated skin and I nuzzle into his chest. He tugs the bond again, playful and light. I whimper at the sensation in my gut.

"Intent and emotions drive your magic, not the other way around. This bond grows strong and intense because my emotions surges when I'm near you, filling me with enough power that I could light up from inside." My throat tightens as his gaze roams over my face. "It may have started our connection but it was never responsible for anything that happened between us after that."

His hands snake up my back and I shudder at the sensation. He leans in again, his nose touching the skin of my neck near my ear. Then he whispers.

"When I touch you, I feel like I have enough power that my magic will burn the world down just to take away your pain." He leans back again and smiles. He swipes a thumb on my cheek, taking away the tear that escapes from my eyes.

I had been hiding behind the Source bond. Blaming it for the feelings I couldn't stop from taking root inside of me. It was a sorry excuse to keep the guilt at bay, for feeling this way when I needed to focus on saving my sister. It was easier to say it was the bond that liked having him around, not me.

"I guess you're voting 'No' to breaking the Source bond, then?" I quip and wiggle my brows at him. He laughs—a rare, genuine one where he throws his head back. His body shakes with mirth. I grin at the accomplishment.

"Oh, Zelle." He murmurs into my ear, his voice full of mischief. "The bond stays."

Chapter 40

Linc and Valera transport us near the border of the wards where they had last seen the Comendeti lurking. The bodies of creatures, some of them are the same ones we saw in the tavern, litter the ground. Their eyes bloodshot and left petrified even in their death. The Comendeti consumed their magic in its mission for vengeance.

The sight makes me sick and I bite down a gag. This is a sick perversion of our Source bond. It's an insult to the sharing of energy and magic. Flynn doesn't look away from the carnage. His body shakes with fury.

We didn't have to travel far. She is much closer to the manor than when we last saw her and I know that if we had delayed a day more, she would have found a way inside. Valera curses under her breath, probably thinking the same thing.

"I have to keep checking the perimeter to keep Ava safe. She powers the wards around Meridian. If harm comes her way the manor falls." She sets her gaze on Linc. "You keep the Triune safe, keeper." Without waiting for a response, she disappears.

Flynn steps closer in front of me blocking my body with his. His fingers laces around mine and I feel much steadier on my feet. Zoha and Zafiya flank me. They do not have enough control of their magic yet. But having them beside me opens up a much wider well of power I hadn't known I had.

If it goes according to plan, we won't even have to risk leaving the protection barriers. Ava stayed behind to continue casting spells to reinforce them. I know her spells are working as the wards thrum with her power. The air shimmers around it and I'm confident nothing will get inside without her knowing.

Zafiya steps back and I look over at her. Her eyes had gone cold and empty.

"I could sense it." She blanches and she bends down. Her fiery hair curtains over his face. "It could sense me, too. It—She knows my scent. She can feel my magic." Zoha is at her side rubbing circles on her back.

"We need more time." She pleads me. Her eyes, the perfect reflection of mine, wide with her fear. She holds Zafiya close. I know she is scared for our sister more than she is for herself. "Maybe we can train more, before—"

"The wards won't last past today. We have to do it now." I tell her. I keep my voice gentle but firm.

We're out in the forest now. Another clearing, one I haven't seen before. The trees here are thicker, older. Their threads pulse at my attention. The ground is damp and rumbling under my feet. Sensing the danger in the air.

I take a deep breath and open myself up to the energy that the Mother is giving to me, it flows through my blood.

I take copious amounts of it and my skin starts to glow from the strain. I let my magic consume it all, let it get drunk on the power now coursing through me. The hair on the back of my neck stands with the tension inside me. The more energy I absorb, the tighter I coil. Ready to explode on command.

"She's here." Flynn murmurs and he steps back from the wards, pressing his back into me. I pull at his arm and he looks at me over his shoulder. I give him a smile and his eyes dart between mine. I incline my head slightly, motioning him to move back. With him, he would trust me enough to take a step back when I ask him to.

This is our battle. Our play. He cannot keep me behind him for this. He frowns but nods as he moves to the side, letting my sisters and I stand on our own.

Fog begins to roil from a distance, thick and bubbling. It moves forward, eating up the ground and I know it's the Hala. I recognize the sickly-sweet music it used to lure me out. I clench my hand, remembering the pain that flooded me when the fog touched my skin. It creeps closer and closer.

"What is that?" Zoha asks, she sidles up a little closer. Her voice leaking with trepidation.

"It's the fog demon that almost took my arm out." I tense as it gets close to the wards and I watch it attempt to go through. It hits the invisible wall and it curves into the sky instead, blanketing us in smoke.

I take my sisters' hands in mine and we form a chain. The contact opens up a flurry of magic inside me, both of them gasp. They feel it, too.

An image of the night of our father's death surfaces in my mind. It had been the same then. We had only been ready to step through that dreadful room when we did it together. When we drew strength from each other.

The same applies today. We can face this as sisters. We are strongest together.

The Comendeti steps out of the fog, materializing from smoke. Its grey skin taut over its bones. What was once skin that reminded me of death, smooth and blank, is now stained with their sin of gluttony.

Cracked and peeling, showing lines of black magic coursing underneath the surface. The evidence of her feeding off of her own minions, of her taking too much too fast.

She snarls at me but she doesn't speak. She flicks her hand and her magic lights up from inside her. The Hala thickens, growing higher and higher over the wards. The wards cannot protect us against the wind now howling at the command of the magic eater. My hair whips around my face and I grip my sisters' hands as I begin to chant.

"Heed us sisters three.

With words of woe we beckon thee.

Magic of blood and magic of three,

Come light the way and burn away,

Let all be gone and be on their way."

Zoha and Zafiya chant along with me. Our voices clear against the wind. Then our intent is heard, my power wanes as it starts siphoning into the Comendeti. When she feels it enter her system she chuckles in delight, her void eyes growing wide. She bares her teeth and a bloody smile.

Again.

I start the chant once more. The power spills out of me, out of my sister and into the monster standing in front of us. My body seizes at the hole opening up inside of me. On instinct, my magic tries to protect me as fear creeps in. The ground bursts with life.

Plants and vines grow and wrap around my legs, grounding me, feeding me with energy. Wind that smells of jasmine envelopes us and hardens around us, a protective shield. I look over at Zafiya and watch as her eyes widen in wonder. This was her magic—I would recognize it anywhere.

Fire. Hot and raging bursts from Zoha's outstretched arm. I flinch when it grows too near me. My eyes widen as it grazes me but it doesn't burn my skin. Goosebumps pebble my skin as the sensation of Zoha's fire remind me so much of our mother's touch. I peer at her subtly.

This is the struggle she is faced with, the denial and the reality she didn't want to deal with. She was our mother's daughter through and through. Their resemblance so uncanny despite her efforts to hide it.

Now, even as a witch she was still the one that's most like mama. They share the same affinity. She has the same fire that consumed our mother on her own command.

Tears line my eyes as I watch her call to it and it burns fervently in front of us. She pours all of it into the Comendeti as if suffocating it with our power.

More, more, more. We give it everything we have. With hands intertwined, the spell leeches our power and siphons it to the magic-eater.

I see the moment it realizes what we're doing. It roars and lunges toward the wards but it flies back at contact. It screeches as her skin starts to crack further, breaking. I see the threads of our power lighting her up from within. It fills her. Drowns her in its potency.

The Comendeti lunges for us again but this time the Hala moves with her. Her hand alight with dark smoke as she feeds the demon more of the power flooding her. The Hala screeches and the ground rumbles as they hit the wards.

The impact shakes me and I lose my footing. Flynn is immediately beside me holding us steady.

"They're going to break through." His eyes stay on our enemy and I watch as the blue shimmering of the wards start the waver. Linc shadow jumps in front of us and puts up his own shield.

My heart hammers in my chest as the Hala and the Comendeti strike again. Linc grunts at the force. No, no. I need more.

"Take it, take it all with you." Flynn tells me. I have not tapped into our Source bond. I do not want to drain him and to subject him to the risk. I've taken too much and he'd given me more than enough.

The cracks in the wards grow wider at each impact. My sisters are barely able to stand as I'm sure their magic is only but a flutter inside them now.

"Do it." He urges. Flynn doesn't wait for me to respond as he pushes on the bond with all his might. I grunt at the rush of power. My head feels like it's splitting into two and my vision is darkening.

I take a deep breath and let go of my sister's hands and I stifle the bond. This was my spell to finish.

So, I chant.

"What is mine is yours to take,

My core, my magic for you to break,

Feed the greed and make it ache."

Flynn protests at my spell and tries to pry open the bond. But it's too late.

I feel my magic rip out of me. The pain searing my bones until I'm screaming. The Comendeti screams with me as all of my essence drowns her. Her skin lighting up and burning from inside.

My core heats up and grows bright. It fights against the spell and I could almost hear it screeching. The battle inside me doesn't last long and I feel my core break. The cracks leaking power into the world and out onto the Comendeti.

The world tilts and my ears start ringing. Blood floods my mouth as the pain from my breaking core fills my body. Knives cut through me, flaying my skin into ribbons and I scream.

I scream until it feels like I've swallowed broken glass but my eyes stay on the Comendeti as I watch her clutch her throat as blood gurgles out of her. All the magic pouring out me, leaking out of my core that's now split open floods her.

She releases one more piercing scream before she explodes in a bright light. A flurry of magic filling the air.

My body deflates and everything turns quiet. Before I hear anything else, I let the abyss inside me take me into the empty darkness.

Chapter 41

There's a hole inside of me now, it makes my chest feel hollow. There's a big gaping void where my core once sat and occupied, where my magic lived and concentrated. Now there's too much space inside.

This is nothing and nowhere. That even if I would try to take in energy it would just go through my body and disappear into this blackness.

It makes me my stomach churn.

I open my eyes and I'm in our room. The curtains are drawn shut, keeping out the light. My limbs protest when I try to move. How long have I been out? I push myself up and I groan at the pain shooting through me.

Zoha and Zafiya are both in bed with me, draped over the bed as if they fell asleep hovering over me. They most likely did.

They don't stir when I push back the covers and try to stand up. I wobble slightly but hands grab me by my shoulders to keep me steady.

I look up to find Linc smiling down at me. His eyes crinkled with worry.

"Hi." He croaks, his voice rough. He wraps his arms around me, taking away some of the ache. He nuzzles into my hair and his chest rumbles as he sighs.

"We've all been so worried." He tightens his arms around me and I squeal softly at the pressure. There's no space for the awkwardness between us now. My best friend rubs small circles around my back, willing warmth into me.

"It's gone." I say into his chest. "I'm not a witch anymore, am I?" He holds me by the chin to tip my head up. Even in the dark, his grey eyes shine so starkly.

"We will get it back." I shake my head, not hopeful. This was different. This nothingness. It's unlike the times I've drained myself where I know I can fill myself up again and my magic will flutter away. Even the bond— *Flynn!*

"Is Flynn okay?" I ask, my voice tight. There was a risk of ripping his magic with mine just because he was tethered to me. I wouldn't be able to live with myself if I took that away from him. I hadn't even told him what I'd plan with that spell, where it even came from.

"He is fine. He was grumbling about his father before we had to pry him from your bedside. He's away on cabal business and he still has his magic." Linc motions to my sleeping sisters. "So do they. You isolated that spell to yourself." The relief floods me and my knees buckle slightly. He takes on my weight and he rests his forehead on mine. "You shouldn't have done that, Z. We promised no heroics."

"I had no choice." I say. At that moment, we would have gotten out. I know Linc would have been able to shadow jump. He would only have a second to spare with that shield. He had put all of his power into taking on the brunt of the Comendeti and the Hala's attacks but we would have escaped.

I was confident that he would have been able to do it and I knew he was about to. He'd take us away to protect us but I couldn't leave after what we had already started.

We've given the magic eater so much power that she would have been able to break those wards with the Hala. It was an all or nothing situation, so I chose the one where everyone else would be safest.

Linc grows quiet and I hug him again.

"It's okay." I cannot say that I regret it despite the longing. In the days since I've let go of my distrust of magic and my resentment towards my mother's decisions. I've learned to understand why she'd chosen a life without magic if the tradeoff is knowing we'd be far away from harm.

Sacrificing that piece of me for my sisters and the safety of everyone else in Meridian including Linc and Flynn was worth it.

I'd do it again if I had to.

"Ava says we can do another ceremony on the next Esbat."

"I don't know why we should even bother." I had full intention in giving the Comendeti all my magic and the spell had obliged me.

Linc straightens and he huffs. Placing his arms on my shoulder so he could look at me with narrowed eyes.

"Stop that." I quirk my eyebrows at the irritation in his voice. I would like to think that I'm being anything but realistic.

"I'm just saying—"

"And I know what you're trying to say but don't shoot it down before we've tried. Magic is give and take. You've given more than what was asked of you and the Mother will recognize this." He eases further back from me when I hear my sisters stir behind us. "Think about it." He gives me a soft kiss on the cheek that makes me smile.

The gesture saying more than his words could. His fierce protectiveness and worries so evident, but he'd learn to take a step back and let me do what I need to. He gives me one last hug and leaves the room.

"You're awake!" Zafiya exclaims as she bounds out of bed and hugs me.

"We were so worried." Zoha stands, her eyes wary. I open my arms and beckon her closer. She obliges and we stand there hugging each other. I could not find the right words to express the emotions coming over me.

I do what feels right and I wrap my arms around them tighter as I let the tears go. Zoha makes soothing noises and Zafiya tugs me closer. Then they cry with me.

In this moment, with tired bodies and minds tucked away in our own room, we let our tears wash over each other. The salt treating the grief, the fear, and the uncertainty. My heart stutters. The void isn't as daunting as it seems now.

Despite what I have lost. What *we* have all lost. We had each other.

Magic or not, we are still sisters. I don't need anything more.

Ava fusses over me as she prepares me for Esbat in her study. We are sprawled on the thick center rug going through crystals and candles. We will be performing the new moon ritual said to heal and recharge witches from across the world in a few weeks and she wants me there to recharge with them.

I know her ridiculously early preparation is just her way of getting me out of bed and back into the practice of magic but I don't complain. I let myself get lost in the motions. The craft. Ava is polishing the crystals across from me, her chocolate brown hair tied in one loose braid behind her.

"If…" My voice wavers and I clear my throat. Ava sets down the one emerald she has in her hand, the one perfectly matching the eyes she flicks to me. "If I don't get my magic back, I'll find our old house. I'd need a bit of time before I can get it fixed and I—"

"The manor is your home. I will not turn you away nor will I let you leave unless you want to." She reaches over and lays her hand on mine. "I may have become a high priestess too late to correct the mistakes this coven had done to Aria and Gab but I can at least make up for it now." A sheen of tears glosses over her eyes and she smiles at me with such sadness. "Let me do that for you. For them."

"They were happy. Despite the exile or maybe even because of it, they were." Ava's throat bobs as she swallows.

"I know. They had three beautiful daughters and they have been blessed greatly." Ava sighs and looks out the window of her study "Still, I have my regrets and I hope to atone for them. I wish you'd stay." I smile at her and nod.

"I'll be your best mortal student." I say lightly and she smiles. I do not tell her that I still do not feel my power come back to me. I don't think it will. The longing is strong but I am not selfish enough to pray and wish it back.

"There's that look again." My face breaks out into a grin at his voice. Flynn steps through the doors bringing with him his smoky scent of pine. His dark hair frames his beautiful face and his eyes sparkle as he sees me. The deep blue grows soft and warm as his gaze rakes over me.

"I told you, magus, I don't have a look." I stand to meet him halfway. His warm hands rests on my waist as I step up to him.

"Hmm." He tilts his head as I look up at him through my lashes. He uses his fingers to brush the pulse at my wrist. With the gentlest of touches, he lifts my arms to wrap around around his neck. "You have a much different one now." He says softly.

I don't answer. Couldn't bring myself to, with him so close. So flush against me. I rise on my toes to place the softest of kisses on his waiting lips. Warmth blooms at the contact, it sears my skin and I sigh. A very small tug in my chest flutters. The familiar sensation flooding me.

Ava walks by to leave the room and she whispers to me.

"There is magic everywhere, Zelle. It will find its way back to you." I look up at Flynn, at the eyes that shimmers so brightly when he watches me.

Maybe magic already has.

About the Author

Krista Eviota

Krista has always found her home within books and stories even as a child. At an early age, stories have been pouring out of her mind as she sees the world from the eyes of a reader. She wrote any chance she could: through handwritten short stories tucked into a private diary, the school newspaper, and fanfiction websites.

Now, even as a full-time corporate employee, the need to read and tell stories never abated. Krista's emotional temperament and childish wonder are her key to writing stories about love, family, and magic.

This is her first novel and hopefully will be the first of many more to come! She lives with her family and two cats in a quiet neighborhood in the Philippines. She is socially awkward and all social media accounts are private.

Acknowledgement

Where do I even begin? Being published as an author is a dream that I conjured and shyly chased after for almost two decades. For those who played a role in my life, no matter how small or big that role may be, thank you. I am here now, in part, because you were in my life.

To my sister, Kimi, who is most prominently the yin to my yang. Thank you for calming the doubts that always crippled me to the point of inaction. Your bluntness is often the remedy I need to pick myself up and just start doing whatever it is I need to do.

To my brother and pillar, Kyle, who gave me stability and assurances through my precarious moods. Thank you for always telling me that it was never too late for me to start. For giving me guidance and holding my hand through tearful nights where my fears overwhelm me.

To my parents and my grandmother, who made sure I always had somewhere and someone to turn to. I may not always ask for help because I wear my independence as a badge of honor but your presence is security. The love and care you give me had allowed me to chase after a dream so grand. Thank you.

To my best friend, Nina, who had become my number one cheerleader in this life. Thank you for the advices and the unabashed support. The rant sessions we have with each other has unburdened me of so much weight that I used to carry on my own. In all the years I stopped writing, our friendship was one of the very reasons I picked up the proverbial pen again. I would not have even started this book if you hadn't believed in me so strongly.

To my alpha reader, beta reader, overall go-to person and the one who had made me believe this book actually deserved to see the light of day, Joanna. The play-by-play reactions you had for Spells and Bindings in its early stages made me giddy and shy. Deep down, it made me so, so hopeful and I held on to that hope like a lifeline. Thank you for peering into this written world and loving it as much as I did.

To my partner and silent supporter, Henston. Thank you for understanding me and my need to explore my passion. You understood me even through the hours I would disappear because I would get so lost in this world. You support me through the freedom you give me to spread my wings and I couldn't ask for anything better.

Thank you to Ukiyoto Team for choosing this title among the many others that may have come your way. I know I had a lot of questions and changes to be made, your patience is appreciated. You have helped me reach a dream I never thought I would in this life.

To my constants, to all the friends and family, I wasn't able to mention. There are so many of you, so many friends that pushed me through the years. Thank you for believing in my skills as a writer more than I ever could. All your words echo and wash over me now. I am overwhelmed with gratitude as I am faced with what I think is both a culmination and beginning.

www.ingramcontent.com/pod-product-compliance
Lightning Source LLC
LaVergne TN
LVHW091713070526
838199LV00050B/2382